HIDDEN MICKEY ADVENTURES 5

The Fifth novel in this Action-Adventure Mystery series about Walt Disney and Disneyland, written for Adults, teens, & tweens (9 and up).

From the author of the acclaimed HIDDEN MICKEY series.

A FAMILY IN CRISIS

When tragedy strikes, Adam and Beth find it more and more difficult to believe in miracles. Will their family ever be whole again?

CAN A MAN FROM THE PAST REALLY HELP A BOY IN THE FUTURE?

Peter, still hurt and angry by the treatment he received at the hands of Nimue, is handed a special message. It is from Walt Disney himself. Can Peter get back his love for Disneyland and fulfill his special Hidden Mickey quest? Or will the absence of his partner be too much for him?

EXTORTION. BLACKMAIL. A FORBIDDEN GLIMPSE INTO THE FUTURE.

Walt exacts a promise from Wolf in exchange for his help. Wolf vowed never to take him on such a dangerous journey. Who will win this ultimate battle of wills?

NOW IS THE TIME TO WISH!

Disneyland—now and in the future—is the backdrop for this exciting tale of hopes, dreams, and discovery. *When You Wish* unites families and friends as they work together to keep the Disney magic alive—both for themselves and for Walt's legacy.

When You Wish

HIDDEN MICKEY
ADVENTURES 5
WHEN YOU WISH

Nancy Temple Rodrigue

Double R Books

HIDDEN MICKEY ADVENTURES 5
WHEN YOU WISH

FIFTH NOVEL IN THE HIDDEN MICKEY ADVENTURES SERIES
SECOND EDITION PAPERBACK, VOLUME 5, JUNE 1, 2017
ISBN 13: 978-1-9383193-4-1

COPYRIGHT © 2016 NANCY RODRIGUE
LIBRARY OF CONGRESS CATALOGING-IN-PUBLICATION DATA ON FILE
www.HIDDENMICKEYBOOK.com
FLESCH-KINCAID GRADE 4.1 - FLESCH READING EASE 83.6

ALL RIGHTS RESERVED
NO PART OF THIS BOOK BE USED OR REPRODUCED IN ANY MANNER WHATSOEVER, ELECTRONIC, MECHANICAL, PHOTOCOPYING, RECORDING, OR OTHERWISE WITHOUT THE PRIOR WRITTEN PERMISSION OF THE PUBLISHER

Double R Books

DOUBLE R BOOKS PUBLISHING
740 N. H STREET, SUITE # 170
LOMPOC, CALIFORNIA, 93436
www.DOUBLERBOOKS.COM
COVER CONCEPT BY NANCY RODRIGUE
www.NANCY.RODRIGUE.org
COVER ARTWORK & COLOR BY CHRISNA RIBEIRO
www.JUHANI.DEVIANTART.com
COVER COPYRIGHT © 2016 BY DOUBLE R BOOKS
www.DOUBLERBOOKS.COM

1ST EDITION eBOOK - APRIL 2016 - ISBN 13: 978-1-9383191-1-2
1ST EDITION HARDBACK - APRIL 2016 - ISBN 13: 978-1-9383192-2-8
1ST EDITION PAPERBACK - APRIL 2016 - ISBN 13: 978-1-9383191-2-9
2ND EDITION PAPERBACK - JUNE 2017 - ISBN 13: 978-1-9383193-4-1

PRINTED IN THE UNITED STATES OF AMERICA

Dedication

*To my husband Russ Rodrigue.
He has read every word I have written,
offered support every step of the way,
and has been there for
almost every book signing
and appearance I have made.
His behind-the-scenes work
has been invaluable to me.
Thank you!*

Nancy Temple Rodrigue

Disclaimer

Walt Disney Company Trademarks: *Hidden Mickey Adventures 5: When You Wish* is in no way authorized by, endorsed by or affiliated with the Walt Disney Company, Inc., Disneyland Park, or WED. Disneyland Park is a registered trademark of the Walt Disney Company. Other trademarks include but are not limited to Adventureland, *Columbia*, Disneyland Paris, Disneyland Railroad, Edison Square, Fantasyland, Finding Nemo Submarines, Fort Wilderness, Frontierland, Golden Oak Ranch, Haunted Mansion, It's a Small World, Jungle Cruise, Liberty Square, Main Street, Market House, *Mark Twain*, Mr. Toad, MouseAdventure, New Orleans Square, Opera House, Phantom Manor, Pinocchio, Pirates of the Caribbean, Sleeping Beauty Castle, Space Mountain, *Swiss Family Robinson*, Tarzan's Treehouse, Tomorrowland, Tom Sawyer Island, Walt Disney Studio, *When You Wish Upon a Star*, and Walt Disney. All references to such trademarked properties are used in accordance with the Fair Use Doctrine and are not meant to imply this book is a Disney product for advertising or other commercial purposes.

While some of the events and persons contained herein are historical facts and figures; other persons named and the events described are purely fictional and a product of the Author's imagination. Any resemblance to actual people is purely coincidental.

The actions depicted within the book are a result of fiction and imagination and are not to be attempted, reproduced or duplicated by the readers of this book. The Publisher and Author assume no responsibility or liability for damages resulting, or alleged to result, directly or indirectly from the use of the information contained herein.

Enjoy all the books from Double R Books
Hardbacks - Paperbacks - eBooks - Apps

Hidden Mickey
1: Sometimes Dead Men DO Tell Tales!
2: It All Started...
3: Wolf! The Legend of Tom Sawyer's Island
4: Wolf! Happily Ever After?
4.5: Unfinished Business-Wals

Hidden Mickey Adventures
1: Peter and the Wolf
2: Peter and the Missing Mansion
3: The Mermaid's Tale
4: Revenge of the Wolf
5: When You Wish

Hidden Mickey Quest books to play inside Disney parks

Hidden Mickey Adventures
In Disneyland ❖ In WDW Magic Kingdom
In Disney California Adventure

Acknowledgements

I would like to thank a few of the people
who have helped this novel come to life:

Dave Smith – Disney Historian
for his help with the Disney Studio

Michael Smyth
for his help with the Disney Studio Ink and Paint Shop

Rebecca Cline – Disney Archives
for her help with the *Columbia Sailing Ship*

Carolyn Hoagland
for her help with the *Columbia Sailing Ship*

Todd Regan – MiceChat
for his help with Disneyland Paris

David Koenig – author *Mouse Tales*
for his help with Jungle Cruise

David W. Smith – co-author *Hidden Mickey 1 & 2*
for his part in the Epilogue

Laura O'Lacy
for her Disneyland knowledge

James D. Keeline
for his help with the Disneyland Railroad

Thanks and Acknowledgements also go to
our proofreader and editor:

Alyssa Colodny

Dear Readers,

In his dedication of Fantasyland, Walt Disney said: "Here is the world of imagination, hopes and dreams. In this timeless land of enchantment, the age of chivalry, magic and make believe are reborn—and fairy tales come true. Fantasyland is dedicated to the young and the young-at-heart—to those who believe that when you wish upon a star, your dreams do come true."

In this special, heart-touching story, we are taken back to the clue-driven storyline of the very first *Hidden Mickey* novels: *Hidden Mickey 1: Sometimes Dead Men Do Tell Tales* and *Hidden Mickey 2: It All Started…* With his partner in peril, Peter must work by himself to solve the riddles that Walt Disney set in place especially for him. As he strives to fulfill his destiny, Peter must learn what is really important—for himself, for his future, and for Walt's Legacy.

Wolf and Omah are on hand, blackmailed by Walt to get what he wants: A glimpse into the future. Will they allow what was never done before—to take Walt with them through time itself?

In *Hidden Mickey Adventures 5: When You Wish*, long-held secrets are divulged as three families try to move forward in the face of extreme distress.

I hope you enjoy this exciting new Adventure.

Nancy Temple Rodrigue

Prologue

Disney Studio, Burbank — 1966

A man stood at a window overlooking the eastern side of the Studio. Reminiscent of an anthill being disturbed, a colorful mass of people flowed in every direction. The Process Lab could be seen, as well as one end of the ever-busy Ink and Paint Building. In the distance, a huge smile painted on his welcoming face, Mickey Mouse watched the goings-on from his perch high overhead on the water tower.

The man, though, hadn't gone to that particular window that day for the view. Truth be told, he hadn't even glanced down. Or up. He just stared outward. Arms folded, head tucked into his chest, he was deep in thought. If someone had dared to interrupt and ask, he probably would have rattled off the latest movie in production, *The Jungle Book*, or the newest attraction that opened at Disneyland, It's a Small World. He might have mentioned the opening of New Orleans Square last month or the exciting new ride, Pirates of the Caribbean, which was being built.

His mind, actually, was focused on more internal matters. Ones he didn't care to share with the anthill of people who moved below.

Dressed for a day at the office, he was in a non-descript brown suit and a striped tie, one of his favorite fedoras perched and ready on a side table. He looked as if he was ready for an on-camera interview or a stroll around the Studio with a visiting dignitary. But there were no interviews and no one scheduled to visit that day. Always the businessman, he could be ready at a moment's notice.

An honest, welcoming smile would transform his tired face as he showed off his thriving Studio.

When he had arrived earlier that day, there was no need to tell his secretary not to disturb him. The frown on his face and the slump of his shoulders had been enough to alert her to his present state of mind. Only the direst of emergencies would get her to push the button on her intercom.

"Walt? Do you have a minute?"

Still facing the window, a small smile turned up one corner of his gray mustache. Only one man would have the temerity to do that. "Wolf. I didn't hear the door."

"I didn't use the door."

Instantly intrigued, Walt Disney turned to face his visitor as the smile spread across his face. "Then that would explain why you weren't announced." His arms were still crossed, but the tired shoulders no longer sagged. *This might prove to be interesting.* As he leaned back against the windowsill, he took a moment to look over his long-time friend and right-hand-man. It was obvious Wolf wasn't dressed as the security guards of that time period. His uniform had a sharper edge to it, a more 'modern' feel to it.

As his boss's scrutiny continued, Wolf took the opportunity to do his own observation. Before he had announced his presence, he had seen Walt's dejected stance. It didn't take a mind-reader to see it was something serious that bothered him. Wolf also noticed Walt's hair was a bit grayer and more lines creased that well-known face. "Did I come at a bad time?"

At the question, Walt let out an amused huff of air as he turned back to the window. He knew he wouldn't be able to throw Wolf off the scent by reciting the latest news of the Studio. "Yes. Well, no, not for you. I'm always glad to see you. Especially when you're dressed like that."

"Like that" meant from the future. It was obvious Wolf had made a trip back in time to see him—even though he still didn't completely understand the how and why of it all. What Wolf and Omah were able to do fascinated him. He just wished one of them would break their hard-fast rule of never taking him along on a trip. Unseen by Wolf, his eyes suddenly narrowed and a small, conspiratorial smile passed over his lips. The look was replaced by a customary frown before he turned to reclaim his seat behind the desk.

He threw in a wheezing cough for good measure.

Unaware of the theatrics, Wolf accepted the gesture of Walt's outstretched hand and sat on one of the nearby chairs. "You look tired today, Walt."

That earned an honest, yet wry chuckle. "Today. Yesterday. Probably tomorrow, too. Not that I would admit it to anyone else, of course."

"Of course." A friendly smile settled on Wolf's face. Sympathy and pity weren't wanted. "The opening of New Orleans Square went well. Everyone loves the addition."

Walt let out a snort. "Glad it's going over well. It cost me as much as the original Louisiana Purchase."

"Worth every penny."

"Lots and lots of pennies." He didn't want to talk about money. Walt rubbed a lined hand over his face and put his head back against his chair. "I am tired, Wolf. I thought the vacation in Vancouver would snap me back, but it didn't." His eyes drifted over to the window again, but, once he settled into the chair, he really didn't feel like getting up to resume his place. "I must be getting old."

A pang surged through Wolf. Walt didn't know yet what would happen in just a few months. He might have an idea in the back of his mind, but he didn't know anything for sure. Wolf knew he couldn't give any hint of the near future and kept things light. "Hey, I'm over 200 years old. Look at me!"

Walt recognized and appreciated the attempt. "You still look 30 and you know it. I know you didn't come to discuss my health, fascinating subject that it is." A cough, a real one this time, suddenly rattled Walt's chest. "Bad timing, that."

"Hey, I thought you only coughed like that to let the animators know you were in the hallway." Wolf noticed the returned sag in the shoulders. The cough took more out of Walt than he would admit, so Wolf changed the subject. "The reason I came was to see about the quest I asked you to make for Peter. I wondered how you were doing with it."

Walt's hand dropped to one of the drawers in his desk. The gesture stopped short and his arm returned to his desk. "Thought that might be the reason for your visit. How is Peter? You had said he was losing his spark toward Disneyland."

"Still the same. I had hoped things would return to normal by now, but they haven't."

"That pendant seems to be more trouble than its worth."

Wolf knew Walt's mumble wasn't meant to be heard and didn't respond to it.

Walt suddenly chuckled as he looked back at Wolf. "It's so odd to talk about someone who hasn't even been born and is the grandson of our good friend who isn't even married yet! And, yet, thanks to you, I've actually met this boy and his mother. Amazing."

Wolf was glad to see some of Walt's customary sparkle come back into his eyes. "And, thanks to Omah, I can now travel without all the bells and whistles."

"Bells and whistles." Walt shook his head and laughed. "That's a pretty poor way to describe thunder and lightning and whatever else you churned up! Omah, huh? So, how's that going?"

Never could pull anything over on Walt. "It's going well. Very well."

Walt waited, but there was no more. Not that that surprised him. Wolf usually kept his cards pretty close to his chest. "So, you want to know about the quest. Well, it's done."

Impressed, Wolf's eyebrows shot up. "Really? That's great. The way you were stalling, I thought you might need more time."

"More time." The phrase seemed to take the spark out of Walt. He wilted in front of Wolf's eyes. "More time. I always need more time, Wolf." With an impatient shove, he pushed his chair away from the desk and returned to the window. Hands on the sill, he leaned forward until his forehead touched the cool glass. "Is there enough time? Have I done enough?" When he felt a warm hand on his shoulder, he lifted his face from the window. "I know I'm not immortal, Wolf. No one is. Well…no one except possibly you and Omah… You know what I mean. I have so many plans, so many ideas all in there," as his finger tapped his temple. "They keep me awake at night. I write them down and file them away for a later day when the time will be right for them." Another cough shook his frame. "Have I done enough?"

"I could tell you yes, but you wouldn't believe me."

Walt looked over his shoulder at the concerned face next to him. "Probably not. I need to see things for myself. Always have. I need to touch them and tinker with them and fix them until they're perfect."

"What can I say that'll help?"

Walt took a deep breath and returned to his desk. *Now's the time.* His hand hovered near the same desk drawer, but he didn't open it. Wolf's question was ignored. "I told you I have Peter's quest finished. Well, I want something from you before I hand it over."

"Anything, Walt." The accommodating look in Wolf's eyes turned cautious when a small smile of victory came over Walt's face. At Walt's next words, Wolf knew he was right to be wary.

"I was hoping you'd say that." His eyes narrowed as he leaned forward and placed his palms flat on his desk. "Before you get what you want, I want you to take me to see the future. I want to see my Park in your time. I want to see for myself that everything's all right. I want to see the changes I saw in my visions." One of his hands shot up when he saw Wolf was going to speak. "No, don't say anything yet, Wolf. This is non-negotiable. I have to *see* that I've done enough. I know you can do it. And, I know I'll be safe, so don't use that old chestnut." He sank back against his chair, his energy suddenly depleted from his strong emotions. "I have to see, Wolf. You have to take me."

"That's blackmail."

"That's unconditional."

Wolf didn't answer immediately. He spent the time studying the man sitting in front of him as he silently went over what it would take out of Walt—both physically and mentally—to do what he demanded. Knowing how much time was really left for Walt, he knew, if he did agree, that they would have to go now.

As the silence stretched, Walt began to think Wolf would tell him what he always told him—no. And he hated to be told no. Before he could make another pitch, Wolf stood from his chair, and Walt's hope crushed. "You're leaving." It was a flat, emotionless statement, one muttered with an unwelcome finality.

"Do you have a warm coat?"

Wolf's seemingly out-of-the-blue question confused Walt. "It's the middle of August."

"You have one in the closet, don't you?"

"I think so. Why?"

"Just get it out. I'm going to go get Omah, and we'll be right back."

"Omah? What does she have to do with this?"

Wolf watched a range of emotions play over Walt's face. Even though the matter of the mermaid statue had long been resolved, it would take some time before he'd fully accept Omah. "Trust me, Walt. I'll do what you ask. I just need Omah's help to make sure it all goes smoothly."

Once it sunk in that Wolf would take him to see Disneyland in the future, Walt relaxed and a lop-sided, silly grin replaced his disappointed frown. "You really mean it, don't you?"

"Yeah, Walt, I do. Just give me a minute…or two…depending on where she is…"

"I'll be right here. Oh, wait a second." Reaching down, a small black book was retrieved from the desk drawer and Walt tossed to Wolf. "For Peter. Hurry back."

Wolf had to smile as the final words guests heard in the future Haunted Mansion just now came out of Walt's mouth. "You're going to love this."

Chapter 1

Fullerton – Current Day

"Who wants to go camping tomorrow?" His hands rubbing together in anticipation of the joyful reception his words would trigger, Lance Brentwood stood in the entryway of their living room. The smile on his face quickly faded.

"Tomorrow, Lance? Don't you have to work?"

"I have plans."

"Me! I wanna go!"

Not to be outdone by his older brother, Andrew's hand shot up. "Me! I wanna go, too"

"You don't even know what camping is, Andrew."

"I do, too, Mikey. We go to that big hotel next to the Grand Canyon."

"We're going all the way to the Grand Canyon, Lance? Isn't this kind of sudden?"

Baffled by the way this had turned on him, Lance looked from one face to another as his wife and three sons all stared at him. Their expressions ranged from excitement to disbelief. "Who said anything about the Grand Canyon?"

"Can we ride the horses down to the bottom again? That was fun, Daddy."

"They were mules, Andrew. Don't you know the difference between a horse and a mule?"

"Honey, wouldn't it be better to go to Arizona in the spring?"

"I have homework."

A piercing whistle from the doorway stopped the ongoing debate. When the desired silence had been achieved, Lance folded his arms across his chest. "Sheesh, guys. Number One: Who said anything about the Grand Canyon?" His finger shot out and pointed at Michael who was about to throw Andrew under the Dad Bus. "Not a word, Michael. Number Two: Staying at the El Tovar is not camping. Number Three: Peter, since when has homework ever stopped you from going anywhere? And, Number Four: Umm, I don't have a Number Four. What I was suggesting was a quick trip out the Golden Oak Ranch."

"Oh, thank goodness."

Lance glanced over at Kimberly's relieved mutter and raised his eyebrows at her.

"Well, I mean, going to Arizona would take a lot more preparation." With a bright smile to diffuse his defensive posture, she patted the sofa cushion next to her.

As Lance moved to join her, nine-year-old Michael got into the spirit of the trip. "Can we ride the horses again, Dad?"

"Are you sure they aren't mules, Mikey?"

"All right, Andrew. That's enough." Lance was glad to see the faces that now looked at him held an eagerness and willingness that hadn't been there before. He had been looking forward to the trip and hated to see it side-railed before it even got started. "Yes, we probably can borrow a few of the horses, Michael. That'd be fun. I was told there's a movie being filmed, so we won't have full range of the...well, range...but there are plenty of other trails to follow."

"Why the sudden trip, honey?"

Lance didn't want to admit that he just really wanted to go, so he used the secondary reason. "Mario, the Ranch's foreman—the one who had known Walt and who's been our contact all these years—is retiring. He wanted us to meet the new man before he goes. I thought we could spend two or three days in our guesthouse and have some fun."

"Are the twins going, too?" Now that it appeared to be established they were actually going, Michael was anxious to know if Adam and Beth Michaels and their twelve-year-old twins, Alex and Catie, would be there, too. For about a year he and Alex had been deep into an ongoing video game contest. They were both always ready for the next round.

"No Michaels and no electronics. Catie is going to Disneyland with a group of her friends and Adam has some kind of trouble on his construction site." He turned to Kimberly and gave her a fake shudder. "I'll bet its Mrs. Anderson again." A long-time customer of Adam's, Rose Anderson had made her interest in Lance known—well known.

Peter's head shot up from his phone. "Why no electronics? What are we supposed to do for a week and a half?"

Lance was disappointed by Peter's irritated response. He had hoped Peter would be more concerned about Catie going to Disneyland without him. "This is family time, Pete, and its only two or three days. We've all been going our own ways for a while, and I thought it would be good for us to do something fun together."

"I think that's a great idea, Sweetheart." Kimberly patted his arm and smiled at the three boys. "Don't you guys agree? We can swim and ride horses and make S'mores over a campfire."

"I love S'mores!"

"I want the black horse again. His name is really John, but I call him Midnight."

"No electronics!?"

At Peter's second outburst, Lance pasted a smile on his face as he turned back to Kimberly. "I think it's going to be a long weekend."

"Anyone home?"

All five surprised faces spun to the doorway at the sound of the deep voice.

"Uncle Wolf!"

"We're going to the Golden Oak Ranch, Uncle Wolf! I get to ride Midnight again!"

"Hey, Wolf. Come on in. I didn't hear the bell."

Before he could enter, Wolf had to untangle himself from Michael's and Andrew's arms and legs that had instantly entwined him. He gave a glance at the silent Peter who merely smiled a brief greeting and returned to his phone. "Hello, all. Golden Oak Ranch, huh? That should be fun. I was actually looking for Omah. Thought she was here."

"Omah? I haven't seen her in a while. Have you, Kimberly?"

"Actually, yes." For a brief moment, Kimberly looked like a deer caught in the headlights. Omah wanted to do something special as a surprise for Wolf and asked for Kimberly's help. The two women had gone to the gazebo out back to put their heads together in privacy. "She left about half an hour ago." In front of the two youngest boys, Kimberly didn't add that Omah had just popped out of sight. At Wolf's questioning stare, she shook her head. "Sorry, Wolf, she didn't say where she was going."

There was a small grunt. "Then that would explain why I was led here." At the curious looks coming from the Michael and Andrew, Wolf knew he should change the subject. Out of the three boys, only Peter knew about his and Omah's ability to travel through time and space merely by concentrating on who they wanted and at what point in time.

At Wolf's uncomfortable silence and inability to come up with another topic, Lance stepped in. "How would you and Omah like to go camping with us? There's more than enough room in the guesthouse." With its one bedroom and a pull-out sofa, they all knew the house was barely large enough for Lance's family, let alone any guests. Adam and Beth always brought along a tent when they joined the Brentwoods.

Wolf gave an amused chuckle. Being a Lakota brave from the 1800's, 'camping' had been his way of life. Whenever he had any desire to do it again, he would just go back in time to visit his family on the River. "Thanks, but, no. But, it'll be a great chance for Andrew and Michael to learn more about the history of the Golden Oak Ranch. How Walt Disney bought it in 1959 and it's one of the last working ranches left in the film industry." He glanced over at Peter with the hope that his former excitement over all things Disney would kick in, but there wasn't even a flicker of interest or sign that he was listening at all. *Good thing I came here first*, he silently told himself. "I need Omah for a, umm, trip I'm going to take. But, since I'm here, Peter..." He stopped talking until the boy looked at him. "I have something for you. Since you're going out to the Ranch, this is a good time as any."

Peter's natural curiosity got the better of him. "Oh? For me? What is it?"

They all watched as Wolf pulled a small black book out of a pocket. Kimberly and Lance felt their hearts speed up. The little book looked familiar. Very familiar. Their eyes flew to Wolf's face, but he was looking only at Peter. Aware of the younger boys, Wolf had to be vague. "It's from an uncle. And it's just for you."

Michael and Andrew let out a disappointed groan. "Why does Peter get all the fun stuff?"

"How do you know its fun?" Peter's retort had been automatic as he stared at the book in his hands. He had immediately seen that it was the same size as all the clues he had found in his Hidden Mickey quests. Curiosity now warred against apathy. After his scare in the Castle, for a year he had kept away from anything remotely Disney. And now Wolf had just placed something Disney in his hands. Without even opening to the first page, he instinctively knew it had something to do with Walt.

He just had to decide if he was going to follow where it led or not.

"Uncle Wolf? Can we go drive your car?"

Michael's question broke the silence that had overtaken the living room. With the exception of Andrew, everyone else was staring at the book in Peter's hands. Since it wasn't meant for him, Michael wasn't overly interested. "Can we? You promised us another lesson."

Hearing the boy, Wolf pulled his eyes off Peter's unreadable face. He couldn't tell what Peter was thinking and looked to Lance for some indication that the book would be accepted.

Lance could only shrug. "He's fourteen."

"He's good at it." Wolf turned back to the eager faces of Michael and Andrew. "Next time, guys. I have to leave. I need to go find Aunt Omah." The classic Mustang wasn't in the driveway and he didn't want to have to explain where it was. "Lance, I need to get going. I might be gone for a while on my…trip."

Understanding Wolf's meaning, Lance put a hand on Michael's shoulder before he could dart out of the room and head for the front door. "Well, have a good time, wherever you're going. We'll take care of things here."

Wolf nodded a good-bye to everyone and turned toward the front of the house. With their attention back on Peter, no one thought to question why they didn't hear the front door open or close.

After a gridlocked hour drive north on Interstate 5, Lance gave a sigh of relief as he merged onto the Antelope Valley Freeway and told the younger boys to look for Placerita Canyon Road. The Brentwood's Escalade was met at the gated entry to the Golden Oak Ranch by a security guard. All the signs read Private Property and No Trespassing. After the necessary identification was given, they were escorted through the winding, dusty roads. They passed the log cabin near Pine Lake, the newer Residential Street, and the Big West Meadow before arriving at the Main Office. North and slightly east was their guest house. Mario, looking much older than when Lance and Adam had first met him over fifteen years ago, eagerly shook their hands. "So good to see you again, Mr. Lance. So, what do you think of our little ranch now, huh? Much bigger now. You think Mr. Walt would approve?"

"I think Walt would like it a lot."

That pleased the old foreman. "Let me introduce you to my replacement, and then you can go to your little house. Will you be wanting horses this time?"

Once introductions had been made and a day and time set for the horses, Lance slowly drove north. There was a strict speed limit so no billowing dust would interfere with any filming that might be going on. The black Escalade already had a gray coat over its surface, so Lance didn't mind the snail's pace. His thoughts were back in time to 2002 when he and Adam had followed one of Walt's clues out to the Ranch. He had been driving a black Mercedes at the time—his pride and joy—and remembered how filthy it too had become. There had been a capsule hidden in the attic of the guest house, and Walt had deeded the small house and pool to whoever discovered the clue. That had been an exciting time for him. He wondered what it was Walt had in store for Peter who remained silent in the rearmost seat.

Andrew and Michael noisily splashed in the small, rectangular pool as their parents relaxed in the shade of a nearby pine tree. A light breeze carried the tangy scent of crushed pine needles as Peter wandered off by himself. The black book, with only about twenty or so pages left inside, was deep in his ever-present backpack and weighed heavier on his mind than it did on his back. The cover had already been opened as the creases on the spine attested, but not by Peter. He had accepted the book from Wolf without any promise of what would be done with it. It had to be a clue search, another Hidden Mickey adventure. Even without looking at the contents, he just knew that would be the case. But, what would he do?

The events of a year ago, when he had been attacked by Maleficent and forced to destroy what he had thought was a priceless animation cel, still troubled him. "It was all fake." That had been his big, disheartening discovery when he found it had all been a trick by Maleficent, or Nimue, as she was also known. It was all done to get him to lead her to something he had never even heard about—a red diamond necklace. He still didn't know what that was. She had put him under a spell. His friend, Lisa, was put under a spell and made to do her bidding. His life had been threatened. His friend Catie had been hurt by his actions and had gone away in tears. He knew that clue search had been construed by Maleficent, not Walt. He knew the animation cel had also been her doing. But, still, a year later, it still bothered him to his core.

"How am I supposed to believe anything is real now?" Alone in the woods, Peter grabbed up a pinecone and tore it apart scale by scale as he continued to mutter out loud. "I couldn't even tell the difference between something from Walt and something from… her." The abused pinecone was hurled into the bush. "How can I believe it now? I know Wolf gave the book to me, but, what if it wasn't really Wolf?" With a disgusted shake of his head, he kicked at a rock. "Ow. Stupid. Of course it was Wolf. She wouldn't dare pretend to be Wolf."

With no one else around in the carefully constructed forest, Peter started to feel a little better as he got his confusing thoughts out in the open. He had talked to his mom. He had talked to his dad. He had talked to Wolf, but none of that had helped. It had been too new, too fresh of a wound. Even a couple of sullen trips back to Disneyland hadn't helped. He was still wary, suspicious of everything around him. "What if this is a real quest from Walt? But, why would Wolf just hand it to me? I thought I was supposed to find the first clue hidden somewhere. That's the way it usually happened."

Peter flung himself onto the leafy ground and was immediately diverted by a line of ants as they worked their way through the jungle of twigs, needles, and leaves. Pulling back his foot, he kept out of their way as they busily went their way preparing for something only they understood. "I'm bored."

No, you're not. He had to smile when his mind instantly corrected his outburst. The whole family loved coming out to the Ranch. Deep inside he looked forward to the horseback riding early tomorrow morning before the heat of the day would settle in. *What if the quest from Walt is really cool?*

A groan would have been heard if anyone had been close enough to his location. "Man, I can't even convince myself that I'm not interested. Okay, one little peek."

Leaning back against the nearest tree, Peter's hand went straight to the stashed book. "I'll just read what it says and then decide what I'm going to do. Nobody has to know one way or another."

Despite his desire to remain aloof, his heart began to speed up when his fingers closed over the cover. *Walt wrote this.* As he began to read, the ants, the vista that spread out below, and his family all faded into the background. Eyes wide, he could only mutter, "OMG."

"***H**ello, Peter,*

I was told you're going through a rough time and I'm sorry to hear that. Sometimes things happen to us that we just don't understand. From what Wolf has said, I know you've learned a lot about me and my life, so you know I've been through the mill a few times, too.

I can tell you this, though, that all the adversity I've had in my life, all my troubles and obstacles have strengthened me. You may not realize it when it happens, but a kick in the teeth may be the best thing in the world for you.

You can overcome whatever it is that's keeping you down. You're young and that's the best time of life! Wish I was young again, knowing what I know now. But, that isn't possible. It's up to the youth of today to take care of tomorrow.

I met you when you were running one of my little Hidden Mickey quests. Catchy name, isn't it? Hidden Mickey. I like that! I saw your determination to finish the quest, even though it meant you had to travel through time with our friend Wolf. Not that I ever imagined something like that was possible—and I have a pretty vivid imagination, if I do say so myself!

This letter and this quest are meant to help you get your determination back again. You will go to many different places that are dear to me. I hope you will look around and appreciate what you see and where you go. Learn from the experiences. What you do with what you see is up to you. You know you can count on Wolf if you get stuck. And probably your mom, too. She looked like she had a pretty good head on her shoulders.

One of my favorite songs is "When You Wish." It tells us that we can follow our dreams and make them come true. Do you want to know the secret to making dreams come true? It can be summarized by Curiosity, Confidence, Courage, and Constancy. To me, the greatest of these is Confidence. When you believe in a thing, believe in it all over, implicitly and unquestioningly.

So, Peter, make your wish, then have the confidence and courage to go after it.

I hope you wish to complete this Hidden Mickey quest I have made just for you.

If you are willing, here is your first clue:

We needed a bridge for the first movie shot at my Ranch, so I built one*.*

Best wishes for you, Walt"

Early in the morning, before anyone else was awake, Peter used his banned phone to access the Internet and research Walt's clue. He now understood why Wolf had given him the little book before their trip. As Wolf knew, he was already at the right spot. The research told him where on the Ranch he needed to go and a handy map showed him how to get there.

When the ranch hands arrived with the horses, Peter was impatient to get moving. His family saw the return of some liveliness and hoped for the best. Communication from Peter had been sparse, if at all.

There was a television commercial being shot in the new Business District, so the family kept to the trails in the north of the Ranch. They wound past the Covered Bridge and the Piney Woods as they headed for Pee Wee's Farmhouse. When the younger boys started to explore the Mess Hall, Peter excused himself and took off at a ground-eating lope due north. There were five points of interest up that way, but he was only interested in one of them: Toby

Tyler Bridge.

Lance and Kimberly watched as he rode off, a look of hope mirrored on their faces. "Stick to the main road," was Lance's hollered comment before he turned back to his family.

Peter had found that *Toby Tyler* was the first movie filmed at the Golden Oak Ranch back in 1960. The bridge had been used for the circus to get over the creek. What he didn't know was what to look for or where.

When he reached the white wooden bridge, he dismounted, took off his riding helmet, and tied his buckskin to a nearby oak tree. The horse immediately dropped her head and started to munch on the abundant green weeds under the tree.

The white gravel road Peter had been following crossed the bridge and turned a sharp right as it continued to the Camp House and Natalie's Cabin. The bridge itself was unimpressive. Two horizontal beams that prevented travelers from falling off the sides of the bridge were held up in place by five posts. Three L-shaped beams stood out from the sides to give the structure strength. Under the bridge was a rocky streambed that probably would have been cool and inviting on that warm day if it had been full of water. But, no water was needed for any movie, so it was dry.

A slow walk across the dusty planks revealed nothing hidden or mysterious to Peter. After another unproductive pass, he jumped down into the rocks. A flashlight was pulled out of a pocket and used to light the beamed underside of the bridge. It was all a uniform, if slightly grayish, white. Under the top layer of rocks, the bed of the stream was hard-packed earth and more rocks. Anything buried would be difficult to locate. Peter aimed the light upward again. His mind on the clue, he ignored the nagging thought that there might be snakes or spiders that had claimed this unused part of the Ranch as their own. His curiosity had gotten the better of him, just as Walt had hoped.

At the halfway point under the bridge he found what he thought he was looking for. A flat container was nailed to the underside and painted in the same white as the bridge. It felt like plastic in contrast to the bridge that was made of wood. A few tugs with his fingertips did nothing but add a splinter to his hand. Going back to the napping horse, Peter picked up his backpack from where he had dropped it. Using the flashlight, he dug through the mess until he found something that might work: a bottle opener.

Back under the bridge, whistling the beloved song from *Pinocchio*, he used the sharp end of the opener to dislodge the container. With a muttered, "Gotcha," it fell into his outstretched hand. The impromptu victory dance was cut short when he banged his head on the lowest beam. "Shoulda left my helmet on."

As he rode sedately back to his family, the opened capsule safely buried in his pack, the next clue circled through his mind. Usually he could tell *something* about the where or what of a clue, but this one stumped him.

"**Which Mask would you choose: Comedy or Tragedy? I'd prefer to laugh.**"

His contemplation ended when his dad came galloping up the road to find him. "Pete. We've got to go. There's been an accident. It's Catie."

Chapter 2

"This isn't Anaheim."

Walt tugged the collar of his jacket tighter against his neck as soft, white snowflakes drifted across his vision. A sense of wonderment filled his mind as the confusion from the abrupt transition dissipated. One minute he was in his office at the Studio, the next he was in some kind of dark tunnel with a curtain of white in front of and behind him.

Wolf took an unobtrusive step closer to make sure Walt was all right. As far as he knew, the trips through time were now fairly painless. Before Omah had showed him a different way to travel, the swirling vortex he always used had been dizzying, disorienting, and usually ended by being unceremoniously dumped onto a cold, wet riverbank. Plus, as an added bonus, he could choose to come out the other end as a man or a full-grown wolf.

Other than his wide, wondering eyes, Walt seemed fine. He had clung to Wolf's arm as instructed, expecting to disappear in a shining, shimmering mass of pink sparkles. Now that they were at the apparent end of the trip—or more correctly, the beginning of something spectacular—he was eager to get moving. It was getting colder by the moment.

"What gave it away, Walt? I wanted to surprise you."

Before Walt could reply, someone riding a small scooter appeared out of the snowflakes. It was Omah, wheeling into the tunnel to greet the two men.

"What happened to your legs?" Concern overcame Walt's eagerness as he hurried over to her.

"Oh, I'm fine, Walt. This is for you. We have a lot of walking to do and thought this would help." Omah got off the bright red, three-wheeled mobility scooter and motioned for Walt to take the seat.

He balked. The glance he shot at Wolf was less-than-cooperative. "I'm quite capable of walking, Wolf, and you know it. I'm not an invalid yet."

"Never said you were, Boss." Wolf knew he had to tread carefully. "As you said, this isn't Anaheim. Out of concern for how tired you've been, we thought this would help. We just wanted you to be able to see everything. That's all. We literally have a lot of ground to cover. There's a heated blanket to go over your legs that's plugged into the battery of the scooter. As you already saw, it's snowing."

"Give it a try, Walt. It's actually fun. If you don't use it, I will."

Wolf and Omah were each on the receiving end of a glare as Walt tried to keep from rubbing his hands together to warm them. "Heated blanket, huh? How come you brought me to the Arctic? What does this have to do with Disneyland?" Without waiting for an answer, he tentatively sat down on the black leather seat, still warm from Omah. The controls were simple enough to figure out as he wheeled back and forth a few times and then did a complete circle around the couple. Like a kid with a new toy, a smile overtook the frown he had been sporting. "Hey, this is kinda fun! Where's that blanket you promised me?"

Crisis averted, Omah helped tuck the blanket around Walt's legs. Just as the warmth started to seep into his legs, a whistle sounded above them. A familiar whistle that echoed through their arched space.

Walt let out a loud, "Ha! I know that whistle. That's the *C. K. Holliday*! Thought you said this wasn't California. So, what happened to California's weather in the future? How'd it get messed up so badly that it's snowing?"

"That probably is the *C. K. Holliday*. But, this isn't California. Come on this way, Walt. And take that scooter off Bunny Speed." Wolf pointed at a small, gray knob on the right side of the control panel. "Put it on Turtle. We don't want to run all day to keep up with you."

A crowd of people suddenly entered their tunnel and ignored the threesome as they headed toward the other end, the same one Wolf had just indicated. Walt watched them go by and could see eagerness and anticipation on each and every one of their faces. "I couldn't understand a word any of them said," he muttered to Omah as they followed at a more sedate pace. "Where are we?"

The snow still fell in lazy flakes as they emerged into the blue light of a winter's afternoon. Walt was silent as he slowly looked around the panorama that had unfolded in front of him. "It's so... so big. It's so...so beautiful."

The scooter inched forward as a wide-eyed Walt took in Town Square covered with an enchanting layer of snow. "Look, the horse-drawn streetcars and there's my Omnibus!" As the first moments of surprise and delight passed, the builder in Walt took over. "I like the design of the buildings. Look how elegant City Hall is. This all seems newer than my Main Street, a little bigger with more frills, like it's a different period in time. Hmmp, not much of a train station, though..."

As they headed down Main Street, Walt read off the names of the different buildings as he passed them. It didn't take him long to spot another similarity. "Hey, they did the window tributes."

As they proceeded, his voice became softer and softer. When he suddenly stopped and fell silent, Wolf came closer. "Something wrong, Walt?"

A tear slowly fell down Walt's cheek as he looked up at one of the windows. "Must be the snow." He swiped at the moisture as his eyes filled again. "I just saw Lilly's Boutique and Flora's Boutique. And, look at that window. Dr. Sherwood. He was the first person to believe in me as an artist. He commissioned a picture when I was very young. It was his horse. And there he is...there they all are...after all these years they're still remembered." He felt a warm hand on his shoulder.

"We remember everything, Walt."

Walt pulled his eyes from the tribute and looked down Main Street at the tall structure that adorned every Park. Now that they were closer, it became more defined through the falling snow.

Wolf smiled over at Omah. She gave him a big grin. "That's what we wanted you to see in the snow. Well, one of the things. Welcome to Paris, Walt."

"Paris? France? I...I got so excited I forgot to ask. We...we made it to Paris?" There was a catch in his voice as the scooter surged toward *Le Chateau de la Belle au Bois Dormant.* "Lillian and I love Paris. I never imagined..."

"That's Sleeping Beauty Castle, Walt. She's 167 feet tall." Omah held hands with Wolf as they approached the towering pink and blue Castle, the colors almost indistinguishable in the layers of snow. Leaning closer, she whispered into his ear. "This was a good thing to do, Wolf. I know we went back and forth about it, but, I think he'll rest easier now. He'll realize he does matter and will be remembered."

Before Walt could zip through the Castle's entry, Wolf called him back. "Hang on a minute, Speedy. There's one last thing I want you to see before we go."

Walt couldn't take his eyes off the Castle. *Roy, we made it to Paris!* "Go? What do you mean go? We just got here. I haven't even ridden the train yet. Do you think they'll let me drive it?"

Wolf took a stand in front of the scooter. By the familiar gleam he could see in Walt's eyes, he figured—correctly—that Walt would just take off. "It's freezing, Walt, and you know it. We only brought you here in January to show you how beautiful one of the Parks looks in the snow. It isn't something you'd ever see in California."

"Then let me stay and enjoy it."

Omah had to hide her grin. She, as well as Wolf, recognized Walt digging in and getting ready for battle. "Boss, we have another plan for that. Once Wolf shows you the next surprise, we'll go..." She held up a hand when Walt was about to object again. "We'll go to the Disneyland Hotel, set up camp, and come back tomorrow. Only it will be in April. You always said you love Paris in the spring."

Walt took a moment to analyze the option just presented to him. "Disneyland Hotel, huh? We'll still be here, but in the spring? And you'll actually let me ride something?"

"Rides, yes. Drive the train, no. And, a different Disneyland Hotel."

There was a distinct grumble when Walt heard he couldn't drive his beloved train. A slight frown on his face, he looked away from the Castle to stare into the distance as an unpleasant realization came over him. His shoulders rose and fell in a silent sigh. "I suppose I'm not really Walt here, am I?"

Wolf nodded that he understood. At this point in time, Walt was gone. His status as a public figure was the stuff of legends, but not as the living, breathing boss. Now he was just another guest amongst the thousands. "You are to us, Boss. Come on. I want to show you something in Adventureland."

"Do I get to ride the Jungle Cruise, Warden?"

That earned a chuckle. "No Jungle Cruise here. We're going to Adventure Isle and you'll see La Cabane des Robinson."

"I understood Robinson out of that. No Jungle Cruise? Why not? Hey, what's that ride? That's new."

"Indiana Jones and the Temple of Peril. We'll go over there later. I wanted you to see…this."

Past rocky outcrops and a bubbling waterfall, a lone, majestic tree rose from the lush landscaping, an active waterwheel carrying bamboo canisters of water up to the highest branches.

"I see why you wanted me to come in the winter. The Swiss Family Treehouse covered in snow! It's beautiful. I don't suppose you'll let me go up there now."

Wolf clapped him on the shoulder. "Tomorrow, Walt. When it's nice and sunny and warm. I just wanted you to see the beauty of the Park in winter." He looked over at Omah. "You all set to take us to the Disneyland Hotel?" Wolf knew to leave the minute details of their trip to Omah. Even though he had been using her traveling technique for over a year now, this trip with Walt was too important, too fragile, to possibly mess up.

"Yes, all set. I already checked into the room so we don't have to go through registration, and the scooter will come with us. We just have to find a quiet spot to, uh, go."

As Wolf and Omah looked around for a good place to vanish from sight, Walt continued to gaze longingly at the Treehouse. 'Tomorrow' seemed like such a long ways away. When he heard "inside Skull Rock," he reluctantly followed them along a smooth walkway. As they meandered behind the Pirate Ship, he was reminded of the Chicken of the Sea ship moored back home in Fantasyland. Once they entered the darkened, empty corridors of Skull Rock, his stomach growled. "Hey, any chance of getting a tuna fish sandwich? I'm hungry."

The Skull vanished from sight before he could get an answer.

"No, it's not right. Omah should have the bedroom. I've slept on sofas before. You've slept on worse."

"It's all right, Boss. The sofa pulls out into a sleeper, just like in your apartment."

"But, you and Wolf can't share…" Walt broke off and looked away. Omah and Wolf were adults and it wasn't up to him to say what they could or couldn't do.

Before Wolf could say anything else, Omah motioned at him. "I think I know what's bothering him." She walked over to the red and white-striped sofa where Walt had positioned himself. Heavy burgundy swags framed the window behind them. As she sat next to him, she held out her left hand. "I guess you'll be the first to know, Walt. Wolf and I got married!" She wiggled her ring finger to show off a two-carat princess-cut diamond nestled in a filigree bed of emeralds.

Walt's face broke out in a wide grin as he took her fingers and examined the beautiful ring. "You did? Why didn't you let me know? I would have sent…" Her hand was dropped as he reached up to scratch his head. "Well, I guess I wouldn't be able to send a wedding present, now would I? Well, anyway, best wishes to you both. Tell me about the ceremony. I love a good story." When Omah started to laugh, he looked at them both with an odd expression on his face. He didn't think he had said anything remotely funny. "Did I miss something?"

Omah waved her hand as she went over to Wolf. He wasn't sure why she found their ceremony so amusing, either. "Oh, don't scowl, Wolf. You'll get worry lines." She took him by the arm and drug him over to the matching sofa across from the one where Walt still sat. "I'll tell it. You would have loved it, Walt. You know about Wolf's family, right? Oh, maybe I should have asked about that first…" She broke off and looked to Wolf for clarification.

"Yeah, Wolf's mentioned his father is the Shaman and how the Friendly Village on the Rivers of America represents them. They're his link to the past. Right, Wolf?" Receiving a nod, Walt had another intriguing thought. "Any chance of meeting them now that you know you can take me places?"

Wolf's groan was accompanied by rolling eyes. "I knew I'd create a monster by allowing you to go with us on one trip. We'll see," was his only answer to Walt's question.

"I've been a dad and a grandfather long enough to recognize that as meaning no."

"Hey, can we get back to my wedding?"

"Our wedding."

"Yes, dear." Omah flashed a bright smile as she pushed her blaze of crimson hair off her shoulder. "Our wedding." She turned back to Walt, her face lit up by the enthusiasm of the telling. "You see, we were just planning to visit with his family and showed up as wolves just for the fun of it. You should have seen his father's face fall when he saw Wolf's big, black body run into camp. He had been so happy his son could travel as a man that he thought something had gone wrong and he'd never get to see Wolf's charming face again. So, we just went into one of the tents and popped back out as humans."

"You can change that quickly?"

The grin on Omah's face had a bit of superiority in it. "Oh, I learned how to do that years ago…"

"A *LOT* of years ago."

Into her story, Omah ignored Wolf's mumble. "Now, the last time I had seen his father, we had a bit of miscommunication. I had mentioned that Wolf and I had been fighting and that Wolf had beaten me…"

"What?"

"Yeah, his father's face looked just like yours, Walt."

"Maybe I should take over the story. You're drifting."

"I am not, Wolf. I'm telling the backstory. Right, Walt?"

Walt still looked disapproving. "What do you mean that Wolf beat you?"

"Well, we were wolves, and you know I've had a bit of a temper…"

"A bit?"

She shot a look at her husband. "Fine. I had a temper. Anyway, it was just the natural thing to do under the circumstances and Wolf ended up the victor due to his larger size…"

"Fighting ability…"

"Don't interrupt, dear. Anyway, as I was saying, his father was happy to see us again and under friendlier terms. When he found out a year had passed since he had seen us, well, one thing led to another, and we told him we were engaged. So, he insisted on us getting married right then. At least, that's what I think he said. I'm still rusty on my Lakota."

Wolf's face was a blank mask of pure innocence. "Yeah, that's what he said."

Eyes narrowed, Omah didn't quite believe him. "The Cooking Woman…"

"The one stirring the big pot?" Engrossed in the tale and the connection to the scene on the River, Walt had to interrupt for clarification.

"Yes, that's the Cooking Woman. She got the women together and hauled me into one of the tipis to get me ready for the wedding." Omah smiled at the remembrance. The whole camp had been so pleased Wolf had finally found someone. She had been dressed in an off-white, fringed dress, and feathers were arranged in her hair. The entranced look on Wolf's face when she emerged was also something she would likewise never forget. "You know the rocky outcrop where the Shaman tells his story, Walt? That's where the ceremony was held. The whole camp stood behind us. I'm not sure what all was said, but Wolf's father united us in holy matrimony. At least, that's what I think he did…"

"Sure thing, honey." Wolf patted her hand as he winked at Walt. "There's nothing my father likes better than long, drawn-out ceremonies. Yep, that's where she promised to love and obey me for the rest of her life."

"Obey? That was in there?"

Wolf put an arm around her shoulders to give her a squeeze. "Yeah, that and a few other things. Hey, don't look at me like that. Maybe you should have brushed up on your Lakota."

Now that the story was over and before they could get into it, Walt stood and yawned. "Well, I'm happy for you both. I think you'll have a grand time together. So, if we're all set on the rooms now, I will go to bed. I want to be ready for tomorrow." Walt headed for the cream-colored door that separated the two rooms. Hand on the golden doorknob, he stopped and turned back. "And, thank you. You have no idea what this means to me."

"**W**hat do you think he's doing now? Think he's asleep?"

Wolf let out a small chuckle. "As excited as he was, I'd bet any amount he's standing at the window staring out at the Park."

"You're probably right." Omah smiled as she looked at the connecting door. "Did you see the look on his face when we pointed out that this suite was called Walt's Apartment? It hadn't sunk in how much it looks like his place over the Fire Station back home."

"We just have to make sure he doesn't grab any souvenirs to take back with him. I don't know what effect that would have on the future."

The fond smile had turned into a worried frown. "Wolf? Do you think we did anything wrong by bringing him here? Do you think there'll be any changes when we take him back?"

Wolf thought for a few moments before he answered. "I hope not. I went over all of that with him before I agreed to make the trip. Walt said he understood the seriousness. If anything is said or done when he goes back, he could affect this whole future." He had to shrug his shoulders. "We'll just have to make sure when this is over."

"You told me what happened when you, Lance, and Peter went back to the Haunted Mansion and met the Gracey's. When you came back to our time, the Mansion was gone."

"Yeah, there was that." Wolf let out a long breath. "We'll have to rely on our memories, too. Last time, no one else realized anything had changed. We won't be able to ask Lance or Kimberly. Even though they're the Guardians, they won't know any different."

"We're taking a big chance."

Wolf glanced over at the closed door. "Yeah, but I think it's worth it. You didn't see how dejected he was when I went to get Peter's quest. He doesn't know how little time he has left. I'd rather give him a happy memory—albeit a secret one—than let him continue to be depressed."

Omah went over for a hug. "I think you're right. We'll just deal with whatever we have to later."

The ringing of Wolf's phone ended their discussion for the moment. After glancing at the caller ID, he put it to his ear. "What's up, Lance?"

Omah listened in the half of the conversation she could hear.

"I wasn't in the Park today... Well, not Disneyland, anyway... Paris...No, Paris, France. Not Paris, Texas." Wolf smiled over at Omah. Apparently Lance hadn't expected that. "Yes, I mean France... With Omah... What do you mean how soon can I be home? Why? What's wrong?" Omah watched as Wolf's grin faded to a look of concern. "What happened to Catie? Is she all right? What... Yes, I can be there in a couple of minutes. Where are you exactly? I need exacts, Lance, or it won't work. What's the date and time... Okay, see you in a few."

"What's wrong? What happened to Catie?"

Wolf still stared at his phone even though Lance had already ended the call. "I...I don't know. There's been some kind of accident. I have to go. I can be back before the morning. I think..." Wolf ran a hand through his hair as he looked at her. "I think I can be back. Can't I?" Usually the one to stay calm in a crisis, Wolf's emotions had begun to cause doubts in his abilities. He had heard Beth and Kimberly in the background and they both had been crying.

Knowing Catie held a soft spot in Wolf's heart, Omah held his hands in a steady grip, a composed expression on her face. "You can do this, Wolf. But, you can't let your sentiments get in the way. You won't end up where you want to." She spoke slowly and clearly. "Focus on Lance and what he just told you. You can react when you get there." She could see Wolf's uneasiness and wondered what he hadn't told her about the situation. Torn by the desire to go to her friends, she looked over at the suite's door. "I want to go with you, but I think I'd better stay here in case Walt wanders out during the night."

"You have your phone, too, right? If I mess up, I can still find you?"

"You'll do fine, Wolf. Go see your friends. They need you."

Wolf took a step away from Omah and closed his eyes in concentration. His focus solely on Lance, he took a deep breath.

Then, in an instant, he was gone.

Chapter 3

Anaheim

Without a sound and barely a movement of air, Wolf appeared inside the sterile hospital room. An unwelcome feeling of déjà vu swept over him as his mind went back to the similar room that had been Walt's—a room from which his boss had never emerged.

With an irritated shake of his head to get rid of that horrible memory, Wolf turned his attention to the small, still person engulfed by white sheets and a labyrinth of tubes and monitors. "Catie."

At the sound of the whispered word, Peter jerked up from his position in the chair next to her bed. "Uncle Wolf? Is that you? Oh, Wolf, it's all my fault."

Wolf, unable to tear his eyes away from the ashen, bandaged-covered face, felt Peter hurl himself against his body. His arms instinctively closed around the boy.

"You're crushing me."

The muffled words filtered through to Wolf's brain and his arms loosened their grip. "What happened? What do you mean it's your fault?" Knowing Peter as well as he did, sensing the boy needed to talk, he looked down into the upturned, troubled face. "How could this possibly be your fault?"

Peter waved a vague hand toward the bed. "Catie...Catie wouldn't be here if it wasn't for me. She should have gone to Disneyland with me, not those other guys. But I didn't want to go to Disneyland any more. I...I pushed her away. She could have been out at the Ranch with us, not with Anne and her brother."

"Slow down, Pete. No matter what, this isn't your fault. You can't think that way."

Peter didn't seem to hear Wolf. "I didn't even tell her about that quest you gave me."

"Can you tell me what happened? Why is she here? Like that..." Wolf again forced himself to look away from the still, pale face to focus back on Peter.

"That idiot brother of Anne, Scott, he did this. They were coming back from the Park and he was showing off what his dad's car could do. It wasn't even his car!"

Wolf could tell Peter was on the verge of getting too worked up again. "Slow down, buddy. Take a deep breath. So, Catie was with Anne and Scott. Then what?"

Angry, Peter shook his head. He had just heard bits and pieces from eaves-dropping on his parents and Uncle Adam and Aunt Beth. They hadn't wanted him to hear the details. But, he did. "He...he was speeding down Harbor and the light on Lincoln turned yellow. Instead of stopping..."

"He ran the red light." Wolf felt his stomach twist into a knot. He knew what was coming.

Peter's eyes filled. "Yeah, he ran the light. I guess the other cars were already moving... The police said he was doing sixty when Catie got T-boned." When Wolf drew in a shocked breath, Peter realized he needed to clarify a point. "Well, the other car hit the back tire on Catie's side, but it was almost the same thing." Peter had to swallow before he could tell the rest of what he knew. "The car spun around, smashing her head into the side window." He swiped at his eyes. "That's why she's all bandaged up like a mummy. Her right arm got broke, too."

Deeply affected, it took an effort to keep his voice calm for Peter's sake. "Has she spoken to anyone? Did she come to?"

A look of confusion swept over the boy's face. "Come to? Uncle Wolf, she...she's in a coma."

The steady *beep, beep, beep* of the heart monitor was the only sound in the room. Wolf took Peter in his arms for another hug, one that he felt he needed as much as Peter might.

"Wolf! I didn't see you come in." Kimberly and Lance had softly pushed open the door to Catie's room. A wave of relief washed over them when they saw Peter in his arms. The boy had claimed sole responsibility for the accident and hadn't listened to a thing they had said. Perhaps Wolf would be able to help. Peter had sworn he wouldn't leave her side until she was better.

With Adam and Beth nowhere in sight, Wolf could tell them, "I came in a different way." At their nod of understanding, he indicated Catie with a tilt of his chin. He didn't want to let go of Peter just yet. "I heard some of the story. When did this happen? Where are Adam and Beth?"

Lance looked over his shoulder at the door. All of their movements seemed stiff and unnatural. "We sent them to the cafeteria for a break. They've been here since midnight. Once the kids were brought here to Anaheim Regional Hospital, it took some time to sort out who was who. The accident happened around 10:30 when the kids were on their way home."

Kimberly had a hard time pulling her eyes away from the bed. They all have known Catie and her brother Alex practically from birth. To her, the kids were an extension of her own family. "The driver, Scott, is only seventeen. I'm not even sure he was supposed to be driving. The only saving grace, if there is one, is that the car was an older Dodge Charger. The thing was built like a tank. Anne, who was in the back seat, and Scott are pretty banged up, but… not like Catie." Her voice cracked. "She got the brunt of it."

"Where are the boys?" Wolf's question earned him a blank stare. Under the high emotions and the shock, he wasn't surprised. "Michael and Andrew? You know, short, have green eyes, brown hair. Live in your house. Make a lot of noise."

The moment of humor helped. Lance walked over and put his hand on Peter's head. "They're with a sitter. This one refused to stay home."

Wolf could tell Lance was proud of his son for wanting to be there for his friend. "I think I'll go down to the cafeteria and see Adam and Beth."

At his words, Peter pulled away from Wolf and silently returned to the chair by Catie's bedside.

Alex, Adam, and Beth sat close together at one of the aluminum tables, assorted drinks forgotten in front of them. When someone approached their table, three pairs of haunted eyes looked upward. Hope flickered across their faces and then vanished. Their smile of recognition barely moved the corners of their mouths.

"Wolf. Thank you for coming." Adam didn't seem to know what else to say. His eyes strayed back to a paper cup filled with cold coffee.

Beth looked like she had aged ten years. The feisty, sarcastic, bubbly personality had been extinguished. "Have you…have you seen Catie?"

Wolf could only nod and held out a hand. In an abrupt move, Beth sprung from her seat to bury her head in his chest. "I'm so sorry, Beth. I don't know what to say."

"My little girl. That's my little girl, Wolf."

His arms tightened. "I know." He looked up at Adam. "Pete said she's in a coma?"

Adam's head bobbed once. It seemed to be the extent of movement he was capable of. "Yeah. When her head…" He broke off, his lower lip between his teeth, and looked away. "When her head hit the window, it caused swelling in her brain." Alex scooted over and leaned against his dad. "The doctors felt a medically-induced coma would be best to let her brain recover. They're giving her controlled anesthetics. At least…at least she can't feel the pain from her broken arm and all the cuts."

"I heard Scott and Anne…" Wolf was stopped by the intense look that came over Adam.

Beth saw it, too, and went back to the table. Picking up Adam's hand, she kissed his knuckles until the furious expression faded from his face. "We've talked with their parents. It's…difficult…for all of us. They're mortified by what happened. Scott and Anne have, gosh, I don't know who has what. There are broken arms and legs, cuts on their faces and bodies. Maybe broken ribs, too. I don't know. This is the first time we've left Catie's room."

"Peter seems to be taking it personally."

A small, fond grin briefly touched Beth's lips. "That sweet, silly boy. He hasn't done much with the twins for almost a year now. You know that." At Wolf's nod, she sighed. "Well, nothing that has to do with Disneyland, anyway. We were invited to go camping with them yesterday." Her eyes filled with tears. "Maybe we should have gone with them and none of this would have happened."

Hearing his wife's distress, Adam came out of his stupor. "We'll kill ourselves with the 'what ifs,' Sweetheart. We can't do that. We have to be strong, as strong as we can, for Catie." He squeezed her shoulders. "All right? I love you. Hey!" He jerked back when Beth wiped her nose on his shirt sleeve.

"I love you, too, Adam."

After giving the family their moment, Wolf wondered where Adam's parents were. As close as the family was, it wasn't like them not to be there, especially in this time of crisis. "John and Margaret?"

Adam glanced up from the mess on his sleeve. "Vacation. I called them early once we knew… something. They'll be here later today."

"Mom? I'm going back to Catie's room."

"That's a good idea, Alex. We'll all go." Beth made a move to clear the table. "Maybe you and Peter can tell her a story. The nurses said we should talk to her as much as we can."

"I'll get that. You guys go ahead. I'll see you a little later." Wolf watched the family as they left the cafeteria. He needed to check in with Omah to tell her what had happened.

It was dark in the hospital room when Wolf reappeared. The clock on the wall indicated it was 3:15. Expecting it to be only an hour or so later than when he left, he pushed his confusion aside for a moment to check on Catie. There seemed to be less tubes and monitors around her bed. The extra bed that had been brought in for Beth had been removed.

A loud sniff from the window drew his attention. Outlined by hazy moonlight, Peter leaned against the windowsill, gazing upward at the night sky. After swiping his sleeve across his eyes, he looked back at the stars.

"Wishing on a star, Peter?"

Even though Wolf had spoken in a whisper, Peter spun around as if someone had shouted, "Boo!" Eyes wide, his hand clamped over his mouth to keep from yelling out. "Gosh, Uncle Wolf, don't do that! My heart's pounding out of my chest."

"Sorry."

Instinctively they both looked at the bed, but there was no reaction from its sleeping occupant. The steady *beep, beep* of the monitor remained unchanged.

"Where've you been, Uncle Wolf? We've missed you."

Wolf felt his mouth fall open and he had to make a conscious effort to close it. Before he answered, he had to recheck the clock. "It was supposed to be just a couple of hours. I seemed to have overshot it somehow."

"Hours? Uncle Wolf, you've been gone for a week."

How'd I mess up again? I was just with Omah. Wasn't I? I haven't even taken Walt back into the Park. Wolf ran a hand through his black, silver-tipped hair. "A week? Well, I'll try to figure that out later. That might explain why Catie looks better."

"Yeah, her bruises started to heal up and they said she didn't need life-support anymore. She's kinda doing better, but she still hasn't woken up." The worried look returned to his face. "She doesn't move or make any sounds. Shouldn't she be up by now?"

Not knowing how to answer the questions that plagued them all, Wolf glanced back at the time and then at the darkness outside the window. He changed the subject. "Are you all taking turns staying with Catie? Is that why you're here at this hour?" His eyes narrowed when Peter suddenly looked sheepish.

Peter's immediate attempt to school his face into innocence failed. "Yeah, sure. It's my turn."

"Peter Percy Brentwood."

There was a dramatic sigh as Peter turned away to roll his eyes. "Why don't you believe me?"

"You're fourteen."

"Oh, and that means I'm a liar?"

"What I mean is that you're only fourteen and your parents wouldn't let you stay here overnight like this. You obviously didn't drive here. So...."

"Okay. Fine. I rode my bike. Hey, it's only five and a half miles from our house." Before Wolf could say anything, Peter surged onward in a desperate effort to keep the criticism at bay. "I come almost every night to talk to Catie." He looked back at the bed. "Aunt Beth said they were going to transfer her to the Placentia-Linda Hospital closer to their house. I...I've just been talking to her about my quest. I really miss her."

Wolf shelved all the objections Peter expected to hear. He could see Peter was slowly trying to work out his feelings of guilt—undeserved as they were—by trying to help his friend. The lecture on safety could wait a bit. "So, how is the quest going? You making progress?"

"Well, I was. Then I got stuck."

"On which clue?"

"The second one." Peter gave a little laugh. "Yeah, I know. Lame. But I just can't figure it out. I come here to talk to Catie about my research and what I've found. I thought it might, I don't know, help her somehow because that's what we used to do together." His shoulders raised in a helpless shrug. "Maybe I'd figure it out if I talked about it out loud. Maybe she'd wake up and help me."

Even in the darkness of the room, Wolf could see his eyes fill with tears. "I think that's a good plan, Pete. But..." He smiled to himself when Peter stiffened at the word. He knew it was coming sooner or later. "But, you can't be riding your bike in the middle of the night like that. You know it isn't safe. I'm guessing your parents don't know where you are, right? How do you think they'd feel if they went into your room and saw that you were gone?"

Still determined that what he was doing was all right, Peter didn't hang his head at the mini-lecture from Wolf. "I know that, Uncle Wolf, but I have to be here. She's my best friend."

Wolf pulled him in for a hug. "You're a good friend, Pete. But, if you want to come like this, let me know so I can bring you."

Peter looked up at his face. "You mean that? Even in the middle of the night?"

"Yeah, I mean it. Catie does need you. She's missed you, too."

"Thanks, Uncle Wolf. So, I can stay?"

Wolf looked back at the clock. "How long have you been here?"

"Umm, since midnight."

"Is there anything else you wanted to talk over with Catie tonight?"

Relieved he wasn't in trouble, Peter shrugged again. "No, I don't think so. That's why I was staring out the window."

"When you wish..."

"Hey, I wasn't wishing on a star! I'm not five."

Wolf gave him a smile. "It might not hurt. So, you ready to go?"

Peter walked back to the bed and touched Catie's undamaged

arm with the lightest of pressure. "I'll see you soon, Catie," he whispered. "Uncle Wolf is going to drive me home. I'll let you know what I find out. Bye." He turned back to Wolf. "So, where's your car?"

"I didn't come in my car."

Peter broke out in a delighted grin.

Chapter 4

Disneyland Paris

"No souvenirs, Walt. They'd be difficult to explain once you got home."

Yvette, the cast member who accepted their passes at the front turnstile, turned to open the small iron gate to allow Walt's scooter to go through. A student of human nature, she had been instantly intrigued by the odd threesome as they approached the Park's entry. It had been obvious that the dark, handsome man was linked to the pretty redhead, but she couldn't figure out their connection to the grumpy older man. The group had been in the middle of an animated, obviously ongoing discussion about the direction their day should go with the man in the scooter being the dissenting vote. The dark one had put out a hand to stop the older one from taking a free park map and had received a glare for his efforts. Focused on the older man, Yvette didn't think he could be the father of either one of them. Their looks were all wrong for that close of a connection. Long-lost uncle? Distant cousin? Were the younger ones caregivers with an attitude? Whatever their relationship, she knew they were all in for a long day. When Yvette gave the gray-headed man a sympathetic smile, she was surprised when he winked back at her. Before the other two could push through the turnstile, he briefly pulled open his jacket to show a brochure securely tucked inside. Eyes twinkling, his forefinger briefly touched his lips to ask for her silence. Yvette had to bite her lips to keep from laughing as he pulled his face back into a scowl. "Have a magical day, mon'ami." As Walt rolled away, she gave an airy wave to Wolf and

Omah as the group headed for the tunnels under the train tracks. *Oui, they're in for it*, she grinned as she turned back to the next guests who waited in the queue.

Emerging from the tunnel, Walt stopped the scooter to fully appreciate the engaging scene that had unfolded in front of his eyes. Now that it was spring, the obscuring layer of snow was gone. He could see the manicured grass and flowers of Town Square and the full effect of the colors on the elaborate Main Street buildings. "This never gets old."

"What's that, Wal...Wally?" Wolf momentarily forgot that they had agreed not to call Walt by his proper name. It was just a precaution in case someone thought he looked familiar.

"This view." Walt rolled over in front of the train station so he had the full perspective all the way down to the Castle. "I'm glad to see the original concept was kept." He fell silent, suddenly overcome by strong emotion. Not sure what year they were in, he had accepted the fact that he was no longer in the picture. In his mind, as he sat there with that grand panorama in front of him, a certain blond-haired man—Kimberly's father—stood next to him. Walt could almost feel the man's hand on his shoulder. "We did it," Walt muttered to his invisible right-hand man. "All our hard work, all the sacrifices we made. We really did it. It's even beyond what we imagined. Thank you, old friend."

"You say something, Wally?" Wolf's sharp hearing had, of course, heard every word. He just wasn't sure if Walt needed a moment. All of it had to be overwhelming, this shift through time and the physical proof of something he hadn't even dreamed possible.

Omah stepped closer to Wolf, a concerned look on her face. She, too, had caught what Walt had said to himself. "Do you think this is too much for him? Do you think we should go back?"

Before Wolf could answer, Walt stood from his scooter and walked over to them. "No, Omah, I'm all right. And, yes, my hearing is still sharp." Whatever they were going to say in their defense was waved away. "No, never mind. I appreciate your concern, but I'm fine." His eyes drifted over to where his apartment would have been over the Fire Station. "I was just saying thanks to a mutual friend of ours." After an appreciative thump on their shoulders, Walt turned to stare at the open, airy train station. He realized, once they went up the steps, that the huge pink and white Disneyland Hotel would be visible. Always comparing, he shook his head in disgust. "My station is better. Let's go ride. You really think they won't let me drive?"

Wolf had to reposition the scooter from where Walt had left it in the middle of the walkway. He grabbed the key before rushing up the steps after Omah's and Walt's retreating figures. The *W. F. Cody* had just come to a steamy stop and Walt didn't want to miss it.

Walt was pointing out the moose painted on the train's large, square lantern. "So, Omah, did you know it all started with a moose?" At her confused look, he let out a light laugh and turned to Wolf. "Have Wolf here tell you that story some day."

"Walt, did you see the names of the carriages? *Silverton, Durango, Denver, Wichita,* and the *Cheyenne*. Each of the trains has themed cars to go with the engines' names."

His boss, however, was more interested in what the engineers were doing inside the cab. Once the passengers had disembarked, the gate was slid open and Walt had to settle on the first carriage behind the bright red coal car. The disappointment dissolved when the train entered a tunnel and Ferd Grofe's *Grand Canyon Suite* began to play. "The murals are wonderful," as he leaned forward to see all the details in the painted Grand Canyon Diorama. "There're more animals, but they got every scene right."

From the tunnel they emerged at the backside of Frontierland and the River, stopped at the rustic station in Frontierland, continued through the tunnel that went over their Pirates of the Caribbean, and stopped next in Fantasyland. Wolf caught Walt's intrigued, "Ooh," before the trip resumed and carried them through the façade of It's a Small World. Discoveryland Station was next and Walt's head seemed to be on a swivel as he tried to take in everything. "What's that? Hey, look, Autopia. What's that green tower? It looks like something out of Jules Verne. I see lots of room for expansion. We're back at that hotel again. Hmmp. Shoulda made the berm higher."

Once Walt was reseated in the scooter, Wolf guided them to the side of Main Street.

"Hey, I want to see the storefronts."

"You will, Wally. I just wanted you to see the Liberty Arcade."

Expecting an arcade like his Penny Arcade filled with novelty games, a Kiss-O-Meter, and the old-time mutoscope movies, Walt's mouth fell open when they entered the covered walkway. He tried to take in all of the elegant designs, hanging lanterns, and arched window displays. "The Statue of Liberty. 1886. This is wonderful. This is like what I wanted to do at Disneyland off of Main Street with Liberty Square and Edison's Corner, but I just didn't have the money at first. And, then, different projects took over and I haven't gotten back to it yet."

"On the other side of Main Street is Discovery Arcade. Edison is over there, along with Westinghouse. You'll love it."

"It's like they knew what I wanted when they built this." Once the words came out of his mouth, Walt glanced up at Wolf. "But, they did know, didn't they?"

Wolf and Omah simply nodded as they slowly progressed through the walkway.

The mobility scooter's speed had been inching faster and faster as they got closer to Fantasyland. Walt thought he had the upper hand until Wolf reached over and put the speed indicator back on Turtle.

"There's something I want you to see before we go through the Castle."

They had stopped in front of the wide, welcoming bridge over the moat. Walt pulled his eyes from the square-cut trees that dotted the green hill sweeping up meet the side of the Castle. It looked as if the beautiful structure had been carved out of the rocky soil. Off to the right, on the other side of the moat, was a small gazebo.

"I saw what looked like a labyrinth from the train."

"Yeah, there's that for later, but that's not what I wanted you to see. Let's go down to the dungeon."

"Dungeon? They have a dungeon?"

Wolf's words had the desired effect. Walt was intrigued.

"Follow us down this path. Welcome to La Tanière du Dragon."

Surrounded by rocky crevices and jagged stalactites, a chained dragon slept near a pool of calm, green water. Her wings tucked back, the horned tail curled out of sight. Bones littered the flat rock on which she slept. Hidden blue, yellow, green and orange lights kept the mood of the cavern dark and eerie. Before Walt could comment, the red, angled eyes slowly opened and steam rose from her tipped nostrils.

"She's seventy-two-feet long and weighs over five thousand pounds. And, no, you can't get closer to check her out!"

Walt grinned over at Omah. "I know. I know. Much as I'd like to." He waved a hand to indicate the subterranean cavern. "Now this is what I would love to do back in California. Think there's any way I can squeeze this in under Sleeping Beauty Castle, Wolf?" Before his companion could answer, Walt headed up the stone walkway. "I want to go check out Merlin's shop."

"How'd he know there was a Merlin's shop, Wolf?"

Wolf's blue eyes narrowed as they watched Walt wheel away. "I think we need to watch him a little closer. He might have slipped in a guide book or map when we weren't looking."

Omah tucked her arm through Wolf's. "At least he's enjoying himself."

"Let's just hope we didn't open Pandora's Box." Wolf pulled her closer. "I'm enjoying myself, too. So, which do you think he'll want to do: Ride le Petit Train du Cirque or go on Le Pays des Contes de Feés?"

"Casey Junior or Storybook Land, right? Still working on my French. Oh, the train, of course. No question."

"Hey, are you two coming or not?"

"Yeah, Wally, we're coming." Omah gave a light laugh as they headed back toward the sunlight.

"**W**ell, I recognized *Snow White*, *Babes in the Woods*, *The Old Mill*, *Fantasia*, *Peter and the Wolf*, and *Sword in the Stone*. Not sure what those other references were."

"They're from some of the newer animated movies that have come out. *Little Mermaid*, *Beauty and the Beast*, *Aladdin*, and one about Rapunzel. How come you're grinning like the Cheshire Cat?"

Walt looked back at the canal boats as they were beginning their trip. The Casey Junior train they had just exited was already in motion again. "You just told me something else about the future. My legacy of animation will continue. Gosh, I always wanted to do *The Little Mermaid*. There's a script somewhere at the Studio." Wolf and Omah heard a bark of laughter as Walt headed back to Le Carrousel de Lancelot. He had been fascinated by the intricate, armor-covered lead horses on the outer row. His carrousel had one lead horse, Jingles, but this one had a whole herd of them. "But, then, you probably found my script by now, right? I want to go on Peter Pan again, too."

"Why in the world did they do that to the flying ships? You don't need a double row of seats. Ruins the design and prevents the guests in the back row from seeing everything."

Wolf put a hand on Walt's shoulder. "Walt..."

"Wally."

"Wally, you're here as a guest, a spectator. You're not going to rebuild it or redesign anything."

"Whenever I go on a ride, I'm always thinking of what's wrong with the thing and how it can be improved."

"I know that, but here you're just a visitor, all right?"

Walt let out a snort as he headed for Les Voyages de Pinocchio. "At least they didn't mess up this one. You know, there is one thing I appreciate."

"What's that, Wally?"

"That the Imagineers honored my request to never have a statue of me anywhere."

Behind Walt's back, Omah gave Wolf a wide-eyed *oh dear* look and hastened to change the subject. They'd have to deal with that later. "How about if we head to Toad Hall? It's over by the train station. I'm getting hungry."

Walt's head whipped around. "What does Mr. Toad's Wild Ride have to do with food?"

"This elegant, Tudor-style mansion is actually a restaurant."

"No Wild Ride? Why not?"

As they got in the short line to order fish and chips, Omah gave a small shrug. "Every Park isn't an exact copy. There are the basic elements, as you saw, like Main Street leading to the Castle and the Lands spreading out from the Hub. There are a lot of the same rides. But there are also different rides and different designs in all the Parks to make them unique."

Walt let that sink in for a moment. "How many Parks are there? Can you tell me that?"

Omah checked with Wolf and got the go-ahead. "There's one in Tokyo, Japan, and they're building one in Shanghai, China. You know about Florida, of course."

"Florida." He flashed her a sly grin. "Surprised you brought that up. Thought it might be a sore spot for you."

Back in the early 1960's when Omah had failed to complete an easy quest Walt had assigned her, he had banished her to the Florida project. In its infancy, she had many years to wait out until the Park was up and running. It had been only recently that she had been able to track down a key element of that quest that had been lost and return it—thanks to her unusual ability—to Walt.

"Yeah, well, let's not go there. That was a long time ago."

"Water under the bridge, right?"

"Lots of water." As they headed for a table by the front windows, her disgruntled mumble could be clearly heard.

"Speaking of water," Wolf interjected to deflect the mood that threatened to descend upon Omah, "how about if we head over to Discoveryland and tour Les Mystères de Nautilus."

"I got Nautilus out of that." Walt looked up from his crunchy fish filets. "Would that be the submarine I saw from the train? I didn't see a lagoon big enough for my submarine fleet."

"No fleet here. They recreated the *20,000 Leagues Under the Sea* exhibit inside of the Nautilus sub you saw."

Uninterested, Walt made a face. "I saw that at home. What's in that big green building over there?"

"That's Space Mountain. It's a high-speed roller coaster."

"A roller coaster inside a dark ride?" Walt suddenly remembered saying those exact words to Wolf as they stood together in Tomorrowland not that long ago. At the time, he had just come out of a deep, long-range vision caused by the red diamond heart pendant. As he had stared up into space that day with Wolf, he recalled fragments of a vision-induced ride—the ride that apparently now stood in Discoveryland. The special ability of that pendant still mystified him, even though he had proof that much of what it foretold about the future had come true. Aware that two pairs of eyes stared at him, Walt shook off the vision that was always there in the back of his mind to tease and tantalize him. "I always wanted to do one of those, but we just don't have the technology. How high-speed?"

As they rose from the table, Wolf wondered what Walt had been thinking. He had seen a look of revelation come and go over his boss's face. "It's pretty intense. It gets up to fifty miles per hour in some spots. I'll bet you can't guess the name of the first passenger." Wolf dumped their trash into a nearby themed trash can. A smug smile crossed Walt's lips when he saw the handy placement of the can. That had been one of the myriads of ideas he had put into place that were obviously still in effect in every Park.

"Considering I still don't know what year this is, I wouldn't take that bet."

"It was Thumper."

That stopped Walt in his tracks. "Thumper? From *Bambi*?"

Wolf grinned at Walt's incredulous expression. "Yep. That Thumper. One of the Imagineers wanted to see what a passenger would go through and what condition he would be in when he returned." He let out a laugh. "So, they strapped in a stuffed Thumper and filmed the whole thing. Thumper's ears would fly up, flatten back, and then move all over the place. That way they could see the experience the riders would have."

Walt nodded. "That's smart thinking. When I wanted to test a ride, they'd make a wooden mock-up of the ride vehicle and then push me through the scenes at whatever pace the ride would run."

"So, what do you think: Frontierland and the *Mark Twain*, or Discoveryland?"

"Well, I'm for both, but let's go see their *Mark Twain*. And I want to get a closer look at what you called Big Thunder. A newer version of my Mine Train, huh?"

They decided to cut through Adventureland first so Walt could ride Pirates of the Caribbean. When they continued their trek to Frontierland, Wolf regaled his boss with the Disneyland Paris backstory of the Phantom Manor. Walt was soon immersed in the tale of the curse of Thunder Mesa, Henry Ravenswood, and his engaged daughter. Once the disapproving Henry had been killed and the daughter's fiancé vanished, she never took off her wedding dress and wandered aimlessly through the Mansion, an evil phantom stalking her every move.

The mobility scooter suddenly veered past the Thunder Mesa Riverboat Landing and headed around the River toward the Manor. "Okay, the *Mark Twain* can wait."

"Wolf! Hey, Wolf. Is that you?"

Stopped in his tracks, Wolf recognized the voice. A foreboding of disaster traveled down his spine. "Get Walt out of here!"

At his hiss, Omah, her fingers laced through Wolf's, glanced over her shoulder to see who it was. "Oh! What's he doing here?"

"He built this Park. I suspect he's a regular visitor. And, there's no doubt in my mind that he'd recognize Walt. There isn't any way we can explain this. Get Walt out of sight and into the Mansion."

Omah hurried to catch up with the scooter. Walt, oblivious to the peril, had stopped to admire Phantom Manor. "I like the dormers on the third floor and the attic. The design looks like it could have come out of the Midwest. Not sure I like the dingy brown wood compared to my white antebellum mansion."

Peeking back over her shoulder, Omah could see that Wolf had used his body to partially block their view. "Hey, the line's not very long. Let's go inside."

"Where's Wolf? Didn't he want to come?"

About to start pushing the scooter herself just to get him moving, Omah fiddled with her purse to give her hands something else to do. "Oh, he'll catch up."

Once Walt and Omah were far enough away, Wolf planted a smile on his face. "Tony."

The Imagineer shook hands with Wolf. "This is a surprise. I don't usually see someone I know here in Paris. Say, who was that with you? I thought I recognized the face."

"You mean my wife, Omah?" Wolf knew that wasn't who Tony meant. But the tactic did seem to work.

"Wife? I didn't know you were married. Congrats, man! Long overdue." Tony looked from the retreating backs as they neared the entrance. "Who's that with her? That's who I thought I recog..."

Wolf had to think fast and blurted out the first name he could think of. "Omah's uncle. Uncle Ninaawa." He had just called Walt 'Uncle Man.'

Before Tony could respond, the spring breeze carried a sound over the two men. It was a sound anyone who ever knew Walt would instantly recognize.

Walt coughed.

Eyes narrowed in suspicion, Tony turned back to Wolf.

Chapter 5

Fullerton

Peter stared at everything he had grouped together on his desk. It wasn't a vast array. This particular collection consisted of a small black book, one piece of paper torn out of said book, a plastic canister half painted white, and an iron key. The key's smallish size belied its importance. His fingers idly played with the cool metal as he recalled all the hidden, forbidden places it had taken him so far. He tapped the key up and down on the desktop as his mind repeated the words 'so far.' He fully discerned that the complete role of the metal object had not yet been fulfilled.

The key had come to him during one of his Hidden Mickey quests—so like the one waiting for his next step. It had been a special gift from Walt to assist him, or whoever found it, in their mission to complete the assigned tasks. The Key to Disneyland. It would open any door, any lock, in the Disneyland Park and the Burbank Studio. There were possibly only three or four in existence. No one knew for sure. As the foremost Guardian of Walt, Wolf, of course, had one. The current president of the Disney Corporation would have one. And, for a little over a year now, Peter, a fourteen-year-old freshman in high school, had one.

The excitement he had felt when he realized what it was had been great. But, his possession had been brief. Deemed too young and impulsive, the key had been hidden until such time as the Guardians felt he was ready and able to assume the responsibility that went with ownership.

In spite of the angst he was going through, Peter's lips turned up into a half-grin. His mom's hiding place had been easy to find. He looked off into the distance, the grin fading. Had she wanted him to find it? She hadn't known much about the quest he and Catie had been following, but had been supportive in the parts she did understand. Perhaps Kimberly had decided having the key to use would have been better than having to force his way into a room or a building.

Catie.

The key dropped onto the wooden desktop with a metallic *ping*. The spark of interest that he had just begun to feel again extinguished. His partner was hurt. Catie wasn't there to bubble over with enthusiasm or send him exclamation point-filled emails when one of them discovered something vital.

He knew, deep down, that Catie's accident wasn't his fault. The realization was also there that the trials they went through at the hands of Nimue were not his fault, either. But, acknowledge them or not, the long-range effects were still in place. Peter had been spooked.

An index finger pushed the small black book around as the same questions again bombarded his mind. Was the book real? Or was it just another trick? Was Wolf under the same type of spell Lisa had been subjected to? Who could he trust?

So far the quest had been fairly straight-forward. The first clue, pretty much solved by Wolf's words, had led to where it was supposed to lead. It had been ridiculously easy. The clues set in place by Nimue hadn't been terribly difficult, either. Should he view that as a red flag and refuse to go any further?

Did he *want to* refuse to go any further?

Peter knew he was at a crossroad. His decision now would dictate his future as either a Guardian of Walt or as a.... *Hmm, what will I become if I don't follow in the footsteps that started with my grandfather? What will I be when I grow up?*

Heady questions. Some of his friends already knew what profession they wanted follow. Tim wanted to be a policeman. Rayne wanted to be a professional dancer. Dawn was into fashion design. Chloe had hopes of getting into law school. The classes they took reflected their determination to make their dreams possible. Other friends, like Jason, Stewart, and Brad, had no direction in mind.

Their focus was on the next weekend.

Up until a year ago, if asked, Peter would have told everyone that he was going to work at Disneyland like his parents. Lance was a security guard partnered with Wolf. His mom used to be a meet-and-greet princess, but now trained the newer, younger women who would fill the tiara. Only the family knew that the posts Lance and Kimberly, and also Wolf, held were façades to cover their more important role as Guardians, to protect Walt and what he had put into place decades ago.

But now? He had no idea. He hadn't even considered any other place he wanted to be but Disneyland.

"It's not supposed to be this hard."

Peter didn't realize he had spoken out loud until the family's Golden Retriever, Dug, awakened at the sound and softly whined. Her plumed tail thumping the carpet, he bent down so he could pat her massive head. "Are you going to help me, Dug? Do you want to go to Disneyland with me and try and find the answer to this clue?"

Excited by the word 'Go' out of all he said, Dug heaved herself to her feet. After turning in a full circle, she planted her paws on his shoulders so she could better lick his face. Her weight almost pulled him out of the chair.

"Okay, okay. Didn't mean for you to get all excited. Down!"

Not the command she wanted, Dug's ears flattened back and her tail drooped as she headed out of Peter's room to look for more agreeable kids. Michael always left some nice, smelly socks on the floor. Maybe he would play with her.

"Was it something I said?" Peter considered calling back the disappointed dog, but sighed instead. Playing with Dug wouldn't solve his dilemma. It would only prolong whatever decision he needed to make. Not that that was such a bad Idea. Procrastination was a longtime friend of Peter's. They had a wonderful understanding between them. Procrastination would be embraced until the very last moment, and then Peter would thrust it aside to do whatever was needed. They both knew the system that had worked so long and so well.

"I could be a professional pitcher for the Angels. Quarterback for the Rams? I know. Driver at Indy." The laugh that spurted from his mouth surprised Peter. He knew those were ridiculous life choices for him. "Can't hit the side of a barn, couldn't throw a straight pass to save my life, and I don't know how to drive." He fingered the black book that teetered on the edge of his desk, ready to fall to the carpet. *This is what you always wanted. Why don't you want it now?*

Walt's book was pushed back to safety. Instead of rereading Walt's personal message, he picked up the clue he had found under Toby Tyler's Bridge. "**Which Mask would you choose: Comedy or Tragedy? I'd prefer to laugh.**"

He still had no idea what that meant. Not knowing on which part to focus—Mask or Comedy or Tragedy—he was stumped. With a disheartened shrug, he turned to his computer.

After typing in 'mask comedy tragedy,' he was inundated with images of two masks apparently from the days of Greek theater. The smiling one, he found, was named after the muse Thalia, and the frowning one was Melpomene. His eyes began to cross the more he read about the origins of the theater masks. "What does that have to do with Walt?"

With a groan of 'duh,' he added Walt to the search engine, but the results were still confusing. "I don't get it. Shouldn't I have to go to Disneyland or the Studio? There are theaters in both places. That's where I went last time."

Frustrated again, he added the word Disneyland to the search. "Oh, that's more like it." Staring at the computer screen, a spark of excitement began to override the apathy of the previous year as Peter felt his heart rate speed up. "Now what do I do?"

The first picture the search engine displayed was the Opera House on Main Street. And, bracketed by Baroque-like ornamental arches on the very apex of the building, were a smiling face and a frowning face. Three stories off the ground, Peter knew this had to be what Walt meant. The Opera House had been the first building completed during the construction of Disneyland and was used a much-needed, on-site lumber mill. Now it was the home of Mr. Lincoln. The offices in use on the second floor had a lovely view of Town Square.

Deep in thought, his fingers idly pushed around the Key to Disneyland on the desktop as the computer screen faded to black. "I can get backstage easily enough with or without Mom or Dad. The doors leading into the buildings back there aren't locked, but any access to the roof should be. I'm pretty sure this key can get me up there." Moving his mouse, he glanced at the clock on the bottom of his computer screen. "I need to talk to Catie. Maybe she'd like to hear what I found." A small smile crossed his face. Catie didn't like heights and wouldn't have wanted to go up there with him—however he would end up accomplishing that feat.

Finding he was leaning close the computer, Peter sat back in his chair. Just then he realized something: He now knew that he was going to follow the clue to see where it led.

The nurses looked up as Peter walked into the High Dependency Unit. Catie had been moved to the HDU when her acute dangers were over. The subdural hematoma was still an issue, so she hadn't been placed in the Pediatrics Ward. He self-consciously raised a hand to greet the nurses as he entered the new room.

"Peter! You should've told me you were coming. We could have picked you up and ridden together." Kimberly, looking agitated, stood from her chair to stretch her back. Michael's eyes remained glued to the TV screen up on the wall, his fingers wrapped around a controller as the game they were playing continued. With an amused snort as she glared at Michael, she thrust her controller into Peter's hands. "Never trust an eight-year old who hands you a Wii stick and says all you have to do is press A."

"Then you won't want to trust Andrew, either." Not there to play games while they waited, Peter tossed the game's controller onto the table.

Kimberly had to smile at his warning. "That's probably true."

"Any news?" Peter indicated the silent Catie with a tilt of his head.

Kimberly's expression fell. "No change today. Catie's vitals are steady. Her brain waves are strong. She's doing better, but she hasn't awakened yet."

Peter took his usual seat next to her bed and looked around at the new flower arrangements in the room. There were also Get Well balloons secured in a far corner and a few stuffed animals, both from home and from her worried friends. She would have loved the bright, cheerful flowers. He, like everyone else, just hoped that she'd open her eyes so she could enjoy them. "Mom, can I, uh, talk to Catie? Alone?"

Kimberly knew better than to embarrass him by teasing. "Sure, honey. I'll bet she'll love to hear your voice." After ruffling Peter's hair, she pried the remaining controller out of oblivious Michael's hands. "Come one, Mikey. Let's go get some ice cream in the cafeteria."

"But we aren't done with our game!"

"Oh, yes, we are." Kimberly herded her middle son out of the room and gave Peter a grin behind the boy's back.

Once his family was out of sight, Peter turned back to the bed. "Hi, Catie. It's me. Peter. Peter Brentwood." He gave a self-conscious chuckle. "You probably knew that, right? How're you doing today? I see you got a new teddy bear from…" He went over to read the card. "Who's Jeffrey? Someone from school…that I don't know?" *Stop it, you sound stupid.* "I, umm, came to tell you something exciting. At least, I think it could be exciting, if I was excited about it…" He shook his head and started over. "I think I found out the answer to the next clue. Remember how it talked about masks and comedy and stuff? I think it means the top of the Opera House on Main Street. There are two faces up there and they look just like the pictures I found on the Internet. There were also some in Bugs Land, but that wasn't there in Walt's time."

As he paused to think about what else he could tell her, he listened to the steady, slow *beep beep* of her heart monitor. It was the only sound in the darkened, quiet room.

He placed a gentle hand on her good arm, the other still mending in a cast. "I just remembered you said you'd been in Drama in school. You were in a play last year. Can't remember which one you told me. Sorry. You probably would have recognized the masks right away, huh? I…uh…" Peter broke off and looked over at the door to make sure no one was standing there. "I miss you, Catie…and I hope you get better soon! I have to go. Mom and Mikey will be back soon. I need to talk Dad into taking me to Disneyland tomorrow. Wish you could come, too."

As he exited the room, he failed to hear Catie's heart monitor. The beeping was noticeably faster.

Disneyland

Lance couldn't read Peter's face. When Peter asked to go with him on his shift the next day, he expected to see some of the old anticipation and eagerness. The face next to him at the Security entrance off Disney Drive was almost expressionless. "You okay to go, Pete? You know what you need to do?"

"What?" Peter's mind was pulled from the mission ahead. He still wasn't sure how he would stay undetected by either the cast members or the thousands of guests milling below. "Yeah, I think so. You aren't going to come with me, are you?"

Lance hid his disappointment. He would have loved to assist his son. Especially a task like this where he needed to keep his wits about him. He and Adam had to recover a hidden clue inside that same building—only it had been inside one of the glass cases in full view of anyone who might have come into the room. *Man, those were fun days!* "Umm, no, not if you're sure about what needs to be done."

Peter's shrug could have meant anything. Yes, I know exactly. No, I don't have a clue. Whatever, I don't want to really be here. Lance merely patted him on the shoulder. "Do what you have to. And, don't get caught. There's only so much I can let you get away with. Uncle Wolf is still on his...well, whatever it is that he's doing. He can't help, either."

"I know." Focused on the rooftop, he didn't want to chat any longer. "Thanks, Dad. I'll call you when I'm done."

Lance grinned at him. "Or, someone else will call me."

Peter had to acknowledge that was a possibility. "See you."

Backpack firmly in place, Key hidden deep in a pocket, annual pass in hand, Peter joined the line of guests as they inched toward the entry turnstiles. He had wanted to be an anonymous tourist and not enter with a family pass. The deep honk of Monorail Blue sounded as it sped past the front entrance. Eager faces peered out of the windows at the floral Mickey face below the train station.

At the sound, Peter looked upward and suddenly wondered if the riders would be able to see the top of the Opera House. He hadn't expected that possibility.

Once he was inside the Park and through the tunnel under the tracks, he looked back. When he couldn't tell one way or the other, he ran up the brick steps to the train station, the highest point in the Park so far. He decided that the monorail track was too far away and not high enough to see over the train station, let alone the top of the building where he would be.

Relieved, he lightly ran down stairs and went to an unoccupied park bench in Town Square that faced the Opera House. From his backpack he pulled out a satellite map of the area that he had printed out at home. Looking back at the ornate building, he didn't see the line of children waiting for the tuxedoed Mickey Mouse standing under the awning of the neighboring Mad Hatter Shop. The horse-drawn carriage pulled by the huge Belgian didn't even get a cursory glance. No, Peter looked solely at the two faces set inside their oval framework. "Wow, that's really high. Okay, inside or outside?"

Peter decided right then to attack his problem from the outside, around back in the cast member-only section. Knowing the crowds that came to see the Lincoln show and the exhibits inside, he felt it would be easier to go in through the back. 'I'm looking for my dad,' would handle anyone questioning him since they were both so well-known in the Park.

At the side of the Disney Gallery, which used to be a Bank of America, was a souvenir stand, a walkway, and an exit for cast members. It was down that shaded, secluded path that he quickly walked. The satellite map reminded him that the building was deceptively larger than what showed from Town Square. About two-thirds of the way, he found a padlocked utility ladder stretching up the side of the white building. With no one in sight, heart pounding, he quickly got the lock opened and scampered up the metal rungs, fully expecting a hand to grab his ankle and pull him back to the ground.

Out of breath from nerves, he reached the top and scurried crablike toward the front of the building on the narrow catwalk. Once he was over the top of the Gallery, he found access to a path used by personnel when they worked on the air conditioning or other equipment on the roof. The masks he wanted were still another level higher than his walkway. It only took a few moments to find another set of steps that took him to a dizzying height.

Always expecting to be discovered, he flattened his body to the level roof and edged closer to the curved arches that protected the masks. "Right or left? Which one was Comedy? Oh, great. I can't remember. Sheesh."

Resisting the urge to peek over the edge to see the masks and what the view of Town Square looked like from up there, Peter concentrated on the back of the huge oval disc. While the faces of the masks were gilded in bright gold, their backing was simply painted white. At the base on the right side, behind Comedy, he found what he wanted. There, secured to the wood and painted to match the surrounding area, was a flat capsule. "Come to papa."

Once the canister was hidden in his backpack, Peter had to decide if he wanted to go back the same way he came, or try to find a safer place to get down, maybe near the hat shop. Feeling exposed due to the height of City Hall on the opposite side of Town Square, he chose the known route. Back at the access ladder, he peered both ways and had to wait for a costumed cast member headed for work at the Emporium. With a sigh of relief he started down the ladder.

"Hey, what are you doing up there?"

Thinking he was in the clear, only two steps to go, Peter's head jerked to the right. One of the Disney Gallery cast members had just come around for a break. Hands on her hips, she didn't look too pleased to see a young boy up on the ladder.

"You! Get down from there!"

Peter had to think fast. The 'I'm looking for my dad' line wouldn't work in this precarious position. "I…uh…thought I saw a cat on the roof."

The cast member, Laura, looked upward, obviously confused. "There're cats everywhere. It's dangerous to be playing around on the ladders. Where are your parents?"

Peter used an old trick. His lower lip began to quiver. "I…I only wanted to help the little kitty. Mom's over in the Emporium shopping. I…I didn't mean to hurt anything."

Laura rushed over to the obviously upset boy and put a kind hand on his arm. "There, there, it's all right. You didn't hurt anything. You just aren't supposed to be back here, honey."

"Oh, I'm sorry! I won't do it again. Thank you. Can I go find my mom now?"

Laura fell for those puppy-dog green eyes. "Yeah. You go find your mom. Here, would you like a Park button?"

Peter accepted the green *I'm Celebrating* balloon-covered button and flashed a smile, one well-honed by his dad. "Oh, thank you! Bye."

"Such a polite young man." Laura checked her watch and saw her break was over, forgetting the part with the boy on the roof access ladder.

Once clear of the cast member-only area, Peter pulled out his phone and called his dad. "Found it. Can I go ride Big Thunder?"

There was a moment of silence. Lance had expected to hear something else. "I guess. So, what did you find?"

"I dunno. Didn't open it."

Disappointed, Lance shook his head. "Yeah, sure. Go have some fun. Be here when I get off, all right?"

"Yeah. Bye." The capsule stuffed in the bottom of his pack, Peter didn't even look at the door to his secret apartment there on Main Street as he headed for Frontierland.

CHAPTER 6

Fullerton

"I found the next clue, Catie." It was just past midnight when Peter turned from the window. Now, thanks to Uncle Wolf, every time he looked up at the night sky the words from *When You Wish Upon a Star* played over and over in his brain. He shook his head in an ineffective effort to change the song. Maybe telling Catie about the heroics he had accomplished would silence Jiminy Cricket's crooning. "You would've hated it. Remember when I had to climb up the side of that pink building in Adventureland? This was worse and in broad daylight! It was just a metal ladder that went straight up to the roof. Did I tell you I almost got caught?" He paused, forgetting she wouldn't answer. With a cough to cover his momentary lapse, he pulled the white and gray capsule from his backpack. "Here it is. I haven't opened it yet. I wanted to do that with you...like we used to."

A surge of disappointment and sorrow suddenly flowed through Peter bringing him to tears. It was only two weeks since the accident, yet he half-hoped she would come around when she heard about something that had been so exciting before. When Catie and her monitors registered no response, the capsule was lowered from in front of her face.

Hopes crushed, his eyes dropped to the object in his hands. His desire to continue with the quest wavered. "I need your help, Catie. It's not the same."

Almost to the point of shoving the container back into his pack, Peter looked at her still features. She looked so peaceful. Sometimes it was difficult to remember why she was still in the hospital and that her major injuries were internal. With a determined sigh, Peter took a firm hold on the sealed end of the capsule. His voice quavered when he declared, "We *are* going to do this together, Catie. This is for you."

Paint covered half of the seal and it had to be loosened by constant back and forth jerks. With one final grunt and a shower of white paint chips all over the floor, the endcap released. In spite of himself, Peter gave a shout of victory. Heads shot up from the nurse's station as he belatedly clamped a hand over his mouth. Mouthing "Sorry," he sheepishly turned back to the bed. Not knowing if it was good or bad, there was no reaction.

Nothing happened when the capsule was upended with a shake. Peering inside, there was only a solitary, rolled-up piece of paper. "No little gift, Catie. Looks like it's just another clue." Leaning toward the open door and the light the nurse's station provided, he could barely make out the written words:

"He'll get the point in the end. Will you?"

Peter let out a snort of laughter. "That has to be the Jungle Cruise, Catie! One of your favorite rides. How about waking up so we can go on it together and see what we can find?"

He hadn't really expected that to work, but it was worth a try. "Okay, fine. Just stay there and rest. I'll do it." He lightly patted her arm. "At least it doesn't sound like I have to climb anything. That's a relief. Wonder if Wolf'll give me a hint. Probably not. He was supposed to drive me here tonight, but never called back. Don't know where he is."

The clue and the capsule were stuffed back into his pack. Another glance at the wall clock made him grimace. "Man, I need to get home. If Mom or Dad find out I snuck out again, they'll ground me for sure. At least the doctor didn't transfer you to the other hospital. This one's closer to my house. I'll be home in about twenty minutes. Rest up, Catie. Bye."

Peter leaned closer to his computer screen as if that would make the image clearer. "Is that the rhino or one of the elephants? Why doesn't this thing zoom in closer?" Frustrated, he shoved back in his chair. The same satellite image that had been so helpful before was now less-than-cooperative. With all the trees and overgrowth, it was impossible to make out what was where. "It's so thick I can't even tell the exact route of the river."

One of the Disneyland reference books Peter took from their library downstairs showed a less-tropical Jungle Cruise. However, the pictures had been taken before 1964 when the ride had undergone a dramatic change. The African Veldt and the Elephant Bathing Pool had been built in 1962, but the animals had to wait until the Imagineers were done with the New York World's Fair in 1964. The rhino that Peter felt was the key to his clue was originally meant to be partly hidden in plants on the berm and only seen from the Disneyland Railroad as the train circled the Park. But Walt had loved the rhino so much he wanted it included inside the Jungle Cruise so more people could enjoy it. It was during these years of change that the skippers were allowed to inject humor into their spiels. At first the skippers created their own material and that eventually led to an official script they all would use. To everyone's relief, the straightforward, educational tone was gone. Walt once said, "I would rather entertain and hope that people learned something than educate people and hope they were entertained." And people were delighted with those changes.

Peter was about to return all the books to their library when he noticed a magazine he had pushed aside. The cover depicted a rendering of the Jungle Cruise, so he quickly flipped through the pages. In the middle he found a two-page, black and white aerial view of the Jungle Cruise, boats and all. The year on the legend said it was taken in 1965, and off to the side was the skeleton of New Orleans Square being built. Peter instantly focused on the lower half of the fascinating shot. The African Veldt and the angry rhino were clearly seen. "Oh, that's not where I thought it was. I thought the rhino backed up to Main Street. It's actually on the lower part of the ride along the train tracks."

Peter stared at the picture as his finger traced the route of the boats. "Then, that's the charging hippo down on that bend, but I can't see Schweitzer Falls. The Falls have to be somewhere in here, because that's the loading dock up there."

The magazine was lowered. "I need to ride the Jungle Cruise."

Disneyland

Still hopeful that Peter would return to his curious, energetic self, Lance readily agreed to take the boy back to the Park. "Anything I can do to help?"

"No, I just need to go on the Jungle Cruise."

Lance's ears perked up. Years ago, he and Kimberly had spent the night in Tarzan's Treehouse during their Hidden Mickey quest. From the height of the middle hut, he had zip-lined into the Jungle and searched for one of Walt's hidden clues. "Did I ever tell you about my hunt to find El Lobo?"

"No."

After waiting a moment, Lance could tell this wasn't the time to go into his tale of daring-do. Peter was obviously only focused on what he needed to do. "Another time, then. Whatever you need to do, just keep out of trouble."

Peter gave him a quick smile. "Thanks, Dad. I'll see you later."

Lance watched his son run off to join the queue inside the boathouse. "Hmmph. I'm more excited about what he might find than he is." With a disappointed shrug, he headed to Tomorrowland to continue his security patrol.

"On your left is the most feared animal in the Jungle: the African Bull Elephant. And, for those of you with a short attention span, on your right is the most feared animal in the Jungle: the African Bull Elephant." There were some giggles as the *Amazon Belle* slid past the twin of the first elephant.

Skipper Lucie pointed ahead to a rocky wall. "Ahead of us is the entrance to the African Veldt. Let's see, those are giraffes and those are gazelles and, hmm, I don't know what those are. They must be gnu. Wow, our zebras are so old they're still in black and white. Aww, look how that pride of lions is protecting that sleeping zebra—the one with his neck bent at such an unusual angle... Hey, there's something you don't see every day. Well, I do. At least the hyenas think it's funny..."

The boat sailed past the Lost Safari as Peter used his phone to snap a couple of pictures. He strained to see the rhino as long as he could before they rounded a bend in the river and had to fight their way through a pool of dangerous hippos that wiggled their ears and blew bubbles. Lost in thought, the blank bullet fired into the air to 'scare that hippo hiding in the tree' startled him back to reality.

After a narrow escape from the whirling piranhas and hearing about the cannibal Trader Sam's marital troubles—"My wife made a terrific stew last night. I'm really going to miss her."—they arrived at the unloading dock. "For those of you who enjoyed my spiel, my name is Lucie. For those of you who didn't enjoy my spiel, well, names really aren't that important, are they? Now that we are safely back, get out. Oh, I'm sorry. That was rude. Please, get out."

Peter was smiling as he exited the boat. Catie would have enjoyed Skipper Lucie. Before he tried to figure things out, and always hungry, he walked over to the nearby Bengal Barbecue to order a chicken skewer. "Bummer," he mumbled when he noticed that all of the tables were occupied. Knowing there were benches along the River, he went around the corner to Frontierland. As he sat facing the River, the *Columbia* had just left the dock and was beginning her journey into the Wilderness. Peter could hear the sea chant playing as the huge boat passed his spot.

The skewer and soft drink were quickly finished; his sticky fingers wiped more on his jeans than the napkin included with the meal. "Now, let's see what the rhino can tell me," as he pulled out his phone.

From the research he had already done, Peter knew the Jungle Cruise animals were now made out of some kind of fiberglass. The rubber and plastic that had been used in the beginning cracked and split too easily. This solid-looking rhino in his picture couldn't possibly have any hidden flaps or holes in which to hide something. Or could it?

Peter looked up from his camera just as one of the rafts began its short, sputtering journey over to Tom Sawyer Island. "Would Walt have hidden the next clue *inside* the rhino? It's the rhino that has the point. Gosh, how am I supposed to find something inside a rhino?" Not realizing he had spoken out loud, he turned red when a passing family gave him a curious look. "Gotta quit doing that."

The next picture was a wider angle and included some of the natives chased up the pole. The last shot was blurred and worthless. A duck swam up to the edge of the River, hoping for some handout from Peter's trash. A loud *quack* got him to look up and smile. "Sorry, buddy, I ate it all." Not getting the desired outcome, the mallard quickly gave up, turned his back, and slowly paddled away, tail feathers shaking off the water.

"I need to see the rhino again." Peter rose from the bench to dump his trash into a nearby can. His steps faltered, though, when he reached the ride's entrance. "I've ridden it, like, a million times. I *know* what it looks like. This isn't going to help. I need to do something else."

There was an empty bench in front of the Adventureland Bazaar and Peter dropped onto it. The two-story boathouse that covered the winding queue of the Jungle Cruise received only a cursory look before he pulled out the magazine he had brought from home. As he stared at the aerial photograph, he began to reason it out. "Well, I can't jump off the boat like I did inside Pirates when that thief chased me. I have to get in there some other way." His face scrunched up. "Too bad it's so far away from Main Street. I might've been able to sneak in through those trees. The only thing the rhino is close to is the train tracks."

Peter felt his heart rate speed up before he actually voiced the thought that suddenly raced through his mind. *What if I got there from the train tracks? I could walk along the tracks... Wait, no, I can't. This picture is too old. There're a lot of buildings along there now...and people. I can't walk the tracks.* He felt his mouth fall open. *I'll have to get there from the back of the train. I'll have to jump.*

Nervous and jittery, Peter sat in the Main Street train station as the different trains came and went. There were three trains running that busy day with approximately seven minutes between each train. As he thought about what he felt he needed to do, he also focused on the passenger cars themselves. Two of the trains had Holiday-style seating that faced inward to the Park for easier, faster loading and unloading. One of the trains, the *E. P. Ripley*, had Excursion-style seating with benches that faced forward. Peter decided that would be the train to use. What he didn't realize, about fifteen or sixteen years earlier, was that his dad and Uncle Adam had gone through the same deliberations and came to the same decision when they, too, had to find a clue somewhere along the rail line.

Jumping onto the last car of the *E. P. Ripley*, Peter's heart drummed in his chest, his mouth dry. "I'm going to get in sooooo much trouble." With a squealing jerk, the train started on its journey round the Magic Kingdom. The quaint buildings of Main Street quickly disappeared from view as the train entered the overgrown trees of the berm. Peter barely heard the recorded voice welcome him and describe the wonders to be seen as the train continued. He heard a shot from a Jungle Cruise skipper and knew he was passing the charging hippo. "The Veldt is next."

Peter tried to peer through the trees to see exactly where he was, but the berm was too high for the low seats on the train. All too soon he was through a short tunnel and stopped at the New Orleans Square station. "Wow, that was fast." He stayed in his seat as the conductor walked the length of the train to assist the guests.

The rest of the trip was a blur. Peter could only focus on what he felt he had to do. The Grand Canyon and the dinosaur panoramas unseen, and back at Main Street, he exited the train. "What do I do now? I can't jump in the middle of the day when someone could see me and I can't jump at night. I wouldn't be able to see anything."

Digging the Key to Disneyland out of a pocket, he let himself into his apartment above the Market House. The lace window coverings hid his presence while he stared down at all the activity. "Do I ask Dad for help? No, he'd never let me do something like that. He wouldn't understand." His mind ran through some of his previous exploits and his parents' reactions when they found out. "They had this weird look when they found out I jumped inside Pirates. I thought they'd get mad, but they just had some kind of secret smile on their faces." *Parents are weird sometimes.* "No, I have to figure this out myself."

As the sun began to set and a few of the sparkling lights lit up the buildings around him, Peter had an idea. "It's still kinda light out. Maybe now would be a good time."

Before he could talk himself out of it, he hurried back to the near-empty train station. A lot of guests were either at dinner within the Park or on their way out to one of the many restaurants around the area. He had to wait for the *Ward Kimball* to depart before the *E. P. Ripley* came to a steamy stop. Most of the tired riders opted for the seats nearest the entry. There were only a few passengers with Peter in his end car.

With only moments before his jump-off point came, his ears were buzzing from nerves. "Don't think. Don't think. Don't think."

He found himself almost at the tunnel before hurling over the backside of the rail. Rolling in the gravel, he came to a stop against the opposite side of the berm, curled into as small a ball as he could. When there were no yells or squealing brakes from the train, he felt it was safe to peek out. All he could see was the back of the train as it continued through the tunnel.

Run! His mind was already in gear before his feet caught up. Using vines and roots, he clawed his way up the berm until he found a thick clump of brush to hide behind. When the pounding in his ears began to lessen and he could actually hear again, the shot from the skipper sounded a long way away. "Man, I really overshot it."

Low to the ground, he kept to the thickest bushes as he worked his way to the rhino's location. Hidden from view, he could hear the sputter and whine of the engines as the boats passed by.

When he finally reached the back of the Veldt, his phone began to loudly play the theme from Star Tours. "Oh shoot! Oh shoot!" as he tried to get it to stop before some sharp-eared guest passing by wondered what that sound was. His voice a muffled gasp, he answered the phone. "Hey, Dad. What's up?"

"Pete? You sound winded. Where are you?"

"Ummm...." He was saved from answering by the shot of a gun.

"Oh, you're on the Jungle Cruise?"

"Umm, yeah, you could say that." Peter wiped the sweat off his forehead with the back of his hand.

"Great. Glad you're having a good time. Listen, I'm on my dinner break and wondered if you wanted to come with me. Blue Bayou? One of your favorites."

Peter's stomach gurgled. "I just ate at the Bengal Barbecue." *Rats, now I'm hungry again.*

"Oh, all right. Then I'll just grab something light. See you in a couple of hours?"

If I'm not in jail. "Yeah, sure, Dad. I'll find you."

"You all right? You sound funny."

"Gotta go. Umm, people are staring." *At the rhino...*

"Oh, right. See you, Pete."

The call ended and Peter slumped back against a tree. This was harder than he thought.

In a secluded nook behind the rhino, surrounded by trees and boulders, Peter peered out as boat after boat went by. "Gosh, don't they ever break down any more?" So far he'd only been able to hurry out once to examine the rhino. The loud spiel of the skippers alerted him when another boat approached. "This is going to take forever."

The latest boat slipped out of view and he ran back to the irritating animal as the hyenas continued to laugh. The point of the rhino's horn went up and down as the natives above him mimicked the movement. "There isn't anything here. That rhino is built like a tank. Oh shoot!"

He dove back under cover just as a boat came into view. "And look at that! Wow, there must be a million rocks on that beach!" as the skipper obviously didn't see the trapped safari waiting for rescue or irate rhino that had caused the problem.

"Okay, one more time." Peter ran his hands over and under the rhino in an attempt to see if a capsule was somehow attached to the body.

"There's the safari I told you to watch out for. See the guy on the bottom? He'll surely get the point in the end! Keep an eye out as we enter the pool of hippopotami…"

In his hiding place, an open-mouthed Peter stared after the unseen boat. "Is that what I missed? It's not the rhino. It's the guys on the pole!"

Peter stepped back into view as he went up to the natives clinging to the pole, stuck there for decades as the persistent rhinoceros stayed in his place. "It has to be one of them. But which one? Man, already??"

Back in the safety of his rocks, Peter pulled out his now-silenced phone to take another look at the pictures. "Which guy would it be and where would Walt hide something?"

It was beginning to get darker and Peter knew the stone-filled beach would soon be lit by hidden spotlights. Plus, the skippers would also use handheld lights to brighten the areas they were spieling. If he was going to find something, it had better be quick.

He didn't want to have to come back and do this again.

Reaching over, he pulled his backpack closer to retrieve his ever-handy flashlight. As he reached into the zippered pouch, his hand froze. Looking at what he held in his hand, his eyes jerked over to the clinging natives. They, too, had backpacks. "It has to be in one of those. But which one? What if it's that guy on top? How would I get up there without a ladder and without being seen?"

Peter shook his head. It was beginning to look impossible.

"...that guy on the bottom will get the point in the end. See? The hyenas like it!"

As the boat rounded the bend, the oft-repeated phrase played over in his mind. "Hey, that's what the clue said. 'He'll get the point in the end.' It has to be the guy on the bottom. Only one way to check."

He had to wait for one more boat to go by. Sprinting to the hapless native, as soon as he was in the 'down' position, Peter felt through the material of the khaki backpack. Something was in there. After the next boat he was back and trying to get open the leather ties. Nerves and sweaty fingers made the easy task more difficult than it needed to be. Deep in concentration, he was almost caught by the next boatload.

"Got it!" Relieved, Peter barely got the ties back into place and himself out of sight before the next boat. He thought he heard the skipper stammer, but could have been mistaken as the spiel continued uninterrupted.

Once back at the dock and unloaded, Skipper Tom swapped placed with one of the loaders. Before he took his place he had something to report to his lead. "I think I saw something out by the rhino. Not sure. It happened so fast. But, I think I saw a kid dive into the bushes."

"Okay, how do I get out of here?" Now that he had what he wanted, Peter relaxed against the tall rocks as he worked it out. Going back to the train tracks wasn't an option. Jumping off a train was one thing. Jumping back on it was another. Whistling softly to himself, he studied the aerial map with the flashlight. "It might take a while, but I think I'd better go to Main Street and come out there. Easier to explain than walking into the train station."

A chuckle died in his throat when he heard sounds rapidly approaching his hiding spot. The crunch of leaves and the snap of twigs could only mean one thing: He had been seen.

"The rhino is just up ahead. Keep an eye out. We don't know how many kids there are. Lance, you circle around to the Veldt. Steve, you come with me to the beach."

With the voices coming from his left—the way he had come in—Peter took off to the right. Keeping low so the passing boats couldn't tip off Security, he wound his way through the thick trees and brush as fast as he could, leaves and branches whipping at his face. Forced to climb partway up the berm to keep undercover, he then worried that a passing train would spot him.

When the sounds of Main Street started to get louder, he knew he was close. Turning away from the train tracks, he pushed through the vines and roots until the vegetation began to thin. He could finally see the back of the Guided Tour Garden and the taller City Hall.

Scrambling down the dirty embankment, catching his foot on a protruding root, he rolled onto the pavement in front of two surprised tour guides. "Cat," he fairly shouted at them before sprinting to the Emporium's back entry. Once inside, he planned to lose himself in the maze of shops and hightail it back to his apartment and safety.

With an attempt to control his rapid breath and mop the moisture from his face, Peter pretended to shop as he calmly strolled through the Emporium. After more than a few glances over his shoulder, he relaxed when there were no signs of alarm or pursuit. He went so far as to buy a bag of toffee peanuts in the Candy Palace before strolling across Main Street to the entry of his apartment.

He stopped dead in his tracks when he saw his dad, arms folded, leaning carelessly against the wall of the stairwell. Lance came down the steps and ambled up to his son. Reaching up, he pulled a leafy eucalyptus twig out of Peter's hair. "So, what'd you find at the rhino?"

CHAPTER 7

Flashback – Disneyland—1956

"That's a real alligator, Harold." Elaine paused at the shaded entrance to the Jungle Cruise to glance inside a chicken-wire pen standing off to the side. Lazily fanning herself with her straw hat, she pushed her white-rimmed sunglasses down her nose. When she leaned closer, a loud hiss came from the three-foot-long reptile inside the cage. Startled, she jumped back. "See? I told you it was real!"

Harold looked up from his guidebook as their son pelted the captive with popcorn. "Don't waste your treat, Marty. It's obviously made out of rubber. That's the sound of the gears inside the jaws. See? They're going up and down just like they do inside the ride." He peered more closely at what he thought was a marvel of engineering. "Amazing. It's practically seamless. Hmm, wonder why there are green pieces of rubber wedged in-between its teeth? It sort of looks like that snake we just bought Marty at that souvenir stand."

Marty was just about to dangle his new green rubber snake into the cage. When the creature became motionless, he lost interest and started his favorite pastime—whining. "Can we go on the ride now? I'm hot! You promised."

Ignoring the persistent drone of his son's voice, Harold consulted the guidebook once again. "Tell you what. This brochure says the Golden Horseshoe is air-conditioned. Why don't we go over there and come back here tonight when it's cooler? Then we can compare this alligator with the ones in the river."

"That's odd, Harold. Wasn't there an alligator in this cage when we were here earlier?"

"Of course there was. We talked about it. Why do you ask?"

Elaine pointed at the cage. One side now had a gaping hole and the chicken-wire was all bent outward. "It's empty now. Wonder if they moved it somewhere else?"

As they moved through the line, Harold thought he had it figured out. He gave an appreciative chuckle. "That's probably just some Disneyland Magic they want us to believe! If we think a 'real' alligator escaped, it would make this ride much more exciting. I'm going to ask one of the guides if that's true or not."

Near the front of the line, the cast members seemed surprised to hear six shots fired from a skipper deep inside the ride. Harold and Elaine could hear them talking. "That was a warning signal. One of the boats either derailed or can't move. We'll have to send out a diver to help if the boat went off the rail."

One of the cast members listening jerked his thumb over his shoulder at the guests in line. "Didn't you hear what that one guy just said? The cage out front is empty! That alligator escaped again."

All heads immediately turned to stare at the murky water. "I ain't going in there. Call the Buena Park Alligator Farm. They're going to have to come and find it."

"Their handler is pretty fast. I don't get it, but he just stands here and makes funny noises in his throat. That dumb gator comes right up to him. You're the diver. Why don't you try it?"

The cast member who should have been on his way to help the stranded boat shook his head. "Nope. That gator is more trouble than he's worth. What would I do with it if it came up to the dock? That little demon is mean. I don't care what the handler says. Let him fix it. And then he can take that thing back to the Alligator Farm with him!"

The men on the dock stood in their places and continued to gaze into the water, alert for a pair of yellow eyes. When another six shots were fired into the air, one of them headed for the rubber rescue boat while another headed for the phone.

Disneyland

"So, how'd you know it was me?"

Lance held up the leafy piece of evidence in his hand. "Oh, I had a pretty good idea when the call came through to Security." After a glance over his shoulder, Lance clasped his son by the shoulder. "Let's get out of sight and then you can tell me all about it."

"I'm not in trouble?"

"Well, if my boss comes by and sees me with a kid with leaves sticking out of his hair, then, yes, you are. But, the faster we get inside and out of sight, the better the odds that the kid in the jungle got away."

Without another word, Peter opened the door on the side of the Market House that seemingly went to nowhere. Once inside the closet-like interior, the door safely closed and locked away from curious eyes, father and son climbed the metal ladder to the second-floor apartment. The rooms, furnished in the same manner as Walt's private apartment above the Fire Station, had been a gift from Walt at the end of one of Peter's previous quests. Outfitted with a small kitchenette and bathroom, it had already been put to good use by the Brentwoods and the Michaels when they wanted to spend the night in the Magic Kingdom.

Seated on the red velvet-covered daybed, Peter pulled out the gray capsule. "I found this in the backpack on the lowest native."

Lance shook his head in wonder. "Amazing it was still there after, what? Forty-some years? You'd think someone would have found it with all the traffic the jungle gets."

"Traffic? What traffic?" Peter's head shot up. Apparently there were a few stories he hadn't yet heard.

That secret smile that so infuriated kids played over his dad's face. "Oh, there've been a few tales that have made their way backstage among the cast members."

"About you and Wolf?"

The smile spread to a huge grin. "No. About your mom and me."

Always ready to deflect any interest in any possible wrongdoing on his part, Peter was all ears. "Tell me."

Lance bit down the urge to let Peter know that he *had* tried to tell him the story, but the boy hadn't been interested. Maybe this was a good sign. "This was just after your mom and I met. Your grandfather was still alive then and he told us that Uncle Adam and I had missed a clue in our first Hidden Mickey hunt. Once we—your mom and I—figured it out, we found we had to search inside the Jungle Cruise for one of the clues." He nodded at the capsule Peter gripped in his hands. "Just like you had to. Well, we felt it was best to do our exploring at night and we worried about the cleaning and repair crews. So...." He paused for dramatic effect and inwardly smiled when Peter leaned forward. "So, we spent the night up in Tarzan's Treehouse and I zip-lined over the Indy queue and into the jungle."

"Zip-line? You? Wow, that must have been something to see."

"Yeah, it was pretty fun." With an upheld hand, Lance felt he had to add, "Not that you are hereby given permission to do *anything* like that. Understand?"

"Umm, sure. But, is the line still there?"

Lance shook his head. "No, I took it down as fast as I could. But, you can still see the hole in the tree if you look hard enough." Before Peter could ask any more, Lance indicated the canister with a tilt of his chin. "So, are you going to open it? I'm curious to see where you have to go next." Inwardly he hoped Peter was likewise as interested.

"Oh." Peter broke eye contact with his dad and looked down at the cool length of plastic. "Umm." A tinge of red crept up his cheeks while Lance waited for a reply. "I kinda told Catie I'd open it with her."

Glad his son was at least engaged enough to want to continue, Lance had to be satisfied. "Okay, that's fair. Maybe your mom and I can drive you over to the hospital after I get off work. That way you won't have to ride your bike over at midnight. Again."

Eyes wide, Peter wisely kept silent. With a brief nod, he merely muttered, "That would be nice."

Fullerton

When Lance and Kimberly suggested a walk outside the hospital with Adam and Beth, Alex stayed behind. Wondering what was up with Peter, he ventured, "You want to play on the Wii with me?

You could take over Michael's racecar. I'm beating him pretty bad so he probably wouldn't mind."

Peter glanced up at the muted television and the animated road race that had been paused. "No, Mikey would be upset. He thinks he's winning."

Alex gave a laugh. "Well, if he wants to think that. So, why'd you stay behind then?"

"I wanted to talk to Catie." Not sure why Alex was so curious, Peter hesitated to see if he was about to be teased.

Alex didn't volunteer the fact that he solely missed his sister. He, too, talked to her whenever they were alone. "That's cool. Can I stay?"

Relieved he didn't have to defend himself, Peter shrugged to indicate he didn't care one way or the other. "Sure. I found another clue in the Jungle Cruise and wanted to open the capsule with her."

The boys approached the silent girl. The bruising on her face had begun to fade from deep purple to tinges of yellow. Alex had already told Catie all about his day, so he waited for Peter.

"Hi, Catie. It's me again. Peter." He half expected Alex to snicker. "I found the next clue. You'll never guess where it was. You know the guys the rhino chased up the tree? Well, it was in the lowest guy's backpack."

Rats, I miss out on all the fun stuff. "How'd you get in there to find that out?" Alex was all ears now.

Peter went silent as his mind began to spin. Catie had been his sole partner on their adventures only because Alex hadn't been interested enough to join them. Now Peter wasn't sure how much he should tell his friend. "Oh, well, you know the Jungle Cruise is right next to Main Street, right?"

Not wanting to appear stupid, Alex had to nod. His field of interest in Disneyland extended to the roller coasters, not the history and demographics. "Oh, yeah. Sure. That makes sense."

Peter let it go with that. He'd fill Catie in on the rest of the details later when no one else was in the room. "Anyway, Catie, I was going to open the next clue with you like I promised. Alex can help me open the capsule and then we'll read it to you."

With a shrug, Alex accepted the container. "It isn't very big. Must not have much inside." The end cap easily twisted off in his hand and revealed a lone piece of notebook paper. "That's weird.

It says: ***Thaddeus Walker gave it his all in 1812. Bring a shovel.***"

Peter's look of interest changed into a frown. "What does 'gave it his all' mean? I don't understand."

"It means that person died in his efforts, whatever it was he had to do. He did his best but didn't live through it."

The boys' heads shot up as their parents returned to the room. After his explanation, Adam went to Catie's side to softly touch her brown hair. The heart-rending gesture was one of reassurance. For a moment, the *beep beep* of her monitor was the only sound in the still room.

Beth went to his side to lean her head against his shoulder. Only Adam could hear her whisper. "She's going to be all right, honey."

To allow the family a moment together, Kimberly herded Lance and Peter out into the hallway. In a similar gesture to acknowledge that her oldest son was fine, she gave him a hug. "So, you found the next clue. Are you excited?"

Peter leaned into the warm embrace for a moment longer before the change of topic gave him the excuse to pull away. "Do you want to see the paper? It's definitely Walt's handwriting. Not sure where I need to go. Do you have any ideas?"

Lance accepted the note to look it over, his heart again speeding up at the prospect. Peter, though, looked as if they were discussing school clothes. *Patience, patience.* "Not sure. I don't recognize the name as someone associated with Walt, but that doesn't mean he isn't." Thinking back to his very first clue with Adam, he suddenly grinned. "But, I do know this: When Walt says to bring a shovel, he means it."

"So I have to dig up something buried in Disneyland?"

"Possibly Disneyland. There are many other places in Walt's history you might have to search."

Peter nodded. "Yeah, like at the Studio where I dug up the Gold Pass to Disneyland."

"Is that how you found the Pass? I never did hear that story." Kimberly took the clue so she could compare it with what she and Lance had found years ago.

Beth's coming out of the hospital room saved Peter from having to explain how he dug up a flowerbed in the Studio's Nunnery.

"So, you found another clue, Peter? How exciting." It became obvious she was struggling with emotion when her eyes filled with tears. After a clearing cough, her smile wavered, but she was able to continue. "I know Catie loves hearing about what you're doing. Thanks for coming to talk to her."

"Maybe she'll wake up and help me with the next one."

Beth gave the boy a hug. "I hope so, honey. You go do us all proud, all right?"

Smothered into her shoulder, Peter's reply was muffled. "I'll do my best."

"So, how many graveyards are there in Disneyland anyway?" Back in his room, safe from any more random hugs, Peter concentrated on the clue. He decided to go with Uncle Adam's explanation that it referred to someone who had died. "Well, that's interesting. There are at least six graveyards in Disneyland. I thought there was only the one in the Haunted Mansion, but there are really three there." His chair scooted closer to the desk. "There's the pet cemetery on the side of the Mansion that most people don't even know about." Picture after picture was brought up and closed. "That can't be it. All the dates are wrong for the clue. They go from 1847 to 1869."

He switched his search the second Mansion graveyard: The tombstones seen in the outside queue. "No dates? How come none of them have dates? Fred, Master Gracey, Brother Claude, Grampa Marc." Five minutes later, Peter found he was reading just to be reading and not doing actual research. "Oh, so that's who they were named after. I knew some of the Imagineers' names but not all of them. Wonder if I need to go to the Park and look for myself. Maybe these pictures missed something."

The graveyard scene at the end of the Haunted Mansion ride was the third. "Gosh, these pictures don't show anything. Yeah, I'll definitely have to go on the ride." He smiled as he clicked off the current screen. "Yeah, that's too bad. I have to ride the Mansion!"

The Frontierland Shootin' Exposition was next on his list of cemeteries. "The only date I can see in Boot Hill is December 1848. That's wrong, too." Peter frowned as he thought. "It can't be there anyway. They're all just targets. How could anything be buried under that?"

The next location earned a groan. "Storybook Land Canal Boats? Really? There's a graveyard in Alice's Village, but, man, they are only, like half an inch tall. I don't want to dig up Storybook Land."

With a shake of his head, Peter dismissed the popular ride to scroll to the next search. "Tom Sawyer Island? Where? At the cabin? No, it was set up behind the old Fort. It says the Fort was torn down and rebuilt in 2007. That's too bad. Is the graveyard still there? Hmm."

Disneyland

Lance and his family had a table waterside in the Blue Bayou Restaurant. Michael and Andrew were more interested in the Pirates of the Caribbean boats slowly floating past their table than their dinner. Lance had eagerly devoured his filet while Peter pushed his Jambalaya around in the bowl. "You going to eat that, Pete?"

"Lance, you just had a huge filet. How can you possibly still be hungry?" Her husband's remarkable hunger always amazed Kimberly. He was still as slender as the day she married him.

"What can I say? I hate seeing something go to waste. Especially the Bayou's Jambalaya."

Peter shoved his bowl closer to his dad and grabbed one of the remaining dinner rolls.

"Can I have a roll to feed the ducks, Mom?"

"There's no ducks in here, Andrew. We're inside."

"I know that, Mikey! I mean the ducks in the River."

Before the two younger ones could get into it, Kimberly sighed. *Just one girl. That's all I ever asked for. One sweet, kind, non-argumentative little daughter.* "All right, you two. That's enough. Andrew, yes, you can have a roll if no one else wants the last one." She threw a look at Lance that told him not to claim the last roll. To change the subject, she turned to Peter. "So, do you think we need to ride the Mansion again? It was so dark it was difficult to see the writing on many of the tombstones. We could give it another go."

Peter wasn't sure. "I don't think that's the right place." In the darkened, moon-lit ambience of the restaurant, amid the soft croaking of frogs and darting fireflies, a sudden bright light caught everyone's attention. Peter glanced over at the lapping water of the Bayou. Someone in the front row of a passing boat just took a flash picture. "That's not going to turn out." He turned back to his mom and her suggestion. "I'd rather go over to Tom Sawyer Island. The picture I saw online was blurry, but the wooden marker thingy looked like it could have said just what the clue said."

Silent all this time, Lance finished up the remaining Jambalaya. "Man, that was good! Did someone order dessert? I can't remember. What?" He stopped when he realized Kimberly and Peter were staring at him. "Do I have something on my face?"

"You never leave enough food to have something on your face, honey."

Lance contentedly patted his flat stomach. "What can I say? I'm a growing boy."

"We were talking about Tom Sawyer Island, Dad. I'd like to go over there before it shuts down for the night."

Lance used the Bayou's flickering darkness to scrutinize Peter's face. What he saw was determination and figured that was good enough for now. "Okay, that's a plan. I'll call two of my security buddies to stand guard. As you know, there're two paths that go up behind the Fort. One from each side of the River. Or we could just come back tonight from the apartment."

Peter surprised him by shaking his head no. "I'd rather do it now. You going to ask Steve and Joe for help?"

"Yeah. They're good for that. They've helped me out before and won't ask any questions later. Plus, they can alert us when the *Mark Twain* or the *Columbia* gets close. I do know the canoes aren't running today."

"You sound like a tour guide, Daddy!"

"You think I'd make a good one, Andrew?"

"I dunno. Can we go feed the ducks now?"

Arms folded over his chest, Peter stood and stared at the small graveyard behind Fort Wilderness. Situated on a tall mound, it was the farthest you walk on the Island before coming to the fenced-off No Man's Land. Thaddeus Walker was indeed there, along with ten others who shared his final resting place. W. Pierre

Feignoux, Lieut. Laurence Clemmings, Sacajawea, and Ebinizer Browne were among the deceased. "Well, I guess it's obvious which grave I want, but what do I do? How much do I have to dig up?"

Lance watched as the *Mark Twain* sailed past, her steam whistle blowing a greeting to the old abandoned Fort. "You have just a couple of minutes before she goes by on the other side. You have to figure it out, son."

"Yeah, but…" Peter sighed as he brought the folding shovel out from his backpack. When he had been at the Studio, he had found a telltale **WED** engraved in the wall above the spot he needed to dig. There was no such marking here. Just hard-packed dirt. "Yeah, yeah, I know. I'll figure it out."

Once the *Mark Twain's* paddlewheel was out of sight on the other side, he knew he should get to work. There would no longer be a danger from any passenger seeing him or what he was about to do.

With a grunt of disgust similar to the one his dad had made back in 2002, the tip of the shovel bit into the ground. Once he broke through the hard top crust, he found the dirt easier to manipulate. Shovelful after shovelful flew to the side.

"Pete? Honey? You're making a mess. You are going to have to fill it back in, you know."

Peter looked over at his mom and noticed the way the dirt had been strewn in every direction. The glimmer of excitement faded. "Maybe Michael can help me."

Michael didn't even look up from his mom's phone. "Nope."

"The *Columbia* just rounded the bend by the canoe dock. We're going to have company soon."

Lance came over from his spot in the shade. "Thanks, Joe. Anything yet, Pete? No? Then hold up until the *Columbia* goes by. You know, we haven't been on her in a long time. Maybe we can ride her when we're done here."

"Ride what, Daddy?" Andrew came back from the happy flock of mallards and mud hens that had just been fed pieces of bread. The ducks went off in a mass of feathers and confusion as the *Columbia's* cannons roared from her deck. Scared by the loud noise, Andrew covered his ears. "I don't want to ride that. It's too loud. Can we go on Pirates again?"

"Andy, there are cannons in there, too, you know."

"I know that, Mikey. But, that's different. Those aren't real."

Peter ignored their ongoing debate on what was real at the Park as he got back to work on the growing hole. Just before the *Columbia* could reach the clearing, his spade hit something hard. "I found something!"

"Hold up." The warning came from Steve as he waved hello and smiled at the guests as the ship slowly sailed by. "All clear."

The family stepped away from their nonchalant protective pose around the hole to see what Peter had found. "I think you got it, Pete. That's definitely plastic and not another rock." Lance stepped over the short wooden railing that encircled the graves to retrieve the find. "Now you can fill it in."

Peter's shoulder sagged. He thought his dad was going to help.

"Lance."

Halfway back over the fence, Lance paused at the one word uttered by his wife. One word, yet so full of meaning. With a roll of his eyes and a dramatic, long-suffering sigh, he tossed the small container to Kimberly. "Fine." Without another word, he took the shovel from Peter and began to fill in the hole.

Unable to believe their eyes, Steve and Joe nudged each other as they left their posts to watch Lance's show. "Wow, he actually does work. I would've lost that bet."

"I know. Did you bring a camera? No one's going to believe us."

Tossing the shovel to the side and tamping down the soft dirt, Lance ignored his fellow security guards. "One word of this and I'll tell Laura what really happened to her family's heirloom vase, Steve."

Steve's tanned face visibly blanched. That monthly poker game had gotten a little rowdier than usual. "Uh, no need to bother Laura. We're good, right, Joe?"

"Hey, I ain't the one who broke it."

Before Lance could prod them any further, cooler heads prevailed. Kimberly stepped between Steve and Joe and thanked them for their help. "Lance is almost done. Do you think you could keep watch for any guests who might wander back here?"

The green-eyed, curvy blonde could have asked them to jump

into the River and they would have happily done it. "You bet, Kimberly. Sorry."

She covered Lance's 'whipped puppies' with a loud cough. Those same green eyes were less-than-mesmerizing when she flashed a warning look at her husband.

Unrepentant, he merely smirked as he called over to his security buddies. "I think we're done here. Thanks, guys. I owe you one. I'll see you at work tomorrow." Turning to his younger sons who started to complain again about their boredom with Peter's stupid job, Lance rubbed his dusty hands together. "So, who's ready for Pirates?"

"Me! Me!"

"Alrighty, then. Let's go catch the last raft before they close the Island for the night. Good work, Pete." He put a hand on Peter's shoulder as they walked the dusty trail back to the dock. Screams from the passengers hurtling down Splash Mountain's flume could be clearly heard from across the River. "Who wants to ride Splash Mountain instead?"

"No."

His other arm snaked around Kimberly's waist when they arrived at the raft dock. "Someone doesn't want to get her hair wet."

"I think Andrew's coming down with a cold. He shouldn't run around the Park with wet feet."

Lance chuckled. "Right."

To Peter, their good-natured banter was merely background noise. He didn't really care what they went on. All the rides were good to him. He just wondered where Walt was going to send him next.

Chapter 8

Disneyland Paris

"We have to get Walt out of here. That was Tony."

Finished with their ride, standing off to the side in the loading room and next to the scooter, Wolf and Omah were in deep discussion. Only half listening, Walt was busy looking at the gothic details of the room as the eerie soundtrack played over and over. "Do I know this Tony?"

Wolf broke off his discussion with his wife to answer Walt, his voice noticeably lower. "Yes, you've met him, but he was a boy in your time. He's gone on to do wonderful things within the company. But," he stressed, "You can't be recognized. You know that."

Even in the darkness of the loading dock, Walt's brief flicker of irritation was easy to read. The Doom Buggy ride vehicles kept moving steadily past them, the occupants either eagerly leaning forward or warily pressed against the back of the black clamshell. "Maybe this Tony wouldn't recognize me." Arms folded across his chest, Walt seemed ready to dig in his feet. He was somewhat surprised when Wolf smiled.

"When was the last time you went anywhere and have not been recognized?"

Walt had to admit the truth of that statement. "Fine. So, now what? I'd like to go on this again. I liked the Frontierland feel of the ghost town. And, we are right here."

Omah stepped forward and motioned for Walt to resume his seat in the scooter. "We'd probably have to wait in line again to ride." She put an understanding hand on his shoulder. "Even for you, Boss."

"Hey, I've never minded waiting in line. That's how you learn things. You see what the guests have to go through and listen to the good and the bad." From his seat, he glanced up at Wolf. "That was easier to do when I wasn't so recognizable, as you pointed out." After one last inspection of the fascinating room, he sighed. "So, can't we just pop over to Discoveryland instead? If Tony is waiting outside, as you seem to think, he wouldn't know to look there."

Wolf knew Walt was just trying to delay the inevitable. "Sorry, Boss, but we can't take the chance. He heard you cough. Everyone who ever knew you knows your cough. Next time I see him, I'm going to have a hard enough time explaining why we seemingly never came out of the Manor."

"What do you think, Wolf? I saw a cast member exit when we brought the scooter in. Maybe we can duck in there and go."

Wolf ignored Walt's grumble as he considered Omah's plan. Company policy was that a cast member escorted a scooter or wheelchair back to the entrance. That wouldn't help their escape. He was fluent enough in French to hopefully persuade the Ghostess to let them go back alone. His Security badge was pulled out of his wallet for good measure. "Here goes nothing," as he turned to their patient cast member.

Burbank Studio

"Hey! I thought we were going to Disneyland." Walt was disappointed to find himself back in his inner office. His mind still whirling with all the wonders he had seen and the effects of the instant transfer, he sank into the chair behind his desk. "What day is this, anyway?"

Omah and Wolf looked at each other and shrugged. "Hopefully it's the same day we left. That was our aim. It should be as if you never left. Should be…" Omah's voice trailed off as she sincerely hoped that to be the case. Even after decades and centuries of travel, it still wasn't an exact science.

Walt glanced at the calendar. It did show him it was the same month, but didn't tell him what he needed to know. "I guess I'll just have to play it by ear and see what's going on today." His eyes narrowed as he turned his attention back to Wolf. "You did promise to take me to Disneyland."

"Wasn't Paris enough?" Wolf tried to keep an innocent expression on his face.

Walt rubbed a tired hand over his face as he snorted. "I guess that sounded pretty ungrateful. I didn't mean it that way." His gesture included Omah. "I do thank you both. I...I never imagined I'd be in Paris or Japan or China." His head slowly shook back and forth as he thought about the future scope of his empire. "Roy and I never even thought that far. After all the money that went into Disneyland and the lack of land we were able to buy in Anaheim, we considered Florida to be our big statement Park. Wish I could tell him what's coming. But, I'd probably be locked up in a loony bin if I tried."

"Best not to, Boss. This was just for you. But, we haven't forgotten our promise. You will get to see Disneyland. Just not today."

"Why... Yeah, I think you're right. I am awfully tired." Walt pushed away from his desk and went to stand by the window. His position was the same as when Wolf first arrived, but his attitude was noticeable brighter than he had been. "Much as I hate to admit it. So, when do you think we can..." His question was interrupted by the intercom. "Excuse me a minute. Don't leave either. I'm not done with you yet." He pushed the button on his desk. "Yes?"

"Walt, The Boys are here to see you."

His head still full of Disneyland Paris, his mind went blank. "Boys?"

His secretary's voice hesitated. Everyone knew who The Boys were. "Umm, the Shermans? You wanted to hear their newest song for *The Jungle Book*."

"Oh, right. Give me moment, will you? I'll come out."

"All right, Walt. I'll tell them."

"I guess that's our cue to leave." After giving Walt a hug, Omah went to sit in the scooter so it would go with them when they went back to their time.

Walt turned to Wolf and held out his hand. "I won't let you forget your promise. You know that, right?"

Wolf had to smile as they shook. "But, Walt, if you see me in the Park tomorrow or the next day and remind me, I won't have any idea what you're talking about. It hasn't happened yet."

"Gosh, how do you keep all this straight?"

"It's one of our burdens, I guess. We won't forget. See you around, Boss."

Walt could see them in his office and, in the next second, they were simply gone. "Amazing. But I do miss all the fireworks and thunder Wolf used to create. Still, I guess it's better than having to explain why my carpet was all wet."

Hand on the doorknob to the outer office, Walt paused. He glanced back at where Wolf and Omah had been a moment before. A sly smile on his face, his hand dipped into his coat's interior pocket. A bright brochure that read Disneyland Paris was pulled partway out before returning to the covering darkness.

Chapter 9

Disney California Adventure

"**One of my favorite colors was Aurora's Golden Yellow hair. Just don't break the glass.**"

"I know the clue, Peter. Gosh, you've told me, like, a million times!"

Peter glanced over at Alex as they walked under the Monorail's bridge in Disney California Adventure. He was beginning to second-guess his decision to ask Alex for his help with the clue he had found buried on Tom Sawyer Island.

Earlier that morning, even though Peter had dreaded it, the boys had gone through the Sleeping Beauty Castle Walkthrough. After Peter had practically sprinted past the dioramas, his heart pounding at the reminder of what he had been put through last year, they had seen nothing. Once he realized he was safe and being silly, they entered the Castle again to do a more thorough search for a possible solution. To Peter, it was the most logical place to see Aurora. Where else would she be behind glass? Walt knew he had a key that would get him into any room, so there would be no need to ruin the display.

After thinking it all through, the animated dioramas didn't hold the answer Peter needed. There was no need to enter and search the locked rooms that held the displays.

After staring at the bronze statue of Sleeping Beauty and Prince Phillip next to the Walkthrough's entry, Peter tried to think of any other place in Disneyland where he might find Aurora. Other than the face character—like his mom had been—who posed for pictures and signed autograph books, he came up empty.

To placate his reluctant partner, Peter had suggested going over to Disneyland's sister park across the Esplanade. Now that they were headed to the Tower of Terror, Peter had expected Alex's attitude to improve. It hadn't. "Why are you biting my head off, Alex? We're going to do something you want to do." When they reached the middle of Buena Vista Street, Peter, as was his custom, patted the bronzed head of Mickey as they passed the Storyteller Statue of Walt and his partner. Designed to match the year 1923 when Walt first arrived in California, this bronzed Walt appeared much younger than how he looked in the Partner's Statue in the Disneyland Hub.

As they turned to the left to enter Hollywood Land, a Red Car Trolley sounded its bell to signal its approach. Moving off the tracks, Alex abruptly stopped in front of the Disney Junior auditorium. Arms folded, he didn't look pleased at the prospect of going on one of his favorite rides. Instead, he looked miserable. "I know where we're going, Peter. You don't have to remind me. I…" Lips pressed together, he looked back toward the towering Carthay Circle Restaurant. His head slowly shook side to side as if he didn't want to put something into words.

"What's wrong? Would you rather go do something else? What?"

"I…" Alex tried to start again. His brown eyes shot back to Peter. "It just doesn't feel right."

Peter had no idea what he was talking—or not talking—about. "I don't get it. What doesn't feel right? I know this," indicating all of California Adventure with a sweep of his hand, "has nothing to do with the clue. I'm just trying to make you happy."

Anger flared up in Alex's eyes. Anger…and something else. "You don't understand, Peter. I don't deserve to be happy!"

Flummoxed, Peter could only stare at him.

Alex balled his hands into fists and, not knowing what to do with them, roughly shoved them into his pockets. The anger faded as quickly as it came. He looked miserable. "I don't deserve to have fun. Not when…not when Catie is still hurt. It isn't right."

Peter suddenly understood his friend and actually shared his feelings. He struggled with the same guilt, but, being fourteen, didn't know how to solve Alex's dilemma. So, he did the next best thing.

"Hey! Why'd you punch me in the arm? That hurt!"

Peter, a silly grin on his face, shrugged. "I don't know. Seemed like the thing to do." A bit of red began to tinge his cheeks. "I do know how you feel, Alex. But, I think Catie would want us to keep working on the clues. Then we go and tell her everything we do."

Still rubbing his arm, Alex slowly nodded. "Mom said the same thing. She says we're doing it for Catie now. I…I just miss her."

"Me, too."

Wary, Alex took a step away. "Just don't hug me or anything, okay, Peter?"

That earned a laugh and broke the mood. "Okay. I promise. Maybe, if you're good, we can go on Heimlich's Chew Chew Train."

Alex groaned at the thought of the slow-moving ride. "I'm not going to Bug's Land."

"Golden Zephyr?"

"Hey, just because you're two years older than I am doesn't mean I'm a baby."

They both heard Peter's stomach growl. "How about some lunch? We're already at Award Wieners."

"We just ate breakfast at Carnation."

"I'm hungry again."

"Peter, you're always hungry."

As the boys devoured their hot dogs and sodas, Peter's mind went back to the clue. "What if the clue doesn't have anything to do with Disneyland? What if it points somewhere else?"

Half-listening, intent on his fries, Alex shrugged. "Where else would you find Aurora?"

"I don't know. In the research I've been doing for days now, I found pictures of her from the Studio in Burbank. But they were just animation cels."

Alex finished off his soda and eyed Peter's. "You going to finish that?" Once handed over, the remainder was noisily slurped down. A small smile turned up Alex's lips after he let out a loud burp. Sometimes it was nice not being there with his mom. "So what if it is an animation cel? Wouldn't they be on display and behind glass?"

"But why would Walt just mention the color of her hair? All of the cels would have the same hair color on them."

Alex's interest was waning. "How much time do we have before our FastPass expires? We need to get going." He could see Peter's mind was not on being dropped from the top of the Tower to the basement. "Maybe it's the paint they used to color her hair. I don't know. Let's go." The food baskets were dumped into a nearby trashcan. Alex hung onto the soda to get the last of the cola-flavored ice as it melted. He stopped when he realized Peter hadn't moved. "What?"

Peter's mouth hung slightly open. "But…that can't be it."

"What?"

Peter turned to face his friend, his eyes not quite in focus. "I looked into the window of the Ink and Paint Department when I was at the Studio a year ago. That can't be it. All the paints were in tall plastic bottles."

"Were they always in plastic?" Two small white tickets were held up in front of Peter's face. "Look. We only have thirty minutes before they expire. We need to get moving."

"It's only two minutes around the corner, Alex, and you know it. We have time to ride Monsters, Inc. first."

"No. After the Tower, we'll get passes for Radiator Springs, and then go on Screamin'. The Wait Time app says there's only a twenty minute wait."

"How would I find that out?"

Glad Peter was at least moving in the right direction, Alex didn't think before he replied. "Find out what?"

"If the paint was always kept in plastic."

"Oh. I thought you were talking about the app. Why don't you ask the animator?" Alex let out a groan when Peter stopped in his tracks.

"What animator?"

Again not considering the consequences, with a tilt of his chin Alex pointed across the street. "The one inside Off the Page. Catie goes in there EVERY TIME we walk past it." Exasperated, he flung his arms out to the side when Peter took off in the wrong direction. "Where are you going?"

"It'll just take a minute. I want to check it out."

"FastPass, Peter. Hey! Man." With the sigh of a martyr, he had no choice but to follow.

Inside the gift shop were numerous art books all about Disney, plus specialized souvenirs and collectibles. But the area that attracted Peter's attention was a small, roped-off section that held a brightly-decorated animator's desk and lamp. There was a thin binder nearby that showed the pictures the artist would be able to draw for the guests.

Busy at work on a drawing of Stitch, the animator, Russ, didn't see the two boys as Peter thumbed through the binder. His head shot up when a voice suddenly asked him a question.

"Can you draw Aurora for us? It's not for us... I mean, it's for a friend."

Russ glanced up at Peter and Alex and smiled. "Sure. Did you see a pose you especially liked?"

Irritated, Alex left it up to Peter to carry on the conversation. He kept looking at his watch to figure how long they could stand there and still get to the Tower of Terror in time.

"Um, no, any is fine. It'll be in color, right?"

"Yes, I can do that, too. It will take a bit longer." He glanced over when the brown-haired boy groaned. "Is that all right?"

Alex turned red when he saw Russ was staring at him. "Yeah, I guess. It's for my sister. She's...sick."

Peter saw his opportunity. "Are there certain colors you have to use, or can you use any color, like any yellow, like, for her hair?"

Eyes back on his new drawing, Russ shook his head. "No, we have specific colors. They have to match what have always been used."

Peter felt his heartrate speed up. He pointed below the drawing table. "Are those the paints you use? Those plastic bottles?"

Russ kept at his work. "Uh huh. I bring in certain colors to match the pictures you saw in the binder. When I have different pictures to draw, I bring in other colors."

"From the Studio?"

Russ wondered about the serious look on the boy's face. "Yes, in Burbank."

Peter had to lick his dry lips. "Have the bottles of paint always been plastic?"

Odd question. They usually want to know how much money I make. "For as long as I've worked for the Studio, yes."

Peter felt his face fall. "Oh. I thought, umm, they might have been, you know, glass or something."

Intent on some close-up work on Aurora's face, Russ grunted. "Oh, that was decades ago. There's still some of the old-time stuff on display in the Paint Room."

Distracted by Alex's tugging on his arm and waving the Fast-Passes, Peter asked if they could pick up the drawing later in the day.

There was a slight hesitation before the animator answered. "Sure. Just go pay at the register now and hang on to your receipt. Did you want this personalized to your friend?"

"Yes. To Catie. With a C. Thank you for all your help."

Russ watched as the boys headed for the register. He had figured they would dart out the door and not pay. As an 'I'm-sorry-for-doubting-you,' he decided to add some of the woodland creatures to the scene for free.

Receipt crammed into his pocket, Peter ran after Alex, making it to the Tower with minutes to spare. As they entered the dusty, dim Hotel lobby, Peter smiled to himself.

He now knew where Walt wanted him to go.

Fullerton Hospital

"Uncle Wolf! You're back from...wherever it was you went. Hi, Omah." Peter and Lance entered Catie's hospital room. With Adam, Beth, and Alex already there, too, it was pretty crowded. The nursing staff, ever hopeful that all the noise would help the cute little girl, looked the other way and ignored the three visitor rule.

Wolf nodded hello to his security partner. "Hey, Lance. Peter. Omah and I just came by to say hello to Catie." The small smile on his lips didn't mask the worry in his eyes when he saw that there had been no change since his last visit.

Omah, still unsure of the reception she would get from the Michaels family, stayed in the background and let her husband do the talking. It greatly pleased her when Peter came over for a hug.

"Where are Kimberly and the boys?" Beth looked over from the chair next to Catie's bed.

"Andrew said he wasn't feeling well. Probably practicing being sick before school starts next week."

At the mention of school, Peter and Alex groaned. "How come

it starts so early? It's only August. It's not fair."

"So, you're what now? A sophomore in college?" Wolf lightly punched Peter.

"Yeah, almost. Freshman in high school, but, same thing." Peter looked proud of himself that he was starting high school this year.

"How are you coming along with the Hidden Mickey quest, Peter?"

Lance and Peter looked surprised that Wolf mentioned it in front of Adam and Beth. The Michaels didn't know Wolf had brought the quest directly from Walt. Lance backed up a step behind Adam and subtly signaled for Wolf to change the subject. He was ignored.

"Umm, it's coming along. Alex here helped me with the last clue. He figured out that it was the Ink and Paint Department at the Studio."

"I did? I mean, yeah, I did. Peter figured out the rest of it."

"Good work, guys." Wolf turned back to Peter. "So, do you know what to do next?"

Peter raised a shoulder in a shrug. "Not yet. Dad and I wanted to talk it over with Uncle Adam."

Holding Catie's inert hand, Adam's head shot up. "Me? Why did you want to talk it over with me?" A spark of interest appeared inside the anguished expression that had become his norm.

"Well, Peter needs a way to get into Ink and Paint. That department is even more off-limits to the public than the whole Studio is. We were going to brainstorm some ideas."

Staring at Lance, Adam knew he didn't need his help in planning anything. Lance was known for being extremely clever. "Really?" The one word sounded rather dry.

Wolf edged to the back of the room to stand with Omah, grinning as he settled back to watch the show.

As he normally did, Lance ignored Adam's obvious disbelief. "Yeah. Even though I, or Wolf for that matter, can get him onto the Studio, he still needs a way to get into that room. Thought maybe you might have some ideas to help."

"Since when did you need my help to plan anything? Remember San Francisco?"

"Which part?"

Adam tilted his head. "Dinner at Ghirardelli Square. Geesh,

what do you mean which part?"

Peter didn't catch the sarcasm that tinged Adam's reply. "What happened in San Francisco?"

"We had to break into a warehouse and rappel from the roof."

Before either of the boys could start hurling questions at them, Adam took over the story. "Yeah, Mr. Master Planner here signed us up for mountain climbing lessons ahead of time. They gave me the most antiquated machinery they could find. Man, I still remember how bad my legs burned for days afterwards."

Lance leaned back against the doorframe, his eyes downcast to hide the amusement in them. "Well, it worked, didn't it? We got in and out just fine."

"Oh, just fine, was it?" Adam suddenly became more animated as he jerked his thumb at his former quest partner. "You hear that, Beth? 'We got out just fine.'"

"Hey, don't look at me. That was before I joined you two misfits."

Adam didn't seem to hear her as he continued with the tale. "Lance here says it was just fine. I had to use the frog rig. Do you have any idea how difficult that is?"

Alex wasn't sure if his dad was upset or amused. He merely shook his head no.

"So here we are in the middle of the night in a darkened warehouse. Suddenly we hear sirens that are getting closer and closer. We had what we needed, so we ran back to the ropes to get back up to the roof." Adam pauses to glare at his friend. "I start struggling with the frog rig—which, by the way—is much harder going up. Anyway, the sirens are almost deafening. I'm struggling and Mr. Helpful here," again indicating Lance, "pulls out an automatic lifter and zips up to the three-story-high roof in seconds. He disappears through the roof and is gone while I expected at any minute to have the police throw the lights on and catch me hanging halfway up in the air!"

"Hey, just because you were too cheap to buy…"

Mouth open, Adam swung around. "Too cheap? They cost $8000! And, by the way, you didn't buy it either. You borrowed it from Hans."

"Who was Hans? I don't remember that name." It was obvious Beth was highly entertained by the interchange.

"He was our climbing instructor. Nice guy. Couldn't figure out why Adam was always upside down in the rigging."

Adam let out a derisive snort. "And Mr. Smooth here made it look *so* easy. Found out later he had trained for two days before I ever got there. He actually told me he could do it better because of superior breeding!"

Peter saw a break in the action and jumped in. "So I get to rappel into the Paint Room? Cool!"

All five adults in the room answered in unison, "No!"

Peter had to take a step backward. "Gosh. I was just kidding. Sorta."

Beth, relieved to see some life come back into Adam, sent a small smile of thanks over to Lance. "I'm sure we'll all come up with something, Peter. Something far less dangerous."

Adam, deep in thought, didn't see her secret smile. When he suddenly snapped his fingers, all eyes turned to him. "Lance, what about Kansas City?"

"You want to go back to Kansas City?"

"No." The word was drawn out into two syllables as Adam held back from strangling his former quest partner. *It would be justifiable homicide. I'd probably get off with a warning.* "I don't want to go back. I was thinking of what you made us do at Walt's first animation studio—the garage."

Lance knew what he meant. He had been leading Adam to that memory all along. But, it still didn't hurt to tweak him a little more. "Oh, that's right. The beam in the roof."

Not realizing he was being pranked, Adam stared at Lance for a long minute. "Have you lost what little remained of your intelligence? I'm amazed Peter turned out so well…" He wondered if he needed to speak slowly so Lance could follow. "No, how we got into the garage in the first place. And don't say by the door."

Lance looked all innocent. "All right. I won't. You must, then, be referring to my brilliant subterfuge of the camera and documentary ploy."

"Ding ding ding. He gets it!" Adam raised his arms in triumph and turned to share the victory with the others. He was met with blank stares and assumed they didn't understand the reference. "Lance brought this huge on-shoulder camera and microphone and told the owners of the house where Walt used to have his little studio that we were shooting a documentary on Walt. Lance was doing the talking…"

"On air talent," Lance helpfully filled in.

"Lance did all the talking, as he usually does," Adam continued, "while I pretended to shoot the whole thing with that heavy camera." He stopped again when he saw the looks on their faces. "What?"

"We know, honey. We know the story."

His eyes narrowed at Beth. "Then why didn't you say so?"

"Because you were having so much fun telling it!"

"Hmmp." Adam stomped back to Catie's bed and picked up her limp hand. "You see what I have to go through, Catie? No respect." He gasped when he felt movement against his palm. "She moved her hand! Beth, she moved her fingers!"

The smile on Beth's face faded a bit. "I know, honey. She's done that a couple of times. The doctor said it was just muscle contractions."

"Why didn't you tell me?"

"Didn't want to get all our hopes up. He said it was a good thing, though. Movement is always good."

Not completely convinced, Adam smoothed Catie's hair from her forehead. "I know she can hear us. I think she was telling us she wants to help on the next clue."

"Speaking of the next clue," Lance broke in before Adam could retreat back into his protective shell, "do you think you can help Peter out, Adam? I'm too well known at the Studio to get away with it."

"Help him do what? I'm not sure—yet again—what you're talking about."

"What I was thinking while you were yapping on and on was that you and Peter could use the same ploy. Only to make it believable, it would have to be bloggers or something like that. You could be filming Peter as he toured the Studio for his online blog."

Adam pushed the immediate objections to the back of his mind. If he really was needed, he wanted to be there for Peter. "I guess I could do it again. I'd need that horrid camera…"

"No, that's outdated." Lance interrupted as he paced the room. "What we could use is Peter's iPad. I think there's a microphone attachment, or we could just plug a mike into it somewhere. Doesn't have to work. You would just follow Peter around the room while he looks for the next clue and pretends to talk about the Studio."

"If you're not coming, how do we get onto the lot? As you said, it is closed to the public."

Thinking of Kimberly and their roles as Guardians of Walt, Lance knew getting onto the lot was no problem. They could easily arrange for Peter as the Boy Wonder Blogger to have access to anything they wanted. "Leave that to me. Are you up for it, Adam? And, Pete, it will have to be quick since it'll be on a work day. You can't tie up that room for too long."

"Why can't we go in on a Sunday when nobody is there?"

"Makes it look more real. Adam?"

Scenes from previous quests slipped through Adam's mind. He realized how much he missed the adrenaline rush. A quick glance at Beth revealed her enthusiastic nod. He felt another movement from Catie's hand. "Yes, I'll help. Just tell me when you need me."

The nurses looked over in their direction they heard the group yell out as one: "Yea!"

Chapter 10

Disney Studio – Burbank

Adam marveled at the ease of getting onto the Studio Lot. Years ago he and Beth had become members of a local Disney Fan Club and were able to join one of their rare, private tours of the Studio. But he was well aware that the average fan walking in off the street would only get as far as the guard station on Buena Vista Street before being politely turned away. Glancing at Peter as they got out of the car, he couldn't help but notice the boy's ease and air of familiarity. There was no wide-eyed sense of wonder he would have expected from a fan as big as Peter. He knew about Peter's escapade in the Studio's Nunnery—so named decades ago because it was a No Man's Land so the many female inkers would be able to relax without male interruption—but thought it had been an isolated incident. Now he was curious.

Adam's curiosity would have to wait, though. Kenneth, the security guard at the entrance gate, had followed them to their parking spot in the visitor lot. Clipboard in hand, he began by pointing at the three soundstages and neighboring trailers over to the right. "We have a lot of production filming going on today, so you need to stay away from those buildings. You might want to begin at the popular signpost at Dopey Drive and then proceed to the front of the Animation Building." Kenneth glanced at the dark suit Peter was wearing. *Very businesslike*. His eyes then paused on the backward-facing baseball cap Adam had shoved onto his blond hair. The pause was just long enough for Adam to uneasily shift under the scrutiny. The hat had been a last-minute addition in an attempt to give him the air of a 'blog filmer' for a young host. Kenneth's eyes shifted away to hide his amusement. "You are also free to film in the Legends Plaza." His look stayed on Peter this time. "Just don't climb all over the statues, all right?"

Trying to keep in the professional mode his dad and Uncle Adam had stressed, Peter held back from rolling his eyes. "Yes, sir. Do we have access to the Archives?"

Kenneth's eyebrows lifted. "No. That's off-limits except by invitation." He consulted his clipboard again. "Which you don't have." When he saw Peter's hopeful look falter, he added, "But you can go into the lobby of the Frank G. Wells Building here," as he pointed to his printed map. "There are some artifacts on display there." He looked from Adam to Peter. "Any other questions? Do you need this map? No? All right. You've been allowed three hours. Have fun." The look on the guard's face indicated anything but fun. "I'll come find you when your time is up." It wasn't an offer.

Forcing a smile, Adam held out his hand. "Thanks for your help. I'm sure we'll get just what we need."

Kenneth shook the proffered hand, his eyes again straying to Adam's hat. "Right."

Letting Peter lead the way, Adam refrained from jerking the cap off his head. "So, do we start on Dopey Drive? It sounded like that was expected. I have my iPad ready. You know what you're going to say?" He was less-than-encouraged by Peter's quick reply.

"Nope. I figured I'd just wing it."

Adam's groan was drowned out by an electric cart zipping by. He recognized one of the stars of a popular television show. "We are so going to jail."

"What'd you say, Uncle Adam?"

"Nothing, Pete. Let's just get this show on the road."

After pretending to film the signpost and Pluto's three paw prints in front of the bright red fire hydrant, Adam began to relax. Peter seemed as full of hot air as his father had been when they did this same ruse in Kansas City back in 2002. Gesturing at the nearby Animation Building that had housed Walt's offices, Peter chattered on and on. Adam had already quit listening and concentrated on holding the iPad level. They had, unfortunately, begun to attract unwanted attention as employees from different departments walked past their position.

When the audience around them had grown, Adam signaled to Peter. "Um, cut! Hey, Peter? I think we have enough footage here. Shall we go on to the next spot?" Adam almost laughed when Peter ran a hand through his hair. His dad had that used that same mannerism when he was in view of 'his adoring public.'

"Yes. Let's go on to the Wells Building."

Adam stifled a chuckle. "Yes. Let's."

As they continued down Minnie Avenue, Peter thought Uncle Adam was acting odd and wondered if something was off. "Did I do something wrong?" He looked down at his clothes to straighten the hated tie.

Adam smiled and put a hand on his shoulder. "No, you're doing just fine. Isn't that the Ink and Paint Department?"

Peter nodded. "Yeah, that's the main entrance. There are other doors on the different streets. We'll have to see which one looks best. This entry seems awfully busy."

"Yeah, I noticed that, too. One of the hazards of coming on a week day. Let's get some footage of the Legends for good measure. I'm not sure if we're being followed or not."

"What?" Peter's head jerked around as they walked. "You think so? What'd you see?"

"Calm down and act professional, Pete. I didn't see anything particular. Just talking out loud." *Which I probably shouldn't do.* "We'll play it by ear. You ready to talk about the Partners Statue?"

The prospect of being able to stand next to the famous statue helped dissipate Peter's concern. In the Disneyland Hub, the identical statue was up on a pedestal, surrounded by flowerbeds and a metal fence. Pictures there could only be taken from a distance. Here, in the Plaza, the statue was ground level. Over on the edge of the Plaza was a park bench that held bronze statues of Roy Disney and Minnie Mouse.

Once Peter had made up enough facts about the statues of the two famous brothers, they edged back toward the Ink and Paint Department. Adam heard Peter gasp when he glanced inside.

"What's wrong, Pete?"

"I...I didn't know there were so many rooms. I only saw the one when I went through the tunnel last year. Look at all those bottles!"

Adam could hear an edge of panic in the boy's voice. "Steady there, Pete. We'll figure it out." His heart sank when he saw that Peter hadn't been exaggerating. There had to be hundreds of bottles in the room they could see. What would they find in the other rooms through those inner doors? "Just remember, we're doing this for Catie. Remember Catie and be calm."

Still staring at the task ahead of him, Peter didn't see Adam swipe at his eyes. "For Catie. I'll do it for her."

Adam had to clear his throat before he could speak. "From what I can see, it looks clear in this room. You want to give it a go? You have something prepared to talk about?"

"Sure."

Shaking his head at the unconvincing tone of Peter's voice, Adam opened the door and urged the boy inside. "Just act like we're supposed to be in here, Pete. People tend to believe you if you act like you know what you're doing." *We are so going to jail.*

"Gotcha." Peter ran a hand through his hair again and shook it back. "Ready, Uncle Adam." His eyes constantly moved around the room while he talked on and on about different Disney movies that might have used these paints. Every time he found a paint bottle that was yellow, he walked over to it and 'accidently' dropped his microphone to look more closely at the bottle. Over and over he only found plastic containers. "Okay, people, let's move into the next room. Here we find the sinks that the animators use to mix the paints to match the exact colors needed for their projects. Just think. Walt Disney himself might have used that very sink."

An artist doing just that was startled to see someone walk in filming. Turning off the water, she excused herself, saying she'd come back in a couple of minutes to allow them some space.

"Why, thank you. That's nice of you." Peter dimpled at her and Adam had to keep from laughing.

"We need to speed it up, Pete." Adam had refrained from speaking until the woman was gone from the room. "She's on the clock and won't want to wait too long. If we upset too many animators, they might call in a complaint. That could bring our friend Kenneth sooner than we want."

Peter had just dropped his mike again. "Rats. There's nothing here. Gosh, how many yellows do they have?" He hurried to the other side of the small room to look at another group of yellow paints. "There's another room over there. Let's try that one and she can get back to the sink."

Adam followed Peter out of the room and thanked the animator for waiting. But, he didn't have Peter's dimples.

"Just don't take too long. People have to work, you know."

"Yes. Sorry." Adam caught up to Peter in the next room. This room had an animator's desk and an overhead ventilation system for the paint fumes. There were another wall of shelving, but there was more than just paint. He could see folder systems and books. Signed artwork was displayed on the upper walls. Peter, he could see, was examining the shelves of glass bottles and animator's brushes. "Is that it, Peter?"

Peter's hands shook as he reached for the bottles. "There aren't any yellows. Look! There isn't even one yellow." He gently pushed a blue bottle aside, his heart pounding. "It isn't here."

"Don't panic, Pete. This has to be the room. There're lots of yellows over on that far wall. Just start talking before someone wonders what we're doing in here." Adam lifted the iPad to eye level again and pushed the record button. "Start talking, Peter."

Running out of material and nerves, Peter started to rattle on about his favorite rides at Disneyland as he edged his way around the room. "Oops, dropped my mike," he announced rather loudly.

"Be careful with the equipment, buddy," Adam automatically replied as he glanced over his shoulder. No one seemed to be paying the least bit of attention to them any longer. "We're clear, Pete. Check out that bottom shelf."

"Uncle Adam! Look! There's a **WED** engraved into the shelf. This is it. It has to be."

Adam hefted the iPad again and hit record, using his body to block anyone from seeing Peter on the floor. "I only see plastic from here, but do what you have to."

Peter didn't take time to reply. There were five different yellows lined up on that shelf, three deep. All of the tall plastic bottles had their elaborate color code facing outward. Peter pulled some of them off the shelf to set them on the floor out of his way. In his hurry, one of them tipped over. He gasped when the bottle's blue endcap slowly rolled away. Canary yellow paint began to ooze all over the floor. Before he could panic further, his eye caught the glint of glass in the back corner. A small, round paint bottle was crammed into the darkest corner behind all the tall containers. And it was yellow. "I found it!"

"Someone's coming. Pocket it and stand up. Hurry. Start talking."

His face flushed, Peter stood just as a different artist came into the room.

"You guys almost done in here?" His mouth went into a deeper frown when he saw the yellow paint spreading over the floor. "What happened here?"

Peter managed to look teary-eyed. "Oh, I'm so sorry. It's all my fault. I was trying to show the bottle to the camera and it just fell out of my hands! I'll clean it up. I'm so sorry."

Adam felt he needed to step in. "We're awfully sorry about the mess. If you show us where the rags are, I'll be glad to clean the floor. Sometimes the boy gets so excited while he's talking. Probably why his blog is so popular." Adam forced his lips to close when he found he was rambling.

The artist looked up from the spill. "No, that's all right. It happens more than you'd think. I'll call for the janitor. He's used to this kind of mess." If he wondered why the young one no longer looked so devastated, he didn't say anything. "You have all you need for your, uh, blog?"

"Yes, we have exactly what we needed. We got just what we came for."

Adam signaled for Peter to tone it down. "Yes, thanks. Everyone has been so helpful. We need to get going, Pete. I think our time's up."

In his excitement, Peter had to hold himself from breaking into a run as they headed for Adam's car. "We did it, Uncle Adam! We found Walt's next clue! Can we go tell Catie?"

Adam put a fond arm around the boy's shoulders. "I think that's a great idea. Do you think we have a minute to shop in the Studio store? I'd like to pick up a souvenir. Or two."

"How about the Commissary? I'm starving."

Just like his dad. "You're always starving. Let's not push our luck. We'll stop somewhere on the way home. How about the Tam O'Shanter on Los Feliz Boulevard? We'll ask for Walt's table."

CHAPTER 11

Fullerton Hospital

"Catie, we got the next clue! Your dad was so cool! It was awesome!"

Adam stood back at the door to watch Peter interact with Catie. The nurses had just finished moving her arms and legs to help keep them limber. After they left, Peter continued their tale of daring-do. Adam was encouraged. Peter seemed a lot more animated and excited about the clue search than he had been. He wondered if this Hidden Mickey hunt would do the trick and get the boy back to his normal excitable self about all things Disney.

"We were just using the iPad and an old microphone and... Oh! Uncle Adam! Her eyes are open! Catie?"

At Peter's startled gasp, Adam leaned out and hollered for the nurse. Adam then rushed to the bed to take up Catie's limp hand. Her unfocused eyes had indeed fluttered open.

The nurse ran in and checked Catie's monitor. But, by the time she pulled out a flashlight to check the retinas, Catie's eyes had slowly closed again.

"That's a good thing, right?" His heart pounding, Adam's voice was full of hope. "Is she coming around?"

"I'll call the doctor right away. Yes, I think this is a very good sign."

Peter pulled out his phone. "I'm going to call Mom and Dad."

As much as Adam wanted to shout from the rooftops, he held out a restraining hand. "Let's just wait and hear what the doctor has to say. This could be like her finger movements and just involuntary." Even though his eyes were wide, Adam took a steadying deep breath. "I don't want to get everyone's hopes up." As Peter's phone was slowly returned to his pocket, Adam smiled at the boy. "But, I think this is very promising. I think we're getting our girl back."

Once the doctor had checked Catie and gone over her brain wave chart, he, too, was optimistic. "That is a good sign that she's coming back to consciousness. Just so you know," he cautioned when Adam looked ready to grab up his phone, "this will still be a slow process. We don't know for sure when she will fully come around. There will probably be some confusion at first while she gets used to the idea of where she is and what happened to her. Catie might not know or remember. Her brain and her body will have to get used to functioning again. It's possible there will have to be some rehabilitation." He hated to see Adam's face fall. "But, there's always the chance that she will come out of it just fine. You just need to know the possibilities. I suggest you all keep doing what you've been doing. Any more questions?"

Adam refused to let the hope within wither. "No. I think you answered everything. Thank you." After shaking hands, and the doctor left, Adam pulled out his phone. "I think we can call the others now. You know what to say, Peter? We don't want them to think she's going to wake up and go home tomorrow."

"I know. But, it would be cool if she did."

Adam had to smile. "Yes, it would be cool....Beth! Honey, guess what? Catie opened her eyes for a couple of moments...Yes, the doctor just left...I know. I'm happy, too...But, here's what he said...."

"Catie, before everyone else gets here, I wanted to open the paint jar with you." Peter pulled the yellow jar out of his backpack and held it up to Catie's face. He knew her eyes would stay closed, but he was still inwardly disappointed when they did. "I found it in the third room of the Paint Department. And, I made a mess. Hard to believe, right?" With a chuckle, he looked over at Uncle Adam.

"Yeah, he sure did, honey. Had to drop one of the brightest yellow paints in the whole room. At least he didn't step in it and have yellow footsteps leading back to our car."

Peter let out a laugh. "That would have been cool!" At the look on Adam's face he felt he had to defend himself. "Well, it would have. If they didn't clean them up, my footprints would be there for everyone to see."

"I don't know if that would be a good thing, Pete."

With a disagreeing shrug, Peter turned back to the paint jar. "Well, anyway, we have the next clue. The jar is pretty small and doesn't make any noise when I shake it. It has to be just the next clue." He twisted off the metal cap and peered inside. "Hey, the inside of the jar was painted yellow. I can see where the brush-strokes stopped. See? They don't even cover the bottom of the jar."

Adam held out his hand so he could examine it. "Well, it would have been difficult to hide a clue in an actual bottle of paint. Maybe this one was specially done just for the clue." The collector in Adam hated to hand the jar back to Peter. He wondered if Walt's finger-prints were on the glass.

"Yep, it's another piece of paper like the other ones. This one says: "**Visit Nevangnewa's house on the cliff.**" Frowning, Peter reread the name on the clue. "Gosh, I wish Uncle Wolf was here. That sounds like something he would know. Uncle Adam?"

Adam didn't answer. He was trying to turn his mind from Catie to focus on the new clue. "Why does that sound so familiar? I should know what that means, but just can't remember."

"Remember what?" Smiles on their faces, Lance and Kimberly came into the room. After a quick hug from Peter, they checked on Catie. "So, our girl's doing better, we hear?"

"You got here fast." Adam checked his watch. Peter had just ended the call to his parents before he finished his update with Beth. "Were you in the area?"

"Took the boys to a play date. So, we just swung over." Lance took the chair by the door, his long legs sprawled out and ankles crossed. "So, what was your feeble mind trying to remember, Adam?"

Adam let it pass. In a better mood than he had been in for a month, he let Lance have his little victory. "We were discussing the next clue Peter found in the paint room."

Lance perked up. "So, you were successful. Wondered if you could pull it off without me…"

"Hey! I was just as much a force in our quest..."

"Boys, boys, boys." Kimberly hid her grin as Lance pushed a few more of Adam's buttons. She could tell Adam was more optimistic than he had been and was thrilled to see it. "Play nice or I'll send you to separate rooms."

Lance pointed at Adam. "He started it."

"I..."

"So, Peter, what did you find?" Kimberly interrupted what could have gone on for hours. "Did you get another clue?"

Peter was sorry the show was over. When his dad and Uncle Adam started to banter, he usually found out more than they intended for him to hear. "Um, yeah." He held up the small jar so they could see it. "We found this and I had just read the clue to Catie." He read it again for his parents.

Kimberly and Adam began to discuss the possible meanings while Lance sat back, a smug look on his face. It didn't take long for the others to notice.

Adam was the first to comment on it. "What? I know that superior look of yours."

"Remember when we were running the MouseAdventure quest when we found the diary?"

Adam waited for a more specific question, but there wasn't anything forthcoming. He knew Lance well enough to know he would make Adam work for it. "Yes. And..."

"We discussed that very name."

"That was over fourteen years ago! I don't have your freaky, abnormal perfect memory."

Lance had always been proud of the fact that he was able to remember everything he ever read. He didn't tell too many people as some tended to treat him like a one-trick pony and use him like a party game. "Eidetic memory, if you want to be precise."

"Lance," Kimberly threw out as a warning.

"Sorry." He looked the exact opposite of contrite as he let out a long-suffering sigh. "We had been discussing possible questions that might come up during the Race. You asked if I remembered the name of the Hopi chief who blessed the Grand Canyon Diorama when it opened in 1958. I answered yes and you, for some reason, dropped it."

"Silly me." Adam shook his head. Remaining friends with

Lance for decades took a lot of work. "Now that you mention it—finally—that does sound right. I think that's your answer, Peter."

Peter, whose head had been swiveling back and forth as if he had been watching a tennis match, looked baffled. "Answer to what? I don't even know what you're talking about any more."

His dad roused himself out of the chair and came over to put his arm around his son's shoulder. "Yeah, I know what you mean. It's like that around Uncle Adam all the time."

"Hey!"

"Lance."

Unabashed, Lance returned to the chair to stretch out again. "What you have, Peter, is the answer to your clue. Nevangnewa was the name of the Hopi chief who was with Walt when he opened the Grand Canyon Diorama. You just have to figure out what Walt meant by his house on the cliff."

"And you aren't going to tell me?"

"Nope. What fun is that?" Lance smiled over at Adam. "Half of the fun of the quests was figuring out the clues and discovering where we needed to go. Right, Adam?"

Adam had to agree with Lance. "Yeah. Much as I hate to admit you're right about anything. You've been doing this for a while now, Pete. Don't you find it more rewarding when you figure it out for yourself?"

Peter was torn. He understood what Uncle Adam meant, but sometimes he still liked the easy way out. He also understood which answer the adults would like to hear. "Yes, I know what you mean. I'll figure it out. You gave me a hint, now I'll find out the rest." With a big smile on his face he turned to his mom. "So, when can I go back to Disneyland?"

"Don't you get tired of that place?" All eyes in the room turned toward the doorway. Wolf and Omah had just arrived.

"Uncle Wolf! Do you know who Nevangnewa was?"

Omah had just gotten a hug from Kimberly and was greeting Peter. She frowned as she looked over at Wolf. "Why does that name sound familiar? It's Hopi, I know that."

"The ninety-six-year old chief who blessed the Grand Canyon Diorama. Nice guy."

Omah snapped her fingers. "That's right! Oh, and remember the little boy, Little White Cloud? He was supposed to represent

Chico, the mascot of the Santa Fe Railroad, but not too many people got that. When Walt and Fred Gurley drove off in the new train, he had to stand by the side of the track and wave at everyone as they went in to see the Diorama for the first time."

"Walt also brought in the Santa Fe All-Indian Band from Winslow, Arizona. It was a big day for Walt. The Diorama was great." Wolf broke off and grinned. "I should say, the Diorama was Grand." There was a disgusted snort when no one seemed to appreciate his humor. "But I think Walt really enjoyed adding another engine to his train collection."

Peter thought he saw an opening to get the answer to the rest of his clue. "Hey, Uncle Wolf, why would Walt say the chief had a house on a cliff?"

Not knowing what had been discussed earlier, Wolf told him, "Hopis were cliff dwellers. He was probably referring to the ruins at the start of the Diorama. What? What'd I say?" He couldn't understand why Adam and Lance groaned and started to signal him behind Peter's back. "Is something wrong?"

Peter was all smiles. "No, not at all. Thanks!"

"You just told Peter the answer to his new clue. We were going to have him look it up himself."

"Oops." Unconcerned, Wolf shrugged it off. "Well, he'll still have to figure out how to reach it."

Picturing the Diorama in his mind, Peter had already been running possible scenarios. Then he started working on it out loud as he paced the short distance around Catie's bed. "Well, I know I can't get in through the front. That's solid glass." The pacing suddenly stopped when he got a brilliant idea. "Hey, I know! I can rappel in from the roof like Dad and Uncle Adam did in San Francisco. They can teach me how."

There was a chorus of "No!" before Lance, a wry grin on his face, could add, "I knew we shouldn't have talked about that in front of you. I don't know where Adam came up with all those dangerous ideas of his. I'm surprised we all weren't killed."

"Hey!"

Chapter 12

Disneyland

    Stuck close to his dad's side, Peter blended in with a large group of cast members who just got off the shuttle from the parking lot. The harried guard at the Harbor Pointe security gate recognized Lance and barely glanced at his identification as they were quickly waved through.

    Once they were safe and out of earshot, Peter was surprised when Lance stopped him. With a hand on the boy's shoulder, Lance glanced back at the gate. He knew what Peter planned to do, but was also well aware of what he would find when he followed that chosen path. "Do you need me to go with you? You know what you're going to do?" The decision to let Peter follow this quest on his own—now that Catie was unable to join him—nagged at the back to Lance's mind. Being a dad, he wanted to help; he wanted his children to succeed in whatever they did. But he realized his desire went against the decision that all of the adults had made. He had to let the boy figure it out for himself.

    Peter stifled an impatient groan and squirmed under the firm hand. Eager to get going and find the next clue, he didn't want to stand around chatting with his dad. "Yes, Dad, I know what I'm doing. I've heard Mom and Aunt Beth talk about Costuming forever. They said over and over how they could hear the trains go by. I know what to do!"

    Biting back what was on the tip of his tongue, Lance could only smile and nod. "All right. If you did your research, then go ahead. Just keep your head down."

Once Lance's hand was lifted from his shoulder, it was Peter who hesitated. It seemed like his dad wanted to say something else but didn't. "Okay. Anything else?"

Lance's smile didn't exactly give the impression of sincerity. "Nope. You're on your own. Just like you wanted."

With the intuition all children learn early on in their lives, Peter knew there was something else behind his dad's words. He waited a moment longer in case Lance decided to enlighten him. When nothing else was said, his right shoulder rose in a slight shrug. *Parents can sure act weird sometimes.* "Okay. I'll see you later, Dad."

Lance said nothing as Peter turned to the left and headed away from him. With a sigh and a "he'll figure it out," Lance headed for the tunnel under the berm and to his assignment.

On his own now, Peter ran at a jog down the long walkway as he headed to Costuming. The building, painted in Walt's favorite No-See-Um Green, blended in with the background trees and shrubs as intended. The eyes of the guests passing overhead on the Monorail wouldn't be drawn to the unobtrusive structures, but instead to the attractions they could see inside the Park. All of the show buildings, Administration, and offices outside of the berm were done in a similar green or gray. Some buildings, such as the show building for Indy, also had a row of tall palm trees to help hide it in plain sight.

Peter's steps slowed as he neared a row of doors and loading bays. From his research, he thought there should have been just three doors: one door would go into general Costuming, one would head upstairs for seasonal and winter costumes, and the third was the exit door. His research said nothing about huge cargo loading doors. Confused, he stared at a burgundy, gold, and green sign that proclaimed: Welcome to the World Famous Cast Costuming. Centered on the sign was one of the mice from *Cinderella* as he stood on a spool of thread and held out a measuring tape. As welcoming as the sign appeared, Peter doubted it would apply to him if he got caught in what he planned to do.

A chatting, noisy group of five young cast members approached the building, their arms full of dirty costumes. One of the college-aged women, Sandy, recognized Peter and noticed the hesitant expression on his face. "Hold up, guys. Hey, I know you!

You're Peter, Lance's boy, aren't you?"

Peter's look immediately went from hesitant to wary. Being unseen and unnoticed had been his plan, not everyone knowing who he was. "Um, yeah, I guess."

"What are you doing out here? This isn't your usual area of exploration."

Mollified by her pleasant, non-demanding demeanor, Peter relaxed a little. He hadn't realized his exploits—like his dad's had been—were better known within the Park than he realized. "I...No, but...I, um, just need to get inside Costuming to check something out." Peter felt his heartrate speed up. The idea that his brilliant, though somewhat vague, plan could come to a screeching halt before it even got started thrust itself into his mind. Falling back on a tried-and-true method, he turned on the charm. "Is there any way you can help me? I don't want to steal anything," he hurried to explain. "I just need to check out what's in the back of the building."

His big green eyes and wide smile seemed to be working. The three women of the group huddled together to see what they could do. Sandy seemed to be the leader, the instigator of the bunch. When she turned back to Peter, her eyes had the spark of anticipation. "Okay, I think we know what we need to do." She waved a hand at the loading dock. "This isn't where you need to be. None of us can get in there. Follow us around the corner. You knew this was the back of the Team Disney Store, right?"

She led the group past the loading bays to a walkway that had vending machines and outdoor lockers. "Okay," Sandy continued as they stood at the end of the long building, "this is the area where you want to go. That first door," she pointed, "goes upstairs, but I don't think you want that." They walked past a row of trees that shaded the area. "Here is where we need to be. Hold on while we drop our costumes into the chutes."

This was new and fascinating to Peter. Aunt Beth and his mom had never explained the details of what they considered an uninteresting routine. He closely watched Sandy as the items of clothing were carefully placed into the chutes so the computer could read the barcode on each piece. "If the computer doesn't read each number, we could get in trouble for a missing costume." As Peter waited, he noticed one of the guys held on to a couple pieces of his Jungle Cruise outfit.

"Everyone ready? Y'all know who does what?" Like a general reviewing her troops, Sandy got the affirmative from her group. Everyone, that is, except Peter who was still in the dark. She next turned to him. "Okay, Peter. Inside that door we expect to find one cast member who is somewhat guarding the entry. We need to get you past him. Shouldn't be too difficult. If he's who I think he is, he likes Cindy here."

"Eww." Apparently Cindy didn't feel the same.

Unmindful, Sandy continued outlining her plans. "Cindy and the two of us girls will block his view while Todd here acts normal and goes to Wall-E to get his costume assignment. Jack will put you behind him, out of sight of our guard. Once you get past the first row of hanging costumes, duck to the right. Jack'll come back and get his costume assignment from Wall-E. Then you're on your own. How does that sound?"

Peter's face lit up. "That sounds great! But, how will I get out again?"

The group exchanged an amused look. "Oh, I have a feeling that will take care of itself. Is, uh, your dad around?"

Not sure he liked the sound of that, Peter just nodded as some of his eagerness faded.

"That's good. Hopefully he'll be the one who responds to the call."

"What call?"

Sandy grinned at him. "The call when you get caught."

Todd, the quiet one of the group, spoke for the first time. "He should be safe from the sensors."

Mouth open, Peter gasped. "Sensors? What sensors? No one said anything about sensors! Are they in the floor or in the walls?"

After a quick glare at Todd, Jack turned to the white-faced boy. "Calm down, buddy. They aren't laser beams. They just detect the barcodes in our costumes. If we have on too many items, the sensor goes off. With over eight hundred costumes to keep track of, they were needed. Keeps theft down. Since you don't have on any costume parts, you should be fine." Jack, who must have been a linebacker in high school football, placed a meaty hand on Peter's shoulder. "Nothing usually gets past the guard at the door or the sensors. But, with a little distraction, you can get a head start. Oh, and keep your head down when you go past the offices right inside. There're windows on each side looking out into Costuming. You ready?"

As anxious as he was, Peter still had a moment of worry for his helpers. "Won't you all get in trouble?"

Big smiles went around the group of Peter's new friends. "Only if we get caught. And we don't plan on getting caught. You girls ready?"

Once in battle formation, Peter's eyes widened when the three women suddenly began a heated argument centered on the mild Todd and the unsuspecting guard inside. As the four friends angrily stormed through the door, Jack and Peter quietly hovered in the back of the scuffle. As planned, all eyes in the cavernous room turned toward the shrill, demanding, angry voices as various pieces of Jungle Cruise costumes flew at the guard under assault. Edging deeper inside, past the offices, Peter ducked down as Jack shielded the boy with his body. Once they were past the first double rack of hanging costumes, Peter felt a slight shove and was off like a scared rabbit. Jack slowly wandered back to the entry, a half-smile on his lips. Once Todd saw Jack was alone, he immediately apologized for all his sins, real or imagined. Sandy then threw her arms around his neck and declared she just knew Todd wasn't a flake and that Cindy liked someone else, not him. The argument ended as quickly as it had started. With bright smiles they presented their identifications to the irritated Lead. Not as easily mollified as Sandy seemed to be, he grumbled as he peeled layers of costumes off himself and the floor and shoved them back at Todd. The now-happy group quietly went to Wall-E to get their printouts for the locations of their replacement clothes. Their cheerful thanks and a wink from Cindy were ignored as the guard turned to the check next cast member who had come in behind them.

Peter had to keep his goal in mind as he hurried through row after glorious row of cast member costumes—Jungle Cruise, Haunted Mansion, Star Tours, Buzz Lightyear, Monorail—all just hanging there in wonderful pressed perfection. Back at the entrance, also distracting him, had been a brown line-drawing of Cinderella sewing her ball dress with the mice clustered around her. The mere glance he had of it wasn't enough, but he knew better than to go back for a better look. Hearing one of the steam train's whistle as it approached the Main Street Station helped him to refocus. "Just like Aunt Beth and Mom said."

The group had entered the room at aisle 18. When he reached the back of the room, aisle 1, he came to an abrupt halt. Expecting to find one or two locked doors that would lead out of the cavernous room and into the Diorama, he only found a wall. His fingers already had curled around the master key hidden in his pocket, just itching to pull it out and get to his desired location. Now all he could do was stare at the back wall.

"You still here, buddy? You need to go!"

Since he had been thus far undetected and lulled by that false sense of security, Peter whirled around at the sound of the urgent voice. Jack stood next to him, taking his time retrieving the last piece to finish off his costume. "But, Jack, there isn't any door back here! Where's the door?"

"Shh! Don't panic. What door? What are you talking about?"

"Into the Grand Canyon Diorama. I...I was sure there was a door back here."

To stall for time, Jack put back what was in his hand and picked up a different one. "I don't know where you got your information, but you're all mixed up. One, there's no door back here. And, two, if there was, it wouldn't be to the Diorama. The Primeval World show building is behind us. And, three, how were you planning on getting past the train tracks?" Hearing something, Jack's head snapped toward the front of the room. "You need to go, man. Head back the way you came. We have Cindy waiting for you up front to get you out. Go!" He could see a look of complete confusion on the boy's face but knew there wasn't any time to discuss it. "You've got the wrong building. Now, get out!"

At Jack's last words, Peter knew he had to leave and regroup. With a hastily muttered, "Thanks," he ran through the racks of clothes. Once he signaled Cindy, she distracted the guard by asking if he was going to the cast member party the next night. Thinking he had a chance for a date, the guard followed her as she backed away from the exit. Peter saw his opportunity and ran for the door, ignoring the sudden yell behind him to stop. Apparently Cindy hadn't been as distracting as she thought she was.

Faced with a long, fruitless run back to the Harbor Pointe station, Peter knew he had to come up with another escape route.

With no other recourse, he took a chance and turned left to run past a row of trees, expecting to be grabbed at any moment. Hearing some mournful barking, he knew he was near the Disneyland Kennel Club for pets not allowed inside the two Parks. Following the corner of the building, he came across a cast member exit. Pushing through the small gate, he passed the kennels. Now in the Esplanade between Disneyland and Disney California Adventure, he kept a steady pace as he dodged through lines of guests waiting to get into Disneyland. Gasping for air, he threw himself down onto a bench in front of Guest Services. Now that he was on the opposite side of the Esplanade Peter tried to calm his wildly-beating heart. Eyes glued to the path he had taken, he kept watch but didn't see any signs of pursuit.

"Wrong building? How could it be the wrong building? Mom said she could hear the train every time it went by." Peter yanked off his backpack and dug through it. On the bottom, hidden from any casual security scan, was a satellite map of the Park that he had printed. Circled was the Costume Department with an arrow that pointed at what he thought was the Grand Canyon Diorama. He smacked his forehead when he realized what Jack had told him: the Costume Department was on the same side of the tunnel as the train. The Diorama, just like the Primeval World, was safe behind huge sheets of glass—on the other side of the track. If he had indeed found a door into the tunnel, he would have only had access to the train, not the Diorama. "I was on the wrong side of the tracks. Any access door would have to be on the other side of the berm. Gosh, how do I miss stuff like this?" The map was lowered into his lap. "I miss Catie. She would've caught this stupid mistake."

With his missing friend, and now his error, he felt deflated. Shoulders sagging, he barely moved when his phone buzzed. A glance at the face showed it was his dad. In another moment of insight, he realized Lance had known all along that he was on the wrong path. But, stubbornly, Peter had wanted to do it himself. For Catie. "Boy, she sure would've been disappointed in me...Hi, Dad," he sighed when he finally answered the phone.

"You in jail yet?"

Peter had to smile at that. "No, not yet. Almost got caught. One of my friends helped me out."

Lance sounded confused. "Friends? Who helped you?"

"Long story."

"I like long stories."

"I'll tell you later, Dad. Where are you?" Peter let out a long groan. He might as well confess since Lance probably already knew. "I had it all wrong. Everything. I didn't find the way into the Diorama."

Lance could hear the discouragement in Peter's voice. "We'll figure it out, son. You want to go for lunch? Corn dog or a slice of pizza?"

At the promise of food, Peter's cheer slowly returned. "Wow. A whole slice of pizza? Do we have to share or do I get it all for myself?"

"I don't know, Pete. How much money do you have on you?"

Before Peter could answer, his dad ended the call. "That's weird. Where am I supposed to meet him?"

"How about here in the Esplanade? And, do you always talk to yourself out loud?"

Peter spun around. "Dad! How'd you know where I was?"

Lance jerked his thumb over his shoulder. "I was patrolling Main Street when I heard the gunshots from the Jungle Cruise and the Monorail horn as it went by. Where else would those two sounds meet? So, pizza?" He left out the fact that Wolf had been posted near the Team Disney Store and had watched the frantic escape.

Peter felt himself relax. Dad was here now and he could regroup. "I'll pay if I can have an advance on my allowance."

Lance put his arm around Peter's shoulder to steer him to the nearby Exit gate. The cast member smiled as she swung open the iron gate for them. Lance nodded his thanks and returned to their negotiations. "How about Carnation Café, no advance, and I'll pay?"

"How about Carnation Café, an advance, and you still pay?"

Once they were seated in a far corner under one of the red and white striped umbrellas, Lance quietly asked, "So, what went wrong, Pete?"

After a long gulp of his lemonade, Peter launched into his tale of new friends and mistakes in reading a map.

Chapter 13

Flashback – Burbank – 1957

"The rebuilding of the *Fred Gurley* is coming right along, Walt"

Walt looked over from the storyboards that filled one of the walls. On that side of the room, the Grand Canyon Diorama was laid out scene-by-scene in the same manner as an animated feature. As the story progressed, guests would experience the Canyon starting from early morning, into a thunder and lightning storm, and end with a beautiful sunset. "Yeah, that train was a good find in Louisiana. And, with the open-sided Narragansett passenger cars that face toward the Park, the guests'll get a better show." Walt turned back to the storyboard, quiet as his head slowly shook back and forth.

That subtle movement from Walt never bode well for the animators or designers. A quick look went around the assembled group to see who would ask. "Something wrong, Boss?"

Walt's eyes didn't leave the colored panels when he finally answered. "I think we can do better. I've seen dioramas in museums in Los Angeles and in New York. I'm going to send Claude to Arizona and then we can start again."

Surprised, the artist/set designer/animator looked up from his notebook. "What!?"

A new set of storyboards covered the wall. Arms folded across his chest, Walt paused in front of one of the panels. "They don't have turkeys in the Grand Canyon, Claude."

"Yes, they do, Walt."

"You saw them."

"No, but I didn't see a mountain lion, either. That doesn't mean they weren't there. I saw the turkeys in a local museum."

Silent, his mind always working, Walt moved on to the next rendering.

Later that week, Walt showed the storyboard to a friend who was visiting the Studio. "Say, did you know they had turkeys at the Grand Canyon?"

"They do? I didn't know that."

Once his friend was out of the room, Walt turned back to Claude. "I'm still not sure about this. Are you positive there are wild turkeys in the Canyon?"

Knowing his boss, Claude was ready for him this time. "Yep. I called the park superintendent responsible for the Canyon and he said the flocks are on the increase!"

On March 31, 1958, after an elaborate dedication ceremony, the first guests got to travel through the Grand Canyon Diorama. They were treated to a 34-foot high, 306-foot long seamless background that had taken more than 300 gallons of paint and over 80,000 man hours to design, paint and construct at a cost of $435,000. The diorama included mountain lions, deer, mountain sheep, skunks, and various birds—including wild turkeys.

Fullerton Hospital

"Catie, you should have seen all the costumes! As far as I could see, they were just hanging here, waiting. It was awesome!" Peter, for the moment alone with his friend, first told her the exciting part of his story. So far he hadn't related his mistake, the one that still ate at him. "They have this computer on the wall that they call Wall-E. It tells them where they need to go to get their costume parts. Your mom said they used to have these cards on the wall like baseball cards. Each costume would have its own card and it would list all the different pieces they needed. Now they have Wall-

E and sensors." Aware he was rambling to stall the inevitable, Peter fingered a pink teddy bear propped up on the stand next to her bed. All of the colorful Get Well balloons had been removed after inadvertently wrapping around her IV bag and setting off an alarm.

Before he could continue, her eyes slowly opened. Her forehead creased with confusion, Catie moved her head to stare straight at Peter. Already told this was a common occurrence now, Peter softly patted her hand. "Hi. It's okay, Catie," he whispered. "You're safe. I'm here. I was just telling you…" He broke off when her eyes closed and she drifted back into the less-muddled darkness. With a silent sigh of disappointment, he had to wait a moment before he was able to continue. "I was just about to tell you about my mistake. I really blew it, Catie. I was totally in the wrong building. Costuming doesn't lead anywhere. But, you probably would have known that, huh?" After a quick glance at the empty door, Peter leaned closer to the bed to finish what he had started to say. "I miss you, Catie. I miss your help and I miss you being there with me. Please wake up so we can work on this together. I know where to go now. Dad helped me figure out the way to get in. But he won't let me rappel in from the ceiling. Go figure." At his little joke, a crooked smile turned up the corners of his mouth in the darkness of the room. It faded when he finished what was in his heart. "I… I just wish you were with me."

Peter moved over to the window to stare into the night sky. Moments later, Wolf came into the room. When he heard the movement, Peter, arms folded across his chest, turned and frowned at his friend. "Don't say it, Uncle Wolf. I'm *not* wishing on a star. You already have that song playing over and over in my head every time I look out a window."

Over by Catie, Wolf's small smile went unseen. In a soft voice, he spoke to the girl in Lakota, his words low and melodic. When he was done, his hand lightly brushed the hair off her forehead. "Rest up, little one. You'll be back with us soon." He looked up to see that Peter still stared at him. The boy's expression, though, had changed from challenging to curious. "What? Can't I say good night to her, too, Pete?"

It wasn't often that someone witnessed the softer side of Wolf. He himself had been on the receiving end, but it still intrigued him. Biting back a grin he knew wouldn't be appreciated, Peter merely shrugged. "That's cool. Are you ready to take me home?"

As they walked through the hospital corridors, they quietly discussed Peter's next move.

"I still don't see why I can't…"

"No."

Peter glanced at his friend. "No what? You don't even know what I was…"

"You are not going to rappel into the building."

A smile passed Peter's lips. "I still don't see…"

"Besides the fact that it's extremely dangerous? You do know that the Diorama building is four stories tall, right? Even if rappelling *was* the only way to get in—which it's not—you would have to know exactly the right spot to enter the roof or you'd be in the wrong part of the room." Wolf knew Peter had just been trying to push his buttons. He had to add one of his own. "You'd never have enough time. Though it would be fun to see you dangling in the air twenty feet from the roof when the next train went by. You were given two other options to get in. I assume you picked the more difficult of the two?"

"Two? Dad only told me about the way in through the building on the Tomorrowland side." Peter heard an amused snort.

"Figures."

"What?" Peter couldn't make out what Wolf had just mumbled. "Mom's going with me Saturday. Did you want to help me, too?"

"I have to work." *And keep an eye on you.*

Peter let it go. He had something more interesting on his mind. When they reached Wolf's car, Peter had to ask. "So, what did you say to Catie? I only understood a couple of the words."

Wolf slid behind the steering wheel. "I just told her you were turning into Jiminy Cricket."

"Hey!"

His amused smile hidden as he checked his side mirror, Wolf had one more question for the eager boy. "So, you figured out what to do about the Intruder Camera in the Diorama?"

"Camera? What camera??"

Disneyland

Kimberly and Peter pushed through a cast member-only door near the Redd Rocket Pizza Port and headed behind the buildings that led to Space Mountain. "Okay, Peter, we're almost there. Now, when we get to the *right* building," she started to kid but then broke off. A glance to her side showed Peter, focused solely on the mission ahead, had missed the intended humor. She could have danced a jig and he wouldn't have noticed. "Cast Health is on the second floor." With an inconspicuous gesture she indicated a plain brown door as they walked passed it. "There's your door. You'll need to get in and out as quickly as you can."

"I know, Mom." Realizing he had been abrupt, he felt he should add something. "You think a headache is enough of a reason to go to Cast Health?"

"I got to know the nurse pretty well when I was expecting your brothers. We're due for a nice chat. I'm just hoping she's working on a Saturday. The headache is just in case I'm questioned."

Peter absently nodded as his mind returned to the task ahead. As his mom entered the long, gray building, he knew the music from the towering Observatron in the middle of Tomorrowland would fade away for her. For him, the blaring, soaring music was part of the mosaic of background sounds from the Park. Peter's goal was at the end of the tunnel nearest the Tomorrowland train station. The Hopi ruins were the first of the features the guests would see when the train started through the Grand Canyon Diorama. This unmarked brown door at the top of a short flight of cement stairs was at least at the correct end of the tunnel.

Peter mentally went over the bits of information he had gathered in his second and third rounds of research. Safe behind glass, safe from any items guests might have attempted to throw into the depths of the display, the attraction required little maintenance. The long room was air conditioned and the climate was held at seventy-four degrees—a measure that also kept the glass windows from fogging over. Thanks to special lighting, the carefully-painted backdrop hadn't faded in all the years it was on exhibition. With an ingenious dust precipitator, the animals preserved inside needed only minimal care now and then. The tree trunks and evergreens were real plants. Following Walt's instructions, they had all been hung upside down for a year to preserve them and retain their unique shapes. The lightning effects were carefully monitored so no burned-out bulb spoiled the illusion of early morning light or a summer storm or the finale of a beautiful sunset. Because of this care and attention, Peter felt only a few access doors inside would be needed—doors that could only be reached after getting past the Intruder Camera.

Peter pulled out his phone and brought up a favorite game. After setting it on Pause, he returned it to his pocket, ready to go. After a quick glance to the right and left, his heart hammering, he brought out the other item in his pocket: his treasured Key to Disneyland. Seeing no one in the vicinity, he was now ready to try the first part of his vague plan. Waiting until he heard one of the trains pass through the tunnel, he ran up the stairs to the brown door. Trying to time it in his mind, he didn't want to open the door too early in case some unwelcome light flooded that part of the display. A quick-thinking conductor might call in the incongruity and stop his plan before it really got started. When he felt it was all right, he unlocked the door, pushed it all the way open, and immediately slammed it shut again. Running back down the stairs, he positioned himself a ways down from the door and checked his watch. With a nonchalant air that belied his sweaty palms, he pulled out the game, leaned back against a rail and started to play, loud pinging and ringing bells obvious.

Within three minutes, a custodian and an unknown security guard came hurrying up the walkway. After a perfunctory glance at Peter, they hurried up the stairs and entered the Diorama. The two men did a thorough search inside the vast room. When they came out five minutes later, they were obviously confused. The security guard came up to Peter who, like most kids these days, he thought, seemed to be engrossed in something on his phone.

"Excuse me. Have you been here a while? Did you by chance see anyone go inside that brown door?"

"Huh?" Peter assumed a confused air. "Where? What door? Oh, that one? Uh, no, I didn't see anyone. Where does it go?"

His last question was ignored. The guard looked over at the custodian and shrugged before turning back to Peter. "You're positive? No one came out of there?"

"I'm just waiting for my mom. She went into Cast Health and

made me stay out here."

"Okay, then. Thanks." The guard returned to the custodian, their voices low as they walked away.

Peter heard the words "malfunction" and "bug." He smiled. The plan had worked so far.

When enough time had elapsed for the two men to get back to wherever they were going, Peter repeated his actions. Only this time, after he ran down the stairs, he hid out of sight but still in view of the door.

The same two men responded to the alarm from inside the Diorama. When they were done with their inspection, they were perplexed. There was no one inside and no sign of any entry. Nothing had been touched or moved. "It has to be a bug in the system, Rob. Do you think we should shut it down and get the camera checked?"

"Good idea." The custodian made the call and then lowered his two-way radio. "I just had the alarm shut off. We can't be running back here every five minutes until it gets fixed. But, the bad news is that the tech guys won't be here for at least an hour." Rob looked around at the area with a critical eye. "There isn't much traffic back here. It should be alright until they get here."

"I don't see that kid anywhere, either. He and his mom must have left."

Rob slapped the guard on the shoulder. "We did what we could, Ken. Let's get back to work."

From his hidden nook, Peter watched until the men were out of sight. Having heard every word, he knew how much time he had. With a confident, cocky smile on his face, he slipped inside the cool room.

From his low vantage point at the bottom of the painted canvas, he looked up to see the edges of the adobe-colored plaster bricks that formed the Hopi homes. Supposed to be ruins, the rounded dwellings were incomplete, jagged. Portions of wooden stick ladders, held together by rope, were part of the authentic-looking display. A short one stuck out of the roof of a square building. Another, longer ladder came up behind the first ruin. Peter was extremely pleased and relieved to see that the longer ladder was a real one. Metal at the bottom, it was, thanks to the magic of Imagineering, finished off at the top to look like wood.

Relaxed, thinking he had plenty of time, he looked all the way across at the uneven top to guess which animal was where. A strong desire came over him to run down to the far end of the Diorama to check and see if the snow really was ground-up Styrofoam. But, after a glance at his watch, he found he had already wasted five minutes gawking. "Better safe than sorry." Grabbing the sides of the ladder, he slowly started to climb the metal rungs.

At the top, he cautiously peered over the ragged edges of the bricks. When there was no train car full of passengers to stare back at him, he finished the ascent. Knowing Walt's way of making everything sturdy, he didn't hesitate to climb over the parapet and onto the rough surface of the ruins. Built with varying heights normal to the time period, Peter had to be careful where he stepped. Tripping over a rough brick and tumbling back down to the bottom of the Canyon was not what he wanted to do.

Standing there with hands on hips, he had to decide which building would be best to explore first. The rounded, open-topped structure was intriguing, but he would be in view of the passing trains. The one that Peter felt was most promising was a ruin that had been built into the side wall. It was the most secluded place, the seemingly perfect spot for Walt to have hidden a clue. All he had to do was get through the window and hope there was a solid floor on the other side.

With only four minutes before the next train would pass by, he carefully walked a few steps to test the strength of the rectangular window. When he found it didn't even wobble, he gave a slight jump and pulled himself through. To his relief there was a solid concrete floor. Now he had to find Walt's clue.

Suddenly he heard the whistle of the train as it set off from the Tomorrowland Station. The train passengers would only have time for a quick view of the old Skyway terminal's location and the back storage buildings before they headed into the first tunnel. What he didn't want them to see was him crouching inside that first brick dwelling. As he waited out the slow train, his back pressed against the wall, he saw flashes of light from hopeful guests attempting to get a photograph of the Canyon. Having tried that himself, he knew they would only be rewarded with pictures of the camera's flash due to the glass dividers. Eyes ever moving around the small area, his noticed something engraved on the base of the window sill. Still down out of sight, he edged over to the brick-like material and smiled. **WED**. There was his indicator.

As the last car, the luxurious Lilly Belle, inched out of sight, Peter's hands were inching over the rough surface around and below those initials. Near the bottom, off to the left side, was a loose plaster brick. Silently congratulating himself, Peter carefully pulled the orange brick out of its home and set it aside so he could reach inside.

He found nothing. "What? Really? Oh, come on." Frowning, he got down on the ground to peer inside the dark hole as best as he could in the soft orange light. What he could see was probably the side of the frame of the viewing window and a wall. Trying again, stretched as far as his arm could go, he could only feel the wall. There was no capsule or container or even a scrap of leftover wood.

Pulling his arm back out of the hole, Peter leaned against the wall as he tried to think. "Why isn't there another clue? Did someone else find it? Wouldn't Wolf have known if something was wrong? Did I miss the real spot?"

Feeling like he must have missed something, Peter leapt to his feet. Even more carefully he examined the rest of the small room, especially the area he had been leaning against. "Hey, that's a door! Shoot. How come I didn't see it when I came in?" He ran his fingers over the simple latch. The lock would be on the other side. "Well, I know how I'm getting out of here, anyway. Sheesh. This must have been what Wolf was hinting at. Coulda just told me."

With a disgusted shake of his head, he decided to search one of the other little buildings. "How long ago did that train go by? Shoot, I forgot to time it. Now I'll have to wait for the next one."

To kill some time, he picked up the brick to return it to its home. As he fingered the rough surface of the face, he found the back was relatively smooth. "Shoulda known it wasn't a real brick. Not sure what it was made…"

Flipping it over, his eyes wide, Peter's mumbling stopped. On the back of the brick was some engraving. He ran his fingers over the carefully-formed words:

"Mind Thy Head – 1787
Look out bellows!"

Chapter 14

Disneyland

"Mom, I'm going out another way. I found a door." The brick safely stashed in his backpack, Peter called Kimberly from a small closet-like space between two doors. Once the door into the Diorama had hissed and sealed shut behind him, he needed to let his mom know the change in plans. "I'm still in the tunnel."

After Kimberly and the nurse had run out of things to talk about, she still hadn't heard from Peter. Becoming more anxious by the moment, Kimberly found herself pacing back and forth outside of the long gray building. She felt it could go two ways. Peter could come walking out of the door, or he could be escorted out by Security. Apparently he had come up with a third option. "You're in the tunnel? Won't you be seen by everyone on the train?"

"No, I'm okay. There's another door I'm hiding behind right now. I can smell the train's smoke so I know the tunnel is right there. I need your help, though."

Those words always made Kimberly's stomach knot. "What happened? Did you get hurt? Did someone see you?"

"No, no, nothing like that. I need to get out of the tunnel, but I'm not sure which end to go to. Or should I go out one of the exit doors on the other side..."

"Hold on, Peter. One thing at a time. You're closest to the Tomorrowland end, right?"

"Yeah. Hold on. The train's going by. I can't hear you."

Through the phone Kimberly could hear the clank and rattle of the train as it passed Peter's hidden location. When the majority of the noise faded, she asked, "Pete? Can you hear me?"

"Yeah, we're good now. Do you think I should go out into Tomorrowland? There's a big gap between the train station and the start of the tunnel, so I could still be seen. And if a Monorail goes by, the pilot might see me, too."

A plan forming in her mind, Kimberly had already started to walk back to the Park. "Let me get to the Tomorrowland train station. I think I can cause a distraction for the conductor. You'll have to move quickly and take your chances with however many guests are waiting for the next train."

"Yeah, and anyone who might be working in the storage buildings."

She hadn't thought of that and groaned. "Listen, I'll call you from the station when I'm in place. The train's already gone, right? So you can at least get to the edge of the tunnel and wait."

"Okay, Mom. Thanks."

Secure in knowing the alarm was still off, Peter eased open the exit door and blinked into the darkness. Once his eyes adjusted, he walked a few hundred feet to peer out of the tunnel. Now a dusky evening, he was further protected by lengthening shadows as he waited. It was only a few minutes before his phone rang again. "Hi, Mom. I don't see anyone in the open doorways. It's clear on my end."

"Good. The station's almost empty. I'm at the far end, close to the Autopia track. I'm waving for the conductor now. Oh, he's looking. He's coming this way." Her voice changed to an excited hiss. "Now! Run, Peter! As quick as you can, get over to the sub entrance. I'll find you there. Gosh, don't know what I'm going to say…Hey, hi, there! Can you help me, uh, Russ?"

Peter heard the phone go silent and knew his mom had ended the call. Thrusting the phone into his pocket, he sprinted out of the tunnel. Leaving the blackened gravel of the tracks, he ran through the dirt and leaped over the low shrubs. Once at the station, head down, he ignored the yells of "Hey!" as he jumped over the metal fence. The sloped walkway he was now on led into Tomorrowland as it curved past Innoventions, rest rooms, a popular vendor stand, and Autopia. He had to veer around a family stopped in front of a height sign to see if their youngest was tall enough to ride Autopia by herself. Not waiting to find out the result, Peter rounded the corner and slowed down only when he neared the Finding Nemo Submarines. Heart pounding and breathing hard from the adrenaline coursing through him, he bounced in place as he waited for his mom.

Fullerton

Homework finished, the orange brick sat on top of it like a paperweight. Lost in thought, Peter idly pushed a pen around the top of his desk. It had been difficult for him to turn off the adrenaline and excitement and come back down to earth and normality. After chattering all the way home telling his mom every detail again, he had been sent to his room to do his ignored homework. Then he could start on the next clue if he so wanted. But after the History and the Calculus were labored through, his energy was spent.

Michael, Andrew, and the hopeful Dug had come in to clamor for his attention. The heavy brick was uninteresting to the younger boys. After an exploratory lick, Dug, too, was sent away disappointed. At this point, Peter just wanted a little solitude.

Now that he was alone, though, he didn't know what to do with himself. Used to a large extended family that included the Michaels and Wolf and Omah, the lack of noise wasn't as welcome as he thought it would be.

Pushing up from his chair, he wandered over to his oak bookcase which contained more souvenirs than books. With no definite plan in mind, he fingered some favorite Disney figurines. When he found himself poking the nose of a stuffed Stitch for no apparent reason, he sighed and looked around his large bedroom. He didn't want to listen to his music. He didn't want to watch a video or a movie. Dinner was over. There was no one he wanted to call or text. At a loss, he slowly wandered over to the window.

The sky overhead had darkened from dusk into night. The first evening star blinked into sight. Peter, head tilted, watched the faraway ball of gas get brighter and brighter, finally joined by a myriad of other twinkles.

"When you wish..."

"Darn it, Wolf!" he angrily thought to himself. "Stop it. I'm *not* wishing on a star. I'm just...I'm just..." He broke off and leaned back from the window, the glass now becoming a mirror. He stared into his own eyes as he completed his rant. "I'm just missing... someone."

The eyes in the window narrowed back at him, the anger spent. "Say it. It's all right. I'm wishing Catie was well again."

As he looked away from his reflection, his gaze stopped on his closed closet door. It was a large closet, a walk-in with floor-to-ceiling shelves, clothing rods, and cubby holes for shoes and packs. Much like the bookcase, the contents the closet were more treasures than clothes. Personal treasures he had already collected for years before the Hidden Mickey searches from Walt had begun. And, after the quests had started, the treasures became more special, more valuable.

Pulling open the paneled oak door, he flipped on the light and stepped into his closet. A quick glance over his shoulder confirmed that he was still alone. The door was clicked shut behind him. The thought of how great the costumes he had seen hanging in that huge room at Disneyland would look in here briefly came and went through his mind. There was something else more important as he reached the cluttered back wall of shelves. Third shelf up from the bottom, stashed under ski goggles, masks and gloves was a smallish box. Unadorned and unlocked, it had been moved to this spot after he felt his under-the-bed hiding place had been compromised. Peter slowly pulled the metal box out from underneath the pile.

His back to the shelves, he sank into a sitting position on the carpeted floor as he stared at the gray box. Already knowing what was inside—mostly treasures from past Hidden Mickey quests—he delayed the simple action of lifting the lid. Did he want to acknowledge what two of those hidden items would mean? Was he ready to do that? Of themselves and by themselves, they were just two of the treats Walt had left to be found. But, if he went through with what he was thinking, they would become something much more personal and lasting.

"I'm only fourteen." His words were whispered as he attempted to work it out internally. "Does that matter? But, when would I know? How old would I have to be?"

His mind returned to all the things he had gone through during the past year. All the anguish, all the uncertainty after what Nimue had done to him. Then, finally, the slow process of healing, of getting his joy back. He knew what this last quest of Walt's had done for him. It was exactly what Walt and Wolf had intended. He *was* excited for the next clue. He *was* interested to see what the future would bring.

Except for that one huge, overpowering thing: Catie was hurt and they weren't sure when, or if, she would ever be the same again.

Peter could now acknowledge how deeply her accident had affected him. They had been friends since birth. The families went on vacations together, out to dinner together, to the Parks together. He couldn't imagine the Michaels—or Catie—not being in his life.

As he lifted the lid of the box, Peter stared at the contents that he had kept hidden away from his family's prying eyes. Most of the handwritten notes from Walt were mixed in with various keys that had come with some of the clues. One of the smaller gray capsules was there. The Gold Pass that everyone else had forgotten about. These and other items were gently pushed aside so Peter could reach what he knew was on the very bottom of the box. One of them had been hidden inside the mermaid that he and Catie had found in the attic of the Haunted Mansion. Peter had figured out the combination of the Chinese puzzle-like mechanics to open the mermaid and reach his next clue—and this small item had fallen out. The other one had been in a small box secured under an awning on the old Motor Boat dock.

He didn't touch either of the items or bring them out of the box. He just stared at them, reassuring himself of what he wanted to do, what he needed to do in the near future.

With a soft click, the box was closed and once again stashed under the ski gear. They were safe and secure.

They would be there when he came to get them.

"Mind Thy Head – 1787. Look out bellows!"

Eyes scrunched, Peter stared at the new clue as his head slowly swung back and forth. "Why does that sounds so familiar? Where have I heard that before? I know I've seen it somewhere." He looked over at his computer, the cursor blinking on and off, waiting for its next command. With a disgusted snort, he shook his head. "Why can't I just look at a clue and know what it means? Why do I have to do so much research? Gosh, I'll bet Dad and

Uncle Adam never had to do this much searching for answers back in the old days."

Falling back to his tried-and-true method, he brought up his favorite search engine and typed in 'mind thy head Disneyland.' "Great. Only 144,000 results. Piece of cake."

It didn't take Peter long to realize that almost all of the search results pointed to the same place: Tarzan's Treehouse. Still, he hesitated. "Okay, I've see that sign a couple of times on the stairs, but…that can't be right. It wasn't called that in Walt's time. It was the Swiss Family Treehouse. Which is in Florida now."

A year ago he would have immediately bounded down the stairs and announce to the family that they needed to go to Walt Disney World. Now, he wasn't so sure. Of course Walt wouldn't know that his treehouse, opened only four years before his death, would be replaced with a different theme. Unless Wolf told him. From what had been said, Peter assumed they worked together on this quest for him.

"No, Wolf wouldn't tell Walt the future. It has to mean something else. What does 'look out below' mean?" A laugh sounded in the still room as he gaped at his computer screen. "That's nice. Only eighty-two million search results." Frustrated, stifling a groan, he ran a hand over his face. "If I go with the obvious, it means something is being dropped from above and the ones down below have to be careful. Okay, that could apply to the Treehouse. What's below the Treehouse? The Jungle Cruise and Indiana Jones and Adventureland and part of New Orleans Square and…" Peter rubbed the bridge of his nose. "There's too many 'ands' here. And why does it say 1787? Great, another and. Was that the year the Robinsons landed on their island?"

Back on the computer, Peter went to one of his favorite sites that was filled with pictures of extinct Disneyland attractions. "If it can be found, the answer will be here." After a virtual tour of the old Treehouse, and a mental promise to go through it again next time they go to Florida, Peter found his answer. According to a plaque at the beginning of the walkways, the Robinsons waded ashore in 1805. "Shoot. That doesn't match at all. So it isn't the old Treehouse. How can it be the new one? Wolf wouldn't tell Walt the future. Would he? So, when was *Tarzan* supposed to have taken place?"

As Peter followed one cold lead after another, his enthusiasm for the thrill of the chase began to wane. "Gosh, how hard is it to find out the time period of *Tarzan*?"

Finding nothing in the Disney-based categories, he switched to the original story of *Tarzan* as written by Edgar Rice Burroughs. An hour later, Peter found himself leaning into the computer screen as he strained to find his answer. "Somebody has to know when *Tarzan* was set, don't they?" For a break, he saw a link to a theory that linked two unrelated Disney movies together. There, at the very bottom of the article, was the date he wanted. Only it wasn't the date he really wanted. It said 'the 1880's,' not 1787. "Great. Now what? It's obviously not the Treehouse. What else could it be?"

Returning to his search engine, Peter typed in '1787 Disneyland' and was rewarded with a surprising answer. "The *Columbia Sailing Ship*? Really?" Already knowing the *Columbia* was the first American ship to circumnavigate the world, Peter bypassed the fascinating history lesson and concentrated on the rest of the clue. "There is a museum downstairs. Wonder if it refers to something down there? Or, maybe I get to climb a mast again! Ooh, is there a crow's nest?" Peter pulled up a different Disneyland-based picture-filled website and got back to work.

In the open doorway, Lance leaned against the frame as he silently watched his son. Peter had been quiet for so long that Lance wondered if he was even awake. As Peter continued to scroll and read and mutter to himself, a fond smile of remembrance flickered over his dad's face. He and Adam had gone through the same frustrating, puzzling, exciting experience when they had started their first Hidden Mickey search. He almost hated to interrupt, but when he heard 'climb a mast,' he had to. "So, how's it going, Pete? Find anything? Can I come in?"

Startled, Peter's head jerked around at the sudden noise. He had been tuned out for a long time. "Dad? Uh, sure, come in. Uh, don't look at the mess…"

Lance picked up the brick. He had already seen it when Kimberly and Peter had gotten home, but he wanted to look at the writing again. It didn't appear to be in Walt's hand. When he had mentioned the possibility to Kimberly, she said it might have been her dad's printing. If it was done late in Walt's life, perhaps he had needed help in getting this quest ready for Peter. "How far have you gotten?"

Peter heaved a dramatic sigh and threw himself back in the chair. "Well, I found out it doesn't refer to the Swiss Family Treehouse or Tarzan's Treehouse. That's where I had seen the 'Mind Thy Head' sign. But, just now I found out that it also is engraved on something called a lintel on the *Columbia* at Disneyland."

"That's a horizontal block that spans the opening between two vertical supports."

"What?"

Lance smiled at the confused look in front of him. "You just asked what a lintel was."

"Oh. Whatever. It's on some board over the stairway that leads down into the museum. What I don't get is why it says to look out below. That doesn't make any sense. Did something fall from the crow's nest?"

Turning the brick over, Lance reread the clue. "Well, for one thing, it doesn't say to look out below. It says 'Look out bellows.'"

Peter repeated the word and frowned. "Did Walt spell it wrong?"

Lance handed the hunk of orange plaster back to his son. "Walt never spelled anything wrong, especially something important. He meant it just as it was written."

Already typing the new word into his computer, Peter didn't reply. "Is that what a bellows is? That wooden pump thing? Where would something like that be on the *Columbia*? Do they use it for the engines?"

"Keep looking. You'll figure it out."

"What?" Peter glanced up from the screen. "You're leaving? You aren't going to help?"

Already in the hallway, Lance leaned back into the room. "You're almost there. And, Pete? You'd better get all those clothes off the floor before your mom sees them."

Eyeing the mess, there was an audible groan. "But I'm doing something important."

Lance threw up his hands. "Hey, just saying. Remember that you're going to want to go to Disneyland again soon."

Peter realized he was being given a fair warning. "Okay, Dad. I'll take care of it," as he turned back to his desk.

Lance knew his son. "Pete?" He waited until he had the boy's full attention. "Shoving them under the bed doesn't count."

"Oh. Rats."

Chapter 15

Flashback – Disneyland – 1957

Sipping his coffee, Dick worked on the weekly cast member schedule as he sat at one of the outside tables at the Chicken Plantation restaurant. A busy Sunday morning, Disneyland's myriads of sounds had receded into pleasant background noise as he continued his work.

"Mind if I join you?"

Recognizing the voice, the manager of Frontierland quickly made one last notation before he looked up. The work schedule would have to wait. "Morning." A welcoming look on his face, he made a motion with his hand. "Pull up a chair, Walt."

Walt signaled for a coffee before they began to discuss what was going on in the Park. He paused when the *Mark Twain* sailed past their secluded corner nook, its steam whistle sounding a salute. A satisfied smile on his face, Walt watched until the pristine white boat rounded the first bend of Tom Sawyer's Island. Getting up from his chair, he walked over to the railing of the restaurant, the business of the day forgotten for now. One of the keel boats, the *Bertha Mae*, full of smiling guests, slowly followed in the *Mark Twain's* wake. Over to the right, the *Gullywhumper* could be seen unloading at the nearby keel boat dock. Three Indian War Canoes overtook the keel boat as they raced past the restaurant to see who would first reach their landing. The sound of laughter drifted over the choppy water to reach his ears before they were out of sight. In the distance Walt could hear the rumble from the engines of the wooden rafts that took guests to and from the Island. Walt did a quick count. Eight different craft were on the River at that moment. Turning back to Dick, he gestured at the River, eyes shining and his voice enthusiastic. "Will you look at that? Now that is a busy River!"

Dick took a sip of his coffee and picked up his pencil to continue with the scheduling. He gave a perfunctory nod to his boss, silently wondering when the other shoe would drop. But, instead of a raised eyebrow or a complaint on how congested the River was, Walt's next words made him lower his pencil.

"You know what we need? We need another big boat!"

Before the amazed Dick could respond, Walt began to tell him what he had recently learned from the Admiral. Joe had already been sent on a mission to find a sailing ship for the River. "Now, it won't be another stern-wheeler." Walt waved in the direction the now-unseen *Mark Twain* had gone. "We've already done that. What I think we should have is a full-scale replica of the *Columbia*. Did you know she was the first American ship to sail around the world? She was also a merchant ship in the Pacific Northwest." Walt then proceeded to fill him in on all the facts and figures of the historical ship and that the *Columbia* would be the first windjammer to be built in America in over a century.

At 110 feet long with the tallest mast reaching 76 feet, the *Columbia* set sail on June 14, 1958. According to maritime tradition, Walt himself had placed a silver dollar under each of the three masts while it was being built.

A few years later, Walt saw a need and wanted to make the show better or 'plus the set,' as he saw the sailing ship. With the assistance of his chief art director from the Studio, they came up with the idea to put an authentic museum below deck. Complete with Galley (kitchen), crew's quarters, and an elaborate Captain's cabin at the stern, it was all lavishly decorated with authentic maritime equipment and details. It showed what life would have been like on a ship in that time period. This museum was opened to the public in 1964 and, for a time, was accessible even when the ship was docked in Fowler's Harbor.

Disneyland

"Hey, she's not running again today. Man, Alex, this is the third time we've tried to ride her."

Peter and Alex, hands on their hips, stood inside Fowler's Harbor and stared up at the docked *Columbia*. The carved masthead towered above them as the ship sat motionless in her mooring.

"How are you supposed to look for the next clue if you can't get into the museum?"

"I don't know, Alex. This is getting old. Why have the ride if they never bring it out?"

Quickly losing interest, Alex tried to see the latest screamers when they hurtled down the slope of the nearby Splash Mountain. The Harbour Galley restaurant blocked his view. With a side glance at Peter, he started to slowly back to the walkway. A question from his friend stopped him in his tracks. "Uh, what'd you say?"

Head tilted to the side, eyes narrowed, Peter stared at the twin. He knew Alex's main interest had always been the thrill rides, not his clue searches. But, Alex had volunteered to go with Peter this time. Peter now wondered why. "I asked if you had any ideas." *Besides riding Splash Mountain or Big Thunder.*

Caught, Alex walked back to the front of the ship. "Sorry. I figured all the boats would be out when it was this busy. There's an hour wait for Splash Mountain. Unless we get a FastPass. I mean, unless *they* get a FastPass." He flashed a fake grin.

Looking down to hide his irritation, Peter fished his passport out of his pocket. "Here. Go get us FastPasses. We might as well ride something while I try to figure out what to do." *Since you obviously don't have any suggestions.* "I'll wait here." He didn't miss the relieved, happy expression on Alex's face as he turned to run off into Critter Country. Turning back to the *Columbia*, Peter stifled a sigh. Catie's willingness and eagerness were sorely missed.

By the time Alex returned, Peter greeted him with a smug smile. "How much time do we have for our FastPasses?"

Wondering what was up, Alex handed him his passport and one of the tickets. "A little over an hour."

"There's no *Fantasmic* tonight, right?"

Alex shook his head. The popular show on the Rivers of America was being refurbished and wouldn't return for another two months. "You have a plan?"

Peter glanced back at the tall ship as he led the way to Frontierland. "Yeah, I do. Let's go have lunch."

Alex hurried to catch up with his taller, fast-walking friend. "We just had breakfast two hours ago."

"I'm hungry."

"You're always hungry. Where are we going?" Alex was hoping Peter would say Big Thunder or, at least, the Haunted Mansion.

"The Golden Horseshoe."

The groan came out of Alex's mouth before he could stop it. But, Peter didn't seem to notice or pay him any attention. "Why there, Pete? There's no show today. It's just a big, empty restaurant."

Big and empty was just what Peter wanted at this moment. "We can share that chocolate cake if you want." He knew Alex's weakness for the eight-layer decadent dessert. Once he saw the look of rebellion fade from his companion's face, he added a little more to tip the scale in his direction. "Then I can tell you what my plans are without anyone else hearing."

The promise of chocolate plus secrets that sounded suspiciously risky got his full attention. Alex was more eager as he followed Peter into the quiet white and gold saloon.

"You sure this will work?" Alex shoveled the last bite of cake into his chocolate-ringed mouth.

"No." Full of cake and soda, Peter pushed back from the table and tried not to belch.

Still focused on the dessert, it took a minute for his answer to sink in. Alex set down the fork after licking off the last possible speck of frosting. "No? What do you mean no?" The worried look came back into his brown eyes. "You're supposed to have it all worked out."

"I *think* it will work, but we won't know until we actually try." Even though he had a minuscule cloud of doubt in the back of his mind, the face he put on for Alex was confident. "Besides, what's the worst they can do? Throw us out of the Park?"

"You make that sound fun. I don't want to get thrown out of anywhere! We promised our parents we wouldn't get into trouble. Why are you smiling?"

Because you sound just like your sister! "I'm not smiling. Listen, I don't want to get into trouble either, but I think this is the only way to do it. Are you in or not? You have the easy job, you know."

Before he answered, Alex thought over the nebulous plan his friend had outlined. What Peter said was true. If something did go wrong, Peter would be the one caught with his hand in the cookie jar, not him. "Yeah, I guess. Just don't screw it up."

Peter flashed him a wide, cocky smile. "What could possibly go wrong?"

Not quite mollified, Alex glanced at his watch. "We need to get to Splash Mountain. It's time for our FastPasses."

Peter collected together the dirty plates and cups before they headed downstairs and out into the warm, autumn sunshine. "You'd better not barf all that chocolate when we get to that last big drop."

Now it was Alex's turn to grin. He'd make sure Peter sat in the seat in front of him.

Evening was a special time at Disneyland. The glare of the sun was gradually replaced with soft mood lighting. All down Main Street the buildings and trees started to twinkle with white lights. Colored spotlights highlighted the turrets and walls of Sleeping Beauty Castle. Tomorrowland became an array of bright neon signs. The lagoon was now a mirror for the soft whites and blues of the Matterhorn, contrasting with the yellow submarines making their slow turn into the shimmering waterfall.

The pace of the guests seemed to slow as the time for dinner approached. Wait times for rides shortened as the lines for the restaurants and food carts became longer. The benches in the Hub that circled the Partners Statue were used more for people watching than a shady place to escape the sunlight.

For Peter, however, evening was turning into a time of concealment. Activities that would be easy to see in the light of day now became more obscured with the darkened sky and long shadows. Heading back to Critter Country with the again-reluctant Alex in tow, Peter ordered a lobster roll and fries at the Harbour Galley. Once the delectable, piled-high sandwich was ready, he went to the last table behind the small restaurant there at Fowler's Harbor. Behind the table was Fowler's Inn where, a couple of years ago, they had located one of Walt's hidden clues. On one side of Fowler's

Inn was a wooden walkway that angled around another seating deck and ended at the canoe dock. On the other side was Peter's goal: the *Columbia*, docked and dark except for the lighting coming from the open windows of the crew quarters below deck.

Peter had positioned Alex be to sitting so he faced the other diners. He grabbed a couple of the fries before checking out the situation. Two tables were occupied and there was a small line of guests waiting for their food. Peter moved a couple of the extra chairs out of sight in an attempt to send any other guests elsewhere with their dinners. The canoes always quit running at dusk and the Island was empty for the night. So, the last thing he had to check was the location of the *Mark Twain*. She was still making cruises and anyone on the second and third decks—not to mention the pilot in the wheelhouse—would have a bird's eye view of what he planned.

The familiar blast of her steam whistle told Peter the *Mark Twain* was on the far side of Tom Sawyer Island. She would be on her way to the dock for unloading. He gave a sigh of relief. That gave him plenty of time before she came by his location again.

"Okay, Alex," he said when he returned to the little round table. "You know what to do?"

"Yeah, I whistle if I see anyone who even looks like they saw you. Or Security."

Adam, Alex's dad, had taught the twins that wonderful, shrill fingers-under-the-tongue whistle that he had never been able master. "Right. Just don't wait too long so I don't have time to hide."

The French fries were pushed around their paper basket. The gesture showed the boy's nervousness even though he tried to maintain a calm appearance for his friend's sake. "I know. I'll watch. You know enough about the museum onboard to be able to hide?"

Peter hesitated. He hadn't ridden the *Columbia* in years, preferring the canoes when he wanted to go on the River. The pictures he had studied were over five years old. "Yeah, I think so. I know what I'm supposed to look for. I just hope it's where I think it is."

Alex guessed Peter was nervous, too, so he just smiled to reassure his friend.

Peter wondered why Alex grimaced at him, but didn't ask. "Okay, here goes nothing."

The seating area and walkway for guests was a full story above the dock for the ships. On the far side of the *Columbia*, away from the tables, a wooden barricade had been built to prevent anyone from stumbling off the end of the walk. Barrels, crates, lobster cages and fishing nets had been used as decorations, but were also strategically placed to ward off intruders in places they didn't belong.

When they had scouted out the area earlier, there had been a green metal gangplank that allowed access to the deck of the ship. No longer needed, the ramp now lay on the wooden dock. As Peter stared at it from his higher elevation, gritting his teeth at his bad luck, he doubted he could put it back in place without plenty of noise and some needed help.

He had already figured out a way to clamor over the barricade and drop down onto the lower dock. Now he saw that wouldn't be necessary. Without the ramp he would face the steep side of the ship. As he looked over the rigging, he saw a second possibility, one that made his stomach drop.

Jutting out from the side of the ship were three light blue platforms called chains that each held ropes connected to the masts. Peter thought if he could stand on top of the wooden railing, he could leap over the narrow distance and grab one of the ropes attached to the nearest chain. *I see four ropes, after all, how could I miss?* Glancing down, he noted the motionless, oil-sheened water. There was a very narrow gap between the dock and the ship. *If I fell straight, I would land in the water. Or bang my head on that wooden pier or...* He quit speculating. It wasn't helping.

A quick glance over his shoulder showed him no one else was in sight. With a pounding pulse, he climbed to the top of the rail and balanced for a moment. Stifling the urge to yell, "Geronimo!" he pushed off with his legs.

The ropes were in his face faster than he anticipated and he made wild grab, wrapping his arms around the thick cable. Knowing he needed to move quickly, he ducked around to the safer backside of the ropes and worked his way over the chain to the opening in the dark blue wood. He climbed over the burgundy railing to drop softly to the deck of the quiet ship.

The elation of his success was short-lived. Now standing on

the most exposed part of the ship, he needed to get out of sight. Anyone looking closely enough would notice him as being out of place and raise an alarm. Scrunched down, he headed for the open walkway that led to the living quarters down below. With a quick smile, he saw the reminder to 'Mind Thy Head' as he disappeared into the safety of the museum.

Breathing easier, he took a bit of time to get his bearings. From the pictures he had studied, he hadn't been able to clearly see what was where. Now that he could look around, he was able to quickly locate the galley where he hoped to find the bellows. His research had told him the bellows would have been used by the cook to keep the fire in the stove and ovens hot enough for cooking and baking as needed.

As he reached the kitchen, his hand fell to the Key to Disneyland safe in his pants pocket. There were a lot of locked doors and crates down here that he itched to open and explore. The cream-colored doors, like the Bos'n's Locker and Sick Bay, had spindle-covered windows so the guests could get a glimpse into what it was like to live on a ship. But Peter, curious as he was, wanted to open each door and see what else was hidden away. Remembering Alex and his own tenuous position, he sighed for missed opportunities and concentrated on his job at hand.

There were four sides to the kitchen display. A thick rope net was strung over part of it to keep the guests at bay. The other sections had a dark brown, waist-high railing. Peter ducked under the railing and studied the brass pots that sat on the stovetop. One of the wide pots was filled with a clear, solid substance to mimic water for a stew, complete with vegetables and garlic pulled from the string hanging off the nearby shelves.

The stove itself was an elaborate cast iron wonder set into the brickwork. Below the railed cooktop were two small ovens with attached pulls to open downward. On the side, also set into the brick, were two larger ovens with doors that swung outward.

Behind the cooktop, on the other side of the brick was what Peter had been seeking. There he instantly recognized the huge wooden bellows that would have kept the galley's fire hot. It was positioned over and behind a massive brick block that had a round, fire-darkened cooking hole. On two of the sides were cast iron doors that he figured were either for fuel or ash removal. There was another long, hinged iron lid on which sat another brass pot.

Peter grabbed the long wooden handle that worked the bellows and marveled that it actually worked. As he lifted it up and down, a metal rod turned and opened, then closed, the leather accordion of the bellows. "Cool!"

As he watched the mechanics, he noticed a thick wood block nailed on the front. There was engraving on it. Just three letters. **W E D**. Becoming more excited, Peter strained to see better but was too far away. Eyeing the solid brick platform of the stove, he hopped up to get a closer look.

Yes, they were Walt's initials and his guiding point. He had left the bellows in the closed position and reached over to grab the handle again. As the pleats bellowed out, he carefully felt around the curved wooden frame. Just as his fingers found an extra 'bump' on the smooth surface of the wood, he heard heavy footsteps on the deck above him. Heart suddenly pounding, he vaguely wondered why he hadn't heard a whistle from Alex. His fingers closed over the capsule and pulled it away from its home of almost fifty years.

He now heard voices as they approached the stairs and frantically tried to find a hiding place. Intent on his discoveries, secure in the protective cover of the ship, he hadn't given hiding a second thought. A quick glance at the locked doors told him that they were too far away and would probably make too much noise. Jumping down from his brick perch, he crouched at the far side and peered around the corner.

He first saw shoes and then pant legs as two security guards came down the stairs. Flashlights aimed at the dim corners of the displays as they began a methodical search. Peter's anxiety didn't cease when he recognized Wolf as one of the guards. He knew he was too far out of the normal realms for a guest for even Wolf to be able to protect him.

Remembering Wolf's eerie sense of hearing, he gave a slight cough and whispered for his friend. "Wolf, it's Peter."

Wolf's head snapped in his direction. "I'll look over here, Joe. That kid could be hiding anywhere." As Wolf stomped over, Peter could clearly see the irritation on his face. "Why didn't you just ask?" His voice was low and angry. "I could have just brought you onboard."

"Oh."

Wolf shook his head and took Peter by the arm, hauling him to his feet. "Just follow my lead and act sorry." Louder, he called to his partner, "Hey, Joe. I found the kid. Let's get him out of here before he damages something."

Joe came over and shined the light in Peter's face. "Wow, I didn't believe it when someone said they saw a kid on the deck."

Wolf pulled Peter along beside him as they went up the stairs to the main deck. Peter was relieved to see the green walkway was again leaning against the side of the ship. He hadn't stopped to think how Wolf and Joe had gotten aboard. As they neared the gangplank, Peter could hear Alex's frantic whistle. "Is that for you?" asked Wolf.

Peter nodded. "Yeah, that would be Alex. He was supposed to warn me. Guess I couldn't hear him inside."

"Apparently not." Wolf kept his voice low as Joe got ahead of them on the walkway. "Just walk past Alex and motion for him to stay back. I'm going to have to throw you out the Main Gate and tell you not to come back. Quit smiling."

Peter wiped the grin off his face. Alex was wide-eyed as Wolf drug Peter past him.

For Alex's benefit, Wolf loudly repeated, "I'm taking you to the Main Gate. You'll have to leave, understand?"

Peter tried to sound contrite. "Yes, sir. I'm awfully sorry. I just wanted…"

"Save it." Joe had taken his other arm and together they escorted Peter through a curious crowd in front of the Mansion and then through Adventureland. To Peter's relief, they took him backstage near the Refreshment Corner and continued behind Main Street to emerge near the entrance of Walt's apartment in the Fire Station. The novelty of being escorted by Security quickly became an embarrassment as more and more people stopped to stare at him and wonder what he did.

"I got this, Joe." Wolf let the other security guard get back to their interrupted patrol as he continued with Peter through the Esplanade toward Harbor Boulevard. "How did you get on the *Columbia* without the gangplank?"

Peter had a sinking feeling his answer wouldn't help the situation. "I, uh, jumped from the railing."

"Are you out of your mind!?" Wolf stopped their march to stare at the boy. "Why didn't you just ask? Your dad or I could have easily taken you aboard." He shook his head in disbelief. "You're just as bad as your dad."

Peter perked up. "What did Dad do?"

"Quit trying to change the subject. Speaking of whom, where is Lance? Or are you here with Adam and Beth?"

"Uncle Adam brought us and then spent the day at the hospital. He's supposed to pick us up when Alex calls him. Which he probably just did…"

"Probably. Where are you meeting him?"

Peter indicated the curved drop-off section just ahead. Before he could speak, Alex came running up, out of breath from hurrying and panic. "Uncle Wolf! Was I glad to see you!" The glare in the sharp blue eyes stopped his effusive remarks. "Um, are we in trouble?"

"Peter jumped from the dock to the ship. What do you think?"

Alex's eyebrows shot up. "You jumped? Is that how you got on? What about that ramp we saw?"

"It was on the dock. I had to think of something else."

"Wow, wish I could have seen that." He broke off again when he sensed Wolf's displeasure. "I mean, how could you do something stupid like that?"

"Okay, you two, knock it off." Wolf glanced over his shoulder as his eyes swept the crowd. "We're being watched by a plainclothes guard. At least act sorry."

Both boys theatrically slumped. "Do you want me to cry, Uncle Wolf?"

Wolf rolled his eyes and had to bite his lip to keep from smiling. *Never a dull moment.* "Adam should be here soon. Crying isn't necessary. Peter, did you get what you were looking for? And, no, don't take it out of your backpack."

Peter lowered his arms. "Oh, right. Yeah, I found it tacked inside the bellow thing. Didn't get a chance to open it."

"Here's Adam." He nodded a greeting as Adam parked and got out of his car. "Hey, Adam. I'm going to have to yell at Peter, all right?"

Alex had given Adam a brief description of what had happened. Hiding a smile, Adam pointed at Peter and started to wave his arms. "What are you doing kicking my kid out?"

Wolf took a step forward and pointed his finger at Adam's chest, being careful not to actually touch him. There was an audience. "And teach your child not to go places he doesn't belong. That won't to be tolerated at Disneyland. He's banned for one month. Don't bring him back until that's over."

Adam got into the spirit. "Yeah, well, we'll just see about that! What's your name? Wolf?" he leaned into read the nametag in the dim light. "Well, Wolf, we'll just see what happens to guards with a bully complex." Adam herded the boys into the car, still having difficulty keeping a straight face.

Wolf watched until they pulled out onto Harbor and disappeared from sight. He managed to wipe his smile off before turning around to assume his duties.

Chapter 16

Fullerton Hospital

"And then I had to jump from the rail and grab a rope before I fell into the water."

"I saw Wolf come running in but he didn't see me. He hauled Peter out by his arms!"

"When Uncle Adam came to pick us up, he and Wolf got into a fake argument 'cause another guard was watching."

Alex and Peter, one on each side of Catie, continued to excitedly talk over each other as they related their adventure. In a corner chair, flipping the pages of a magazine, sat Kimberly, her head slowly shaking back and forth at what she was hearing. By silently listening, she found she learned more than had been related at the house. She hadn't yet discussed with Lance what they should do about Peter's reckless actions Perhaps Wolf's threat of a ban might be the best way to go. If Peter had found the next clue, having to wait a month to follow up on it would definitely be a punishment.

"Wolf said I was banned for a month, but I think that was just for show. Well, I hope he was kidding."

"I kept whistling for Peter like I was supposed to, but he never came out."

"I never heard you, Alex! Hmmph, I thought that whistle of yours was supposed to be loud."

When Kimberly saw Alex put his fingers under his tongue, she had to say something. "Alex, honey, that's not a good idea inside a hospital room. Save the demonstration for when we get home."

And hopefully by then you'll forget all about it.

Alex had learned enough not to roll his eyes. "Yes, Aunt Kimberly. Sorry." He turned back to the bed. "And then... Hey, Catie! Look, guys, her eyes are open again. Hi, sis."

Catie tilted her head so she could face her brother, her lips forming into a crooked smile.

"Did you hear us, Catie? We were telling you about the latest clue Peter found."

Wanting his share of attention, Peter put a gentle hand on her shoulder. "You would have loved it, Catie." Her focus, though, was solely on her twin. Swallowing his disappointment when she didn't look at him, he turned back to Alex. "I think she misses you. Keep talking."

"I miss you, too." Biting his lower lip, Alex's voice lowered as emotion took over. "Can you talk, Catie? Is there anything special you want to hear about? School sucks."

Her smile widened a little. Under the covers, unnoticed by the others, her undamaged arm tried to rise from the bed. Hampered by the blanket covering her, the movement and the frustration seemed to deplete all her energy. The smile slowly faded as her brown eyes closed once again.

Kimberly had come over to the bed to softly stroke Catie's hair. It was a soothing motion she had used on her boys when they had trouble sleeping. "That was the longest she's been awake. That's a good sign." Tears stung the back of her eyes. "I think she's going to be all right. You know, maybe we'd better go and let her sleep. We'll want to tell your mom and dad, Alex."

"She didn't even look at me." Peter had stepped back from the bed as they gathered up their things to leave.

Kimberly put her arm around her son's drooping shoulders. *When did he get to be this tall?* "She's making progress, Pete. Good progress. I know she was happy to hear from both of you. But, Alex is her twin brother. They've always had a special bond."

He merely nodded, not wanting to pursue the subject. "If we're going home, I need to open the capsule and see where I have to go next."

Now wasn't the time to mention any ramifications from his stunt. Kimberly waited for Alex to say his goodbyes before she herded them down to her car.

Peter stared at the handwritten note in his hand. Confusion wiped out the anxious anticipation he had felt. "That's not right. It can't be right. It wasn't even built yet. How could Walt know? He was gone before it opened."

The next clue in the Hidden Mickey search contained only three words:

"**Don't be cheeken.**"

Flashback – Disneyland – January 3, 1965

Watercolor paintings hung on the wall behind Walt and Julie. In the forefront was a table filled with a small town of miniature buildings, wrought iron balconies, and curving streets. Walt's hand, holding a small box camera with a flashcube attached, gestured at the wall. It seemed like the movie camera had caught them in mid-conversation. "This is what we call New Orleans Square." Walt turned from the wall to the model, his finger running through the streets as the camera followed his movement. "See all these streets? It's going to be very interesting with little shops and restaurants and people can wander around in there.

"Now over here," as Walt indicated a lovely nighttime scene painted in dark blues and purples, "we have the special attraction called the Blue Bayou Lagoon. People will actually get on a boat here and ride through the lagoon." When he turned from the painting to his companion, his voice revealed his excitement for the project. "Here we send them down a waterfall and take them back into the past to the days of the pirates and the old Caribbean. Those pirates were always sacking towns... You believe in pirates, of course?"

Intent on the description, Julie seemed surprised to be asked a question. "Oh, yes, Walt. I do!"

"Good, good. Then come over here with me." They walked a short distance into a model room filled with maquettes and busts and mock-ups of different scenes. Walt stopped next to a man busily at work on the head of a pirate, a blue bandana wrapped around the white clay. "Blaine, tell her what you're working on."

The artist looked up with a smile. "This here will be a full-size pirate," as he turned the head for a better view.

"He looks kind of mean."

Blaine gave a short laugh. "You're right there, Julie. Well, the pirates were a pretty tough bunch."

Walt took over the conversation. "We'll have him animated in the show with all kinds of body movements. We call it Audio-Animatronics. But, before Blaine worked on the full-scale pirate, he worked on the miniature. Come over here with me."

There were a dozen foot-tall statues on the table and Walt picked up one of the pirates. He held it up to a drawing on the wall behind the table. It was a perfect match. "We do the drawing to get the characters right, then Blaine takes them and puts them into dimension."

The camera panned the wall of drawings. "Here we have different pirates and the scenes that will happen in the ride. Like this fellow who is covered with loot!" Walt picked up a colorful pirate who had about eight hats piled on his head, his arms also full of clothing. The statue appeared to be rocking back and forth to mimic the movement of the boat he was trying to get into. "Now we'll go around and see the town the pirates are sacking."

The next room was filled with draped tables, each one holding a different scene. Walt and Julie stopped next to an Imagineer who was positioning a small pirate onto a large pirate ship. Behind them could be seen the stone-work of a fortress.

Claude set down the small figure amid the rest of the crew. "We've been restaging this walking-the-plank scene. We've got the water below and this fellow," as the camera zoomed in on a scared townsman teetering on the edge of the plank, "well, he's in a pretty bad way."

"I'm going to take Julie to see the town, Claude."

"All right, Walt."

They turned to another mock-up of the Spanish-styled town. Walt stopped in front of one scene. He let out an appreciative chuckle as the camera slowly panned an elaborate, detailed courtyard. A small group of pirates, holding cutlasses and flintlock rifles, were lowering a tied-up man into a stone well. Up above, the nightcapped head of an angry woman poked out of a window.

Walt pointed at a small metal ring that stood up on the edge of the table. "Now, if you look through that ring, you'll see what the audience gets. Here you see the pirates dunking the mayor in the well, trying to force him to reveal the hiding place of town's treasure."

The camera continued past the pirates and stacks of kegged gunpowder. "All of this will be seen from a boat, you know, and all the characters will be life-size and lifelike in their movements." A stack of barrels came next, holes shot into them, as streams of rum were frozen in the air. The pirates who lounged or staggered about had drunk their stolen find.

"Even though these fellows found the town's rum supply, they are more interested in what is happening across the river."

The camera panned to three tiers of pirates who leaned forward to see what was happening across the river. There, a line of women in various signs of distress were all tied together at the waist. A beautiful redhead in a scarlet dress stood out from the rest of them, seemingly uncaring of her predicament. "Here they are auctioned off, all the town's beauties."

Julie beamed at the all the scenes she's seen so far. "That's absolutely fantastic, Walt!"

Walt held up a cautionary finger. "You haven't even seen the grand climactic scene."

"How could you possibly top this?"

Walt rocked back on his heels, obviously enjoying his tale. "Well, we set the place on fire and have our audience trapped down there in the flaming city!"

"How do they get out?"

"Well, you got into this mess by going down a waterfall. Now, how would you suppose we get out?"

Julie tilted her head, an unsure smile on her face. "By going *up* a waterfall?"

Walt gave a laugh as he turned to look into the camera. "That's right! Anything's possible at Disneyland!"

Fullerton

"I guess anything's possible at Disneyland." Peter sat back from his computer. He had just watched the tenth anniversary show from *Walt Disney's Wonderful World of Color*. The details of the upcoming Pirate ride had captured his attention. Walt had indeed known all about the attraction and what would be included in it. "Now that I know where to go I just need to figure out how." A grimace replaced his smile. Still smarting from the set-down he had received from his last stunt, he knew he'd have to plan this next one more carefully. "Guess I won't be jumping from a boat any time soon. They're too far away from the Well Scene anyway. I'll just have to figure out another way to get there."

Closing his eyes and leaning back in his chair, Peter pictured the Pirates of the Caribbean ride in his mind. From the moment he would step onto the flat-bottom boat in Laffite's Landing to the final chain-driven ascent up the last waterfall, he followed the winding course. Each scene, each turn in the river was as clear to him as if he was actually there. He could hear the *boom* of the cannons on the *Wicked Wench* as she fought against the fort. Between the turrets on the fort on the left were the silhouettes of a sword fight. The sounds of the battle muted as the boat turned left and entered the pillaged Spanish town. Their knees shaking in fear, prisoners still in their nightclothes watched in horror as the mayor was again and again lowered into the well, the sound of his gurgling floated over the water. As the mayor was raised again, a stream of water shot out of his mouth and his wife appeared in an upper window. "Do not tell him, Carlos. Don't be cheeken." One of watching pirates fired his flintlock at her and she fell screaming back into their house.

Peter's memory kept the ride going as the boat next went past a dress shop with a particular Captain hiding from the pirates who were seeking him. The following auction and the popular redhead took up both sides of the waterway. He pictured the pirates who looked down from an arch as the boat slowly sailed under. After the auction was the sacked town with a pirate teetering on top of a stack of rum barrels outside the wrecked cantina.

Peter stopped just as he got to the minstrels singing about their wayward lifestyle. His eyes popped open as he leaned forward in his chair. Though not exactly sure, he thought he might have discovered a way to reach the mayor. There were two more weeks to go in his detention, so he had to rely on the Internet to check out his new theory. With renewed energy, he got to work.

"I'm going to need Aunt Beth's help to get to the next clue."

Lance glanced over from the stove where he was scrambling eggs for their breakfast. "Oh? I don't think she's gone back to work yet." The excited look on Peter's face fell. "What did you need? Anything I can do? Or Wolf?"

At the mention of Wolf, Peter had to grimace. What he had thought was a joke had turned into reality. He had been banned from the Park for a month. Not sure if Wolf would help him, Peter's shrug was wary. "I don't know. How much do you know about the backstage area of Pirates?"

The question caught him off-guard, causing Lance to pause. Turning back to the stovetop to cover his discomfort, he fiddled with the eggs. It had happened over a decade ago, but the memory of what he had done still haunted him. In their first Hidden Mickey treasure hunt, he, Adam, and Beth had found a secret tunnel behind the massive bed in the Captain's Quarters. It led to a subterranean cavern beneath the Treasure Room. There they had found the final door and the final clue to their treasure. In a state of desperation and greed, Lance had actually pulled a gun on his two friends and demanded the treasure—whatever it was—for himself. That impulsive, stupid move had cost him his two friends and, ultimately, the treasure behind that door. He still didn't know what it was Adam and Beth had found. He never asked. Taken in another direction, he had followed what he thought was the answer to the clue. In the end, he had come across a different cavern and a different find that had led him to Kimberly. It had taken years and years to win back his friends. It wasn't a warm, fuzzy memory for Lance.

Peter still waited for an answer so Lance swallowed his shame and shoveled the eggs onto plates. "Call your brothers. Breakfast is ready." When he recovered his composure, he answered his son. "Yeah, I know a little about the backstage area on the New Orleans side. It's like a maze back there. Very easy to get lost. But, I think you know that."

Peter joined Michael and Andrew at the table and thoughtfully chewed on a piece of toast. "Yeah, that's why I wondered if Aunt Beth could help. You know I need to get to the Mayor in the Well, right?"

Lance took a sip of orange juice and nodded. "That area of the ride is outside the berm, of course, and on the other side of the water. I can't help you back there. Wolf might. I don't know."

"I'd rather ask Aunt Beth."

Munching on a piece of bacon hid Lance's smile. "Wolf isn't mad at you."

Silently listening, Michael's radar kicked in. "What'd Peter do? Why's Uncle Wolf mad at him?"

"He isn't mad at me. Didn't you hear Dad?"

"Boys, stop. Sorry I'm late." Kimberly came into the kitchen and took her chair. "This looks great, honey. I could smell the bacon upstairs."

"Well, I knew you had to work today. New batch of princesses to train?"

Peter's head shot up. "You're going to Disneyland?"

"I am. You're not." Kimberly's tone held an apology even though she didn't voice it. "You only have a few more days to go. You can wait that long." The grumble she received as a reply wasn't understandable.

Lance filled her in on the conversation she had missed. "Peter thinks he knows how to get to the Mayor, but will need Beth's help."

"She hasn't gone back to work since…since Catie got hurt."

"I know, Mom. I was just hoping she could help me. I have a plan all worked out."

Neither Lance nor Kimberly liked the gleam in his eyes. "Well, maybe you can lay it all out for us tonight when I get home and we'll go from there."

Realizing he had to be satisfied with that, Peter merely nodded. It was going to be a long day.

Chapter 17

Fullerton

Lance stared at the printout Peter had handed him. It was rough layout of the entire Pirate ride flume with the scenes reduced to minimal words like Treasure Cache, Fort, Jail. Just after the *Wicked Wench*, though, was another flume Peter had highlighted with three arrows. There were also a double row of lines over the flume that seemed to connect the land areas.

Lance pointed at the second set of lines. "What's that one?"

In his excitement, Peter was bouncing up and down on his toes. "The Hairy Leg Pirate."

Picturing the scene, Lance knew if you looked up as you sailed under that bridge, the hairy leg of a pirate slowly swung back and forth. "It's an arch over the water."

Nodding, Peter pointed at the first set of double lines. "So's that one." He then indicated the other waterway that made a large curve behind the Auction and the Chase. "That's why I need Aunt Beth's help."

"Ah, I'd forgotten all about that place." The words Boat Storage were printed inside the secondary flume. "You know? I think you're right. Do you want me to call Beth for you?"

"You mean I can go ahead with it?"

Lance studied the drawing a little longer. When he nodded, Peter let out a *Whoop!* "I think this is a good idea, Pete. Your usual place to jump is too far away." He glanced up at his son. "You do know you'll have to do this during the day while the ride is operating."

"Oh. I thought Aunt Beth could get me in after it closes."

"You'd be putting her job at risk if she was caught there after hours helping you. Well, I guess you still are, but there's less of a chance this way. If you're not seen, that is. It is a job they have to do every day, so its possible Beth can arrange to do it."

"I was thinking I needed to wear all black since that part of the ride is pretty dark." Peter paused.

"What's wrong? It seems like you have it all worked out."

"I'm just not sure exactly where to look. It's pretty big and everyone in the boats will be able to see me." Peter's enthusiasm and confidence was starting to wane the more he thought about it.

"That's why you need to figure it out before you get Beth involved. Look at the clue again and come to a decision."

Peter eyed his dad. "Where would you look first?"

Lance handed the map back to his son. "This is your clue search. You need to figure that out for yourself."

"But you have an idea, right?"

Lance smiled at the boy's persistence. "Yes, I do."

"And you won't tell me."

"Nope."

Disneyland

"**O**kay, Peter, this is what's going to happen." Dressed in her pirate costume at the loading position on the Landing, Beth felt both excited and guilty. She hadn't been to work since the accident and missed all of her friends on the attraction. But, a major part of her happiness was overshadowed by guilt at not being by Catie's side in case she was needed. She pushed the guilt to the back of her mind. This is just what she would have done if her daughter was with Peter on this search. "Since it's late in the evening and not very busy, we need to take four of the boats off the flume. There are too many empty boats going through." She paused to help the next group of guests into their boat. When the two launches were on their way into the dark waters of the Bayou, she lowered her voice. "I'm going to get you into the last boat to be taken offline. Once your boat gets into the water, immediately duck down onto the floor and stay there until you hear me call you. I want the dispatcher to think this one is empty too. Got it?"

The Lead of the ride signaled Beth to hold back the guests so the next four boats could be sent out empty. A friend of Beth's, she looked the other way when Peter got into the last boat and took a seat. As soon as the first two boats were underway, Beth went up the stairs to the dispatcher's office. Here was the wall of monitors that showed different parts of the ride. When the second set of boats—the ones that held Peter—was sent forward, Beth interrupted Scott before the boat would drift into his view. She silently hoped Peter did what he was told. "Hey, Scott, I'm going down to gets those boats offline. Cloe is there to take my place. Be back soon."

"Nice to have you with us again, Beth. That's fine. Let me know when you're back." Scott turned back to the monitors and waited for the green light that indicated all the guests were seated properly. Once the light came on, he punched a button that released them into the flume.

Peter had immediately pretended to drop something, bent down to pick it up, and never resurfaced. He had an odd ride of just watching the sky as he floated along. The waterfalls were interesting when he banged around and then deluged with water at the bottom. Not daring to peek over the side, he could tell where he was just by the sounds. When he went through the misty curtain and into the Fort scene, he tensed. He was almost there.

Beth had to hurry down a flight of stairs and wind through the tunnels until she reached the battle scene. She shook her head. Peter never would have been able to navigate this by himself. Just past the Fort and the ship, she reached the operation panel. Watching the boats, she saw the last one loaded with guests. After it drifted by, she pushed a button that stopped the next boats and raised a black curtain that was invisible in the darkness of the ride. Once ready, she flipped an electrical switch that rerouted the next four boats backstage. When they were safely out of sight, the curtain was back in place and the ride flume opened for the boats to continue as normal.

Beth hurried into the boat storage area. It was a dark room with a low, black ceiling and narrow wooden walkways next to the motionless boats. Lit by a few fluorescent bulbs, there were wires and cables snaking through the curved waterway. "Peter?" Her voice was low. Even though there was a lot of action going on out in the ride, she didn't want to be accidently overheard. "You can come out now."

His head popped up from the empty boat. A wide smile covered his face as he examined the storage area. "Wow, this is so cool!"

Beth looked around at the stark, unadorned wooden walls. "If you say so. Not so loud, please. I need to get back to work. You know what you need to do?"

He slowly nodded. "Yeah, I think so. Where's that door into the Auction?"

Beth pointed behind her. "Follow me. I need to go that way to get back to the Landing." She ran a critical eye over his black clothes. "Pull your cap a little lower. Your blond hair is like a beacon."

"Thanks for your help, Aunt Beth! I couldn't have done this without you."

She gave him an impromptu hug, Catie's missing presence unexpectedly washing over her. "You're welcome, honey. Just keep your head down and wait for the break between the boats. There isn't anything else I can do for you. Just meet me back here in two hours when its time to take more boats offline. You set?"

Suddenly nervous, he just nodded. He had it all worked out in his mind, but, as he had found, not everything went as planned.

Seeing his hesitation, Beth took him by the shoulders and looked into his wide eyes. "You don't have to do this, Pete. We can figure something else out if you want."

Shooting for bravado, he gave her a wavering smile. "I got this. What can possibly go wrong?"

Folding her arms over her chest, Beth tilted her head. "Isn't that what you said to Alex before Wolf dragged you off the *Columbia*?"

Gosh, Alex told her everything! "Yeah, well, this is different. Alex isn't here."

"Not totally reassuring. We can call this off."

"No, I'm good. Just a little nervous. Don't you have to get back to work?"

Beth let out a loud laugh and then clamped her hand over her mouth. "Oh, you are so much like your dad! Yes, I have to get back, punk. Thanks for reminding me. See you in two hours?"

When he realized she had asked a question, Peter gave a brief nod and followed her to his entry point.

"Shift yer cargo, dearie. Show 'em your larboard side."

"We wants the redhead! We wants the redhead!"

Peter had crawled through the back of the Auction set, the familiar dialogue drifting over him. Behind the tied-up prospective brides was the huge Mercado building. To fill the set were bales of goods, baskets and barrels, and a random goat that cluttered the floor. A few of the doors of the façade were open, an orange glow of fire coming from within. Peter knew he had to get behind the Auctioneer and the lady with whom he was trying to entice the drunken pirates.

A small set of stairs went up to the next level that brought him even with the open door directly under the Mercado lettering. There was only a short distance to cover to get behind the Auctioneer, but it would be in full view of the oncoming boats. On his hands and knees, Peter cautiously stuck his head out of the open doorway. A camera immediately flashed in his eyes. "Oh, that's probably not good." He threw himself backward just as a disembodied voice came out of nowhere. "No flash photography, please."

Heart pounding, he waited until he thought the second boat would be gone. The scene beyond the auction was enticing enough that he didn't worry about people looking backward and seeing him. Instead of sprinting as he had first planned, he crawled behind the blue-dressed bride and her captor. Once past those two figures, he threw himself flat on the curved archway. The goat perched on the topmost post towering overhead didn't seem too concerned by his abrupt appearance

"It's gold I be after!"

"Yeah, you and me both, Captain," Peter mumbled to himself as he eyed the length of the bridge. It didn't look that long in the pictures. There were two more pirates and a chicken on the bridge. He knew he would have to be careful not to bump the Audio-Animatronic figures as it might cause them to malfunction. As he stared at the goat, he thought it felt odd to be the only human—the only *real* human—in the scene. The figures kept on with their programmed movements as if he was invisible.

Just under the goat was another pirate, this one really fearsome in appearance, pistol in hand as he kept watch over the drunken bidders. Peter peeked out over his bald head to see the position of the next boats. "Gosh, there's an endless stream of them. Maybe if I just keep my butt down I can make it across."

Slowly inching forward, Peter held his breath as if that would make him smaller. Just as he got to the second pirate on the bridge, it suddenly moved, jerking forward and waving the rum bottle in his hand. Biting down the urge to shout, Peter stopped and dropped fully on the arch. "Wow, that's spooky. Forgot he did that." The chicken perched on the end of the bridge seemed to turn to look at him. "Spookier and spookier."

When he finally edged to the end of the arch, he still had a few feet of open space before he could duck behind the set. With three tiers of bidding pirates, crates of chickens, a donkey, and various boxes, Peter knew he would have plenty of cover to reach the Mayor's well. Just after the second boat drifted by, he sprinted for the La Cantina's arched doorway. Fluttering overhead was the *Buy A Bride* banner that seemed to be printed on a large petticoat.

The pirates, still intent on the auction across the river, paid Peter no mind as he quickly worked his way through the façade of the Caribbean town. A rooster seemed to think it was dawn and crowed as he went by, a bullet fired by the second-in-command across the river pinged harmlessly overhead.

Much to his relief he found the sets were all connected behind the façades. He had wondered how he would work his way through the Costurera with Captain Jack. The searching pirates might not have seen the Captain as he hid behind a mannequin, but Peter knew he wouldn't have been so invisible.

Once he reached the Well scene, he had to stop and think. Where did he want to go? A quick glance at his watch showed more time had passed than he realized. He still had to find the next clue and work his way back to where Aunt Beth would be waiting.

Thinking about the clue itself, it had basically included only two people: the mayor and his wife. The words were for the mayor, but spoken by the woman. With a sinking feeling, much like what the mayor probably felt as he was lowered into the well again, Peter thought he should first check out the well. "Oh, gosh."

On his stomach again, he worked his way to the middle of the scene. The five pirates on the left and the townsmen on the right, guarded by another pirate, didn't interest him. Just the stone well. In the exact middle of the scene. The first thing everyone looked at when they came around the bend after the Fort.

Crouched down in the orange glow of the torchlight, Peter waited. He was directly behind the pirate Captain as he questioned the hapless mayor. About to make a dash for it, Peter noticed some arches under the wife's window. They were a lot closer to the action than where he was. There was also a short stone wall or planter that connected to the well, probably built to hide some of the wires and cable.

Now safe behind the stonework, Peter waited for the mayor to come up for air. Hoping he timed it right, he raised enough to look into the depths of the well. Only there was no depth to it, other than the length needed to hide the Mayor and send water into his mouth. Peter could see no place for a capsule to be hidden. As the mayor dropped into the well once more, Peter dropped to his haunches behind him.

That left the mayor's helpful wife. As another set of boats went by, Peter worked his way around the broken furniture piled in the arches. Facing the edge of the set was another arch. Beyond this was a stairway that hugged the wall shared by the main part of the attacking Fort.

Almost at the top of the stairs, Peter noticed an open doorway lit by a hanging lantern. That doorway, though, didn't seem to lead into the wife's room. With the hope of another door and being shielded enough by his dark clothes, Peter saw a gap in the floating boats and ran for the stairs. Narrow as they were, he managed to keep his balance. Holding his breath, facing the wall, he had to stay motionless when two more boats came into view.

His hand now held the Key to Disneyland and Walt's special gift did its trick. He eased into the darkened room and quickly closed the door behind him.

Heaving a sigh of relief, he slumped against the door and took a moment to catch his breath. Now all the boats in the whole ride could go by and he didn't care. He was safe as long as he was in this room.

"Do not tell him, Carlos. Don't be cheeken."

The mayor's wife flew forward, pushed open the shuttered window, and tried to support her husband. With a shriek, she came backwards again as the sound of a bullet ricocheted in the air.

"Still spooky."

Peter now had time to examine the brave woman and soon wished he hadn't. This wasn't a full-body Audio-Animatronic like most of the ones below. The woman was literally half a person dressed in a pink nightgown with a white cap on her head. Nails polished, her fingers held onto the metal handles of the shutters. The lower part of the body consisted on two metal pipes that held her aloft from a framework of wires and cables that moved out and back on a small trolley. Towels and rags were piled around her to catch any hydraulic fluid that might leak out of her gears.

"Ewww. Should've given us a spoiler alert with this one." Peter shook his head and then remembered why he was there. "Clue, clue, here, clue." Peter whistled softly as the wife shot forward again to warn Carlos.

There were a couple of electrical boxes in that small room. Peter kept away from them because they were something that would be used if Maintenance or a set dresser came in. No, Walt would hide a capsule somewhere more out-of-the-way.

As the wife slammed the shutters shut, he noticed the golden curtains next to the window as they fluttered back into place. They looked old and had a darker satin edging all around. Careful not to damage the fragile drapes, Peter gently moved them aside. He also made sure he was out of the way of her trolley system. Close to the floor was a dark, round capsule. When the curtains were in place, it was completely hidden. When the wife was out shouting at the pirates, it looked like any cover for any piece of equipment. It was the **W E D** on it that told Peter he found what he sought.

Because of foreseen height problems, Peter had not brought his trusty backpack. He might have been crouched down out of sight, but that pack would have stuck up in plain sight. Not knowing what else to do, Peter tucked in his shirt and dropped the cold capsule inside next to his chest. "This one is bigger than the last few. Wonder where Walt will send me next?"

The urge to open the capsule was strong, but Peter knew he had to repeat all his previous stealth, Ninja-like moves to get back to Beth in time. Taking a deep breath to steady his nerves, Peter edged open the door and waited for three boatloads of guests to drift away. Running down the stairs took a moment and then he was safe behind the façade of the sacked town, leaving the poor mayor and fellow townsmen to the pirates.

"You made it!"

Peter found himself engulfed in another hug. "Yeah, it was... interesting."

"What? I couldn't hear you." Beth realized she was strangling the boy. "Are you ready to get home?"

"Yeah. You never did tell me how I was going to get back. Do I get to ride a boat back to the dock?" Peter tried to look down the length of the boat storage. It was so long it almost reached the Burning Town.

"No, we're putting boats away for the night. I'm going to have to turn you in to Security."

Peter didn't think he heard her right. "What?" His head jerked around expecting to see a squadron of guards grab him.

Seeing he didn't understand, Beth put a calming hand on his shoulder. "I called for Wolf, honey. He's going to escort you through the maze and take you out at Downtown Disney. Lance will meet you at the Rainforest Cafe."

Peter looked disappointed. "Oh, I thought I'd have some time in the Park."

"Well, you might get dinner and a volcano."

The possibility of the multi-layered chocolate cake and ice cream dessert softened his disappointment. "A volcano would be good."

"Ah, here he is. Hello, Wolf."

After a greeting to Beth, Wolf turned to Peter. He wondered why the boy shrank back a little. "What's wrong?"

"I thought you were mad at me."

"I was. But, it's been over a month. You served your time. And," as he gestured around, a motion that included Beth, "you seemed to have learned your lesson by asking for help."

"Yes, I really did."

"Don't overplay it, Peter. You ready to go? You found the capsule up in the window?"

Peter's eyes narrowed. "You knew where it was?"

"Of course I did."

Peter just shook his head. "Yeah, yeah, I know. It was my job to find it. You probably know where I go next, too."

Wolf just smiled at him, a smile that usually made the recipient nervous. It worked.

"Okay, fine. Don't tell me. I'll figure it out."

"You ready?"

"Yeah. Thanks, Aunt Beth. I appreciate your help."

She was grinning at the by-play between them. "You're welcome. Let me know what you find in the capsule. Adam, Alex and I will want to know. And you can tell Catie next time you see her."

Wolf led Peter out through a different way and they wound through the backways of the Pirate outbuilding. Already outside the berm, too soon Peter found himself back in the main stream of people. "You know your way now, Pete?"

Peter gave a laugh. "Yeah, I think I can find my way ten feet into Downtown Disney. Isn't that what they call the Monorail going by overhead?"

Wolf ignored the sarcasm. "You know, Pete, I'm proud of you for working it all out for yourself. Walt worked hard on this quest for you. He even resorted to blackmail to get something from me in exchange." He motioned for Peter to not ask his burning questions. "He'd be pleased in how far you've come."

"So, how far do I still have to go?"

"That, too, is for you to find out."

Peter knew that was all he was going to get out of their friend. He would have to be content with Wolf's praise. He'd wait and bring up that interesting blackmail bit later. "Are you going to join us for dinner?"

"No, I'm going out with Omah."

"Ooh, big date night?"

Again he was ignored. "I'll give her your regards."

Peter had a big grin plastered on his face. "Okay, thanks again, Wolf. I'll let you know when I figure out the next clue."

"Tell your dad I'll see him tomorrow at work."

"Night."

CHAPTER 18

Fullerton

Upending the gray container, Peter was surprised when two items came sliding out into his waiting hand. Up to this point, Walt hadn't included any special gifts to accompany the next clue as he had done in most of the previous Hidden Mickey searches. And, from the length of the written note, Peter began to wonder what kind of clue could possibly require so much of an explanation. As he started to read the familiar writing, though, a whole new outlook for the future opened up.

"*Hello, Peter,*

I'm proud that you have reached this final point in your special quest. I must say, it was refreshing to develop these clues with a specific person in mind. All the quests before—and the ones to follow—I knew would be designed for some faceless, unknown person. In any one of those cases, I wouldn't know if he or she would follow through or not. It's hard to believe that someone might find a tempting clue and not follow through to the end, but you never know.

Having met you and your mother through Wolf's wonderful ability, it was a pleasure to make this search just for you. You might have had some trouble nagging at you from a past experience, but I had no doubt that you would go all the way until the end. Were you able to do as I asked? Did you look around at each location? Could you see the special hand of my Imagineers in the different places you went? Did you appreciate what you were seeing? To me, the journey is as important as the final destination.

Even though I might not like it, I've always known I wouldn't live forever—well, not in body, anyway. My decision to set up these quests was to find people who would carry out my intentions, my desires, my legacy. In that way, what I strived so hard to create would survive long after I am gone. These dedicated people, starting with your grandfather, have become my Guardians.

Since you have completed the course I set out for you, it is my belief that you qualify to join this elite group. You might be young in age, but you have shown courage and dedication. I believe your enthusiasm for my legacy will continue to grow as you do. I want men like you to help guide the future. I want you to join the Guardians and take your deserved place alongside the others.

The other item in this small canister is a rough copy of an unfinished Alice comedy from many years ago. The actual script was a treasure included in a previous quest. You get to see the movie. It is an eight-millimeter film that I watched once on my Bell and Howell movie projector. No one else has seen this little gem. Unfortunately, the series ended before it could be finished and released. I hope you enjoy it. Those were wonderful days!

You will find something else that no one else has. No, don't tip the container on its ear again. It isn't there. I arranged with your grandfather to leave it somewhere where he knew you would find it. He told me to say 'Look in back of the smaller filing cabinet for a folder named Peter.' He said you'd know where to go.

I will leave you now with my thanks. Now, if you got to know many of my men here in the Studio, you would know that isn't said very often. But, on special occasions I drag the word out. This, to me, is a special occasion.

Perhaps some day, if Wolf will allow it, I'll get to see you again.

Just remember to keep wishing and all your dreams will come true!

Best wishes,
Walt Disney."

Peter sat back in his chair and let the handwritten pages drop to his lap. *A personal letter from Walt Disney! Wow.* His next thought was that he wanted to share this with Catie. He tapped the small canister of film with his index finger. Not sure if they had a projector capable of handling the small gauge film, he hesitated on opening the round metal tin. He had seen film like that before. At the slightest touch it could spring out of its tight coil and unwind before he could stop it. No, he'd save that gem for later.

One particular part of the letter was reread—the part that said his grandfather had hidden something for him. He knew it had to be in that small green filing cabinet up in the War Room, but he still didn't have unlimited access to the fascinating room. With a cocky smile, Peter wondered if whatever Walt had left for him might change that. "He said I was a Guardian now. Mom and Dad will have to let me in."

A glance at his clock told him it was only seven in the evening. His family was probably downstairs in the living room watching television. He was torn. He wanted to go read the letter to Catie, but he also wanted to see what he could find in the filing cabinet. That would require Mom or Dad, without letting either of his brothers know what they were doing.

Peter grabbed up the film canister and headed for the stairs.

"Give me fifteen minutes, Pete. My show's almost over."

"But this is important, Dad!"

"You've been upstairs all day. It can wait fifteen minutes."

"But..."

"Honey, have a seat. Have some popcorn. You know this is your dad's favorite show."

Peter threw himself on the sofa, the force causing some popcorn to fly out of the bowl. Dug, always nearby, jumped at the chance to grab a few stray kernels before they were cleaned up.

"You know corn isn't good for dogs. Mikey, help clear the floor, will you?"

"Peter made the mess."

One nice, pretty little girl. That's all I ever asked for. Give me strength not to kill them. Taking a calming breath, Kimberly chose not to pursue that battle. "All of you will... Well, never mind. Dug beat us to it."

A long, golden tail thumped happily on the clean floor. Not quite content, the Golden Retriever steadily eyed the youngest, Andrew, waiting for the next handful to miss his mouth.

There was a chorus of "Hey!" when Lance clicked off the television. "Hey yourself. How can I watch with all this noise?" He glanced at the now-empty, buttery bowl. "And you all ate all the popcorn. How can I watch a show without popcorn? So, Pete, what was so important?"

All eyes in the room instantly turned to Peter. The youngest two were silently blaming Peter for the shortened television program. The older two were wondering what he had found in the gray canister from Pirates. "Um, can I talk to you, Dad?"

"Sure, go ahead."

"Not here. Upstairs."

Lance threw a questioning glance at Kimberly. Not having any idea what was going on, she gave a slight shrug. "I'll be right back, honey." When they had reached Peter's room, he asked, "So, what's up? What did you find?"

Peter drew Walt's letter out of his top desk drawer and handed it to Lance. "Walt wrote me this letter."

"Letter? No clue?"

Peter shook his head and indicated the metal film can that was back on his desk. "He left me this *Alice* comedy he said no one else has ever seen."

Lance's eyes lit up. "Oooh, that's pretty interesting."

"Not as interesting as what might be upstairs. In the War Room." Peter made sure he stressed the location.

Lance's head shot up from the canister. "In the War Room? Why do you think there's something for you in there? We surely would have found it by now."

Peter pointed at that passage in Walt's letter. "He said grandpa hid something for me."

"Well, let's go see what we can find."

Peter was all smiles as his dad led the way up the stairs that took them to the third floor of their house. To most people, the stairs ended in an attic filled with cartons of cast-off clothes, furniture, and various Disney items yet to be placed in the main part of the house. However, next to the seldom-used elevator was a door. It was difficult to see because it was covered by the same Victorian wallpaper as the walls around it. Hidden in plain sight. Also concealed was the elaborate alarm system that Lance now disengaged.

With a quick glance at the holographic map of Disneyland suspended in the middle of the room, Peter went straight to the small filing cabinet.

"We've been in that cabinet many times over the years, Pete. There never was a folder with your name on it. We would've remembered it."

Not answering, Peter held his breath as he pulled out the squeaky drawer and started to riffle through the files inside. "It has to be here. Walt said it would."

Lance's reply was cut off when Peter let out a triumphant yell. "What'd you find?"

Peter held up a thin manila folder. "See? It says Peter on it! Just like Walt said."

"I don't understand." Lance didn't reach out to take the folder from Peter. The confused look on his face said it all. "That can't be there."

"But it is." Peter looked away for a moment as he tried to figure out some logical explanation. "Maybe it's the time travel thingy. You know, it might not have been there before because it wasn't put there before when all this other stuff was. Maybe Grandpa just added it recently in their time…" He rubbed a hand over his eyes. "Man, this is hard to keep straight."

"You know, you might be right. We can ask Wolf about it later. So, no matter how or when it got there, what's inside?"

"Oh, yeah. I forgot to look." Peter eagerly parted the sides of the folder. "There's only one piece of paper in here."

"You sound disappointed. What were you expecting? What does it say?"

Peter didn't know what he had been expecting. Having already received a Gold Pass, his own apartment over Main Street, and the Key to Disneyland, he assumed it would be something more significant than a single piece of paper. "Oh!"

Lance could see that Peter's face had transformed into sheer joy. "What is it? Can you show me?"

"Sure, Partner."

Lance frowned at his choice of words. "Partner? Let me see."

Peter turned the thick piece of paper around. It was an elaborate certificate, its borders filled with filigree and Disney characters. In the center was a detailed depiction of Sleeping Beauty Castle. Lance could tell it had been hand-drawn and printed by Walt himself. The flowery lettering proclaimed that Peter Percy Brentwood was now a full-fledged, acknowledged Guardian of Walt.

"Well, congratulations, Pete. This is quite a day for you. You've been working toward it for a long time."

"So, do I get my own key to this War Room?"

"Don't push it, son."

Peter knew when to drop it. "Can we go tell Catie? I know she'd love to hear about it."

Lance was glad to see the excited look on his son's face. After a long, angst-filled year, it was a relief to see him happy again and looking forward to his duties as a Guardian—even though he knew Peter was still vague on what exactly this entailed. But, enough time for that in the future. "I think that's a great idea. I'll go tell your mom and see if they all want to go."

For some reason, Peter became subdued. "All right. I need to get something from my room. I'll be right down."

When his dad closed up the War Room and set the alarm, Peter followed him down the first set of stairs. He turned to go into his room, checking back over his shoulder to make sure he wasn't followed. Slipping into his closet, he pulled the door shut and went to the back wall. Working quickly, he uncovered his hidden treasure box and opened its lid. Lips suddenly dry, he pulled out one small item from the very bottom. Staring at it, heart pounding in his chest, his head slowly nodded. "This is the time."

Andrew claimed he had "a 'fectious cough" and Michael didn't want to leave the television, so Lance and Peter made the short drive to the Fullerton Hospital. Lance noticed Peter was unusually quiet. After two major finds he figured Peter would be jumping out of his seat and retelling every detail of his last trek into Pirates. But, the boy was still. "You all right, son?"

Peter acted like a firecracker had gone off under his feet. "What!? Oh, uhm, yeah. Sorry, Dad, what'd you ask?"

Lance's glance into his side mirror hid his amusement. "I just asked if you were all right."

"Yeah. Fine. Great! Why wouldn't I?" *Gosh, shut up, Peter!*

"You just seem jumpy. That's all."

"Oh. No, I, uhm, just thinking about what I'm going to tell Catie."

Lance let it slide as he pulled into a parking spot. "I know she'll be proud of you, too. Just like your Mom and I are."

Peter hadn't really heard him, but realized he needed to make some kind of a reply. "Thanks?" When Lance didn't say anything else, Peter figured that must have been appropriate.

As they got closer to Catie's room, Peter seemed to get more and more nervous. He pulled up short when he saw Adam and Beth were already inside. Lance, on the other hand, was glad to see them.

"Hey, you two. Nice to see you. How's our girl doing today? Any more action?"

"She has more color today. Her eyes were open again and she followed us while we were talking to her. That was encouraging." Beth turned to greet Peter who was still hovering by the door. "Hello, Peter. Did you open the canister yet? We're excited to hear what you found."

Eyes wide, seemingly startled to be singled out, his hand fell to his jeans pocket. "What? Oh, yeah, I did. It was, um, a letter. From Walt. Disney."

When he said nothing else, Adam and Beth looked to Lance for more of an explanation. Lance could only shrug. "I'm sure he'll fill you in later. I think he wanted to tell Catie first."

"Oh, well, how about if we go down to the cafeteria? I could use a coffee right about now. Adam? You two want to come with me?"

Not sure why Peter was acting so oddly, the men followed Beth out of the room. "We'll be back in about twenty minutes. That good for you, Pete?"

His eyes on a fresh flower arrangement across the room, Peter nodded. "Yeah, thanks, Dad. I'll…" He didn't finish his sentence as the adults filed out of the room.

Now that he was alone, he first walked over to the window to peer out into the night sky. He seemed to be drawing either strength or courage from the blinking stars overhead. Wolf's teasing voice crept into his head. "Fine," he ground out, "I'm wishing on a star, Wolf. You happy?"

Mind made up, he went up to the hospital bed. "Hi, Catie. It's me, Peter." His abrupt chuckle broke the serious demeanor. "I guess you probably knew that. Listen, Catie. I wanted to tell you something. I did find that last clue inside the Pirates ride. It was really cool and kinda weird to walk around in there. I got a letter from Walt, too. He made me a Guardian, Catie! I even found an official certificate in the filing cabinet." Peter broke off and looked away. Catie didn't know about the War Room. She had been in their attic, but had never noticed or commented on that hidden door. "Uhm, that's cool news, isn't it? But, I have something else I want to tell you." A quick look at the door showed him he was still alone, but the clock on the wall said he didn't have that much more time alone with her. "You know how much I've missed you, right? It seemed really strange for you to not be there with me when I was running these clues. It made me realize something, Catie." He took a deep breath and shoved a hand in his pocket. His fingers closed around the small object as he drew it out. "I know we're still young, but I...I don't want to do these things without you again. I thought that if I gave you this, it would be like a promise between us. I wish you could talk to me and tell me if it was okay with you."

Peter reached for Catie's hand that was resting on top of the blanket. Into it he pressed the gold Claddagh ring he had found inside the wooden mermaid. Two hands reached around the gold band and met in the middle to hold a diamond-inlaid heart. The crown above the small heart also was encrusted with small diamonds. Walt and his wife Lillian had each worn a ring like that. Even the Partners Statue in Disneyland depicts the ring on Walt's hand. "I know you can't hold onto this right now. You don't have any pockets, do you? No, I guess not. I just want you to feel it in your hand. I know you remember the ring. That was a fun time when we found it, wasn't it?" He smiled at the memory, the pleasure dimmed momentarily by the remembrance of Omah and her part in it. But, that all worked out to everyone's benefit, especially Wolf's. She was one of the family now.

He left the ring in her weak grasp while he ran a shaky hand through his hair and let out a huge *whoosh* of air. It had been difficult to open his heart like that. He just wished she had been conscious to hear it. With a slight groan he realized he'd probably have to repeat the process all over again at a later date. "Wonder if it will be any easier the second time?"

When his allotted twenty minutes was almost up, Peter retrieved the small ring from Catie's hand. It was warm from her touch and he held it tightly in his palm before returning it to his pocket.

"I'll see you again soon, Catie. Maybe I'll get a thin chain so you can wear it around your neck. I wish you could talk to me and tell me you heard what I said. And…how you'd react to it. But, don't worry," he whispered. "You'll be all right. I'll keep it safe. Bye now."

With a heavy sigh Peter turned from the bed to head for the door. He planned to meet his parents downstairs in the cafeteria and then leave from there. His thoughts on tomorrow and having the Guardian certificate framed, it was so faint he almost missed it.

"Peter?"

Spinning on his heels, his face was engulfed by a huge grin.

"Catie! You're awake!"

Epilogue

Disneyland – 2042

Big Red, the Mark XII Monorail, silently glided through the Esplanade of the Disneyland Resort. Hovering electromagnetically a foot above the rail, it had just come from its fourth stop at the Disneyland Hotel and headed for the Tomorrowland Station. After picking up new passengers at the California Adventure Station and at the Paradise Pier Hotel, all the seats in the six cars were taken. Some of the new arrivals would head to the newly-opened apartments in the Sleeping Beauty Castle Towers; others were eager to continue their adventures within the Park. A ten-year old boy sitting in the co-pilot seat pushed the button for the air horn and energetically waved to the people on the moving walkways below.

The remodeled, larger Sleeping Beauty Castle with its furnished towers wasn't the only place Park visitors could spend the night. After much popular demand, the Swiss Family Treehouse had returned to Adventureland. The three original huts were back in refurnished glory. The largest, most popular hut—the Main Bedroom that had belonged to Mother and Father in the 1960 film *Swiss Family Robinson*—was complete with its own lavatory. The 'tortoise-shell' sink's running water was seemingly supplied by the large, turning waterwheel made out of realistic-looking bamboo. Most guests loved the special tasseled pull-rope that hung over the opulent king-sized bed. Just like in the movie, guests pulled on the rope and the thatched ceiling opened on hidden levers. Lying in bed, in their own secluded privacy, the occupants could watch the

9:30 fireworks show with the music piped through hidden speakers.

In the movie, the two smaller huts had been the boys' rooms. Now, less opulent than the Main Bedroom, they were more fun for visitors. The lower hut had a private waterfall slide that ended up in the pool below. Guarded over by Ellie the baby elephant, she would playfully squirt each rider as they curved along the bottom portion of the slide.

The uppermost hut had the best view. High above the Park, guests sat on their own private wooden deck to watch the nighttime show of *Fantasmic!* or the interactive water show in California Adventure. The fireworks seemed to be so close that they could almost reach out to touch them.

One of the newer attractions that was visible from the upper hut was the Mine Train through Nature's Wonderland. Overlapping the Big Thunder rollercoaster that boasted a new 360-degree loop, guests could once again travel through the balancing rocks and colorful Rainbow Caverns in the backmost portion of Frontierland. At one point in the ride, the Big Thunder train looked as if it was going to crash right into the slower-moving Mine Train. Seemingly coming out of nowhere, the Big Thunder train would screech out of a hidden cavern and race toward the other train. Then, at the last minute, Old Unfaithful Geyser would erupt and the Big Thunder cars would veer sharply away, narrowly avoiding disaster. Careening around the Bubbling Pots of Mud, the train would vanish down a steep incline, its passengers screaming in delight as they narrowly missed being crushed by an avalanche of rocks. The Mine Train would continue on its more sedate journey through Bear Country, Elk Meadow, and under the misty water of Cascade Peaks. Once back at Rainbow Ridge and its interactive displays of the Old West, kids of all ages could replicate gunfights and watch a spectacular stunt show in the street just in front of the popular attraction.

Back on Main Street, a line had formed for the Main Street Cinema. As original cartoons of Mickey Mouse played on the old-fashioned flat-screen televisions, guests could enter private, red-curtained booths that lined the walls—much like the old-time telephone booths—that comfortably accommodated a family of four. Each guest was given a special mouse-eared Virtual Reality headset to fit over their eyes and plug into their ears. With the push of a button on a pop-up menu, they would be 'transported' into any attraction in Disneyland's history that they wanted to relive. Older guests especially loved to visit the Disneyland of their childhood. Instantly seated in an Atomobile, they relived their personal Adventure through Inner Space, or climbed into a Skyway Cab for a roundtrip flight over Fantasyland, ending back at the Swiss chalet nestled up and behind the Storybook Land Canal Boats. The Mike Fink Keelboats came alive for them once again, with Beth Roberts as their holographic pilot. As they listened to her humorous spiel, they could turn their head in any direction and see Tom Sawyer Island as it was way back in 1996. Or they could go further back in time when the surrounding trees didn't hide Fort Wilderness and the Native American shows were held in the nearby Village. The Country Bear Jamboree or the Carousel of Progress, the original Sleeping Beauty Walk-Through or the Submarine Voyage, America Sings or the Lion King Parade; they were all there in vivid virtual clarity.

The Jungle Cruise now offered two tracks for its passengers. One track provided entertainment from a skipper as he took them through underground caverns of Middle Asia before emerging back into the bright light and onto the rivers of Africa and South America.

The second track let the guests skipper their own boat. Bringing along as many guests as they wanted, the entertainment was theirs to provide. Those who always felt 'they could do it better' now had the opportunity to do so. Riding along the original guide rail set in 1955 and timed so the boats never ran side-by-side, each track was immersed in the Jungle all their own.

Lance guided his granddaughter through the bricked arch of the entry tunnel, holding her hand, feeling her squeeze his hand tighter as she emerged onto Main Street. He smiled as he heard her sharp intake of breath as the grand panorama opened up before her wide green eyes. The Castle, the shops, the people, all signified something fantastic to the little five-year-old.

They walked into the Town Square, toward the tall, shiny flagpole that stood among beautifully manicured flowers. The two stopped and gazed down the street. The trolley car was slowly moving toward the pink and white Castle, the *clop-clop-clop* of the Belgium horse's hooves easily heard over the sounds of the crowd. The muted honk of the Omnibus drew her excited attention as it started on its own electric journey down Main Street. A small group of guests took pictures of the *E.P. Ripley* steam train as it waited at the Train Station for its next load of guests, sounding its whistle in hello. The sounds were as plentiful as the sights and smells.

Smiling to himself, Lance looked down at his granddaughter, enjoying the emotional memory of the first time he had seen Disneyland. As they stood there, other memories of Disneyland came flooding back. Memories of good times with friends, exciting adventures, and romantic moments with a certain green-eyed, blonde beauty. He looked toward the Fire House and the apartment in the upper story. The light was still burning bright in the window. He let the memories wash through him. *Had it really been forty years?* he asked himself with a shake of his head in wonderment. *It seemed like just yesterday.*

An excited tug on his arm brought him out of his memories. "Well, what do you think, Lilly?" Lance glanced down at the wide-eyed, blonde little girl. Having just moved back from a three-year sabbatical in Paris with Peter and Catie, this was Lilly's first time visiting Disneyland.

"It's a dream!" Her answer was breathless, her eyes not moving from the tall, golden spires of the Castle in the distance.

Lance smiled and looked over to his right. There were a few inquisitive guests reading the bronze plaque imbedded in the base of the flagpole.

Kneeling down to her level, Lance gave Lilly a kiss. "Stay here with Grandma, Lilly." He transferred the small hand to his wife Kimberly's grasp. "I'll be right back." Expecting this, she just nodded as he walked off toward the flagpole.

"Where's Papa going!? I wanna go with Papa!" Not wanting to miss anything, Lilly began to get worried.

Looking down at the little hand that was placed in her own, Kimberly's heart suddenly began to pound as her mouth formed an 'O'. A memory, a vision rushed back into her mind, one that she experienced forty years ago not far away from where they stood. She had forgotten about the vision that was given to her by the red diamond heart. Lance had never been told about it; it was too personal at the time she had received it. 'How you get there is up to you', had been written on the note from Walt. Her relationship with Lance had been too new, too fresh then. How could she casually throw into the conversation, "Oh, by the way, I just saw myself holding the hand of a beautiful blonde-headed little girl. She looked around five or six years old and she was *our* granddaughter. So, where would you like to go for dinner?" No, she buried the vision deep inside her heart, safe to take out and cherish whenever she wanted to see it again. But, time and reality came—as they always did—and she eventually forgot about it as her life with Lance started. She had found her reality with him was quite wonderful and very real. Now, forty years later, holding Lilly's hand, the vision returned. Because she and Lance had had three boys, until now, the vision had remained deeply buried with nothing to prick at the memory. Now, she looked down at the little hand in hers and the beautiful, concerned face that peered up into her own. The amazement on Kimberly's face faded into a loving smile at her granddaughter. This was the lovely child she had seen. Her future had come true.

"Thank you, Walt."

"Grandma?" Not understanding her, Lilly pulled on Kimberly's hand and pointed at Lance. "He's getting away!"

"It's okay, honey. Papa has something he needs to do." Kimberly tried to soothe the girl and looked for a diversion. "Let's go say hi to Mickey at the Opera House."

Following her Grandmother's pointing finger, Lilly bounced up and down. "Is that the real Mickey!?"

With a laugh, Kimberly led her over toward the ornate white building. "Well, let's go ask him."

Lance, honoring his long-standing tradition, approached the flagpole to pay his respects. The other guests had moved on and a lone man stood there now, looking down at the raised letters. After giving the older man a mere glance, Lance's head suddenly shot back to his face, his heart pounding in his ears. *No. It can't be. How come we weren't told?* Unanswerable questions bounced back and forth in his mind as he took a step back, his eyes still glued on the man.

Unaware of the scrutiny, the man's fingers moved over the bronze words, reading as he went. Noticing a red button just above the plaque, he pushed it and jumped back, startled. A three-dimensional Walt Disney appeared in front of the flagpole. "To all who come to this happy place, welcome..." Disney's familiar voice boomed out as he recited the Opening Day Speech.

The older man leaned toward the transparent, but still somehow solid figure as the speech continued. He poked a finger through the apparition and began to chuckle to himself.

Wondering if he should get her, Lance looked back toward his wife and Lilly, easily finding their shining heads in the crowd surrounding Mickey. For a moment he became diverted and smiled as he thought about all the 'first times' Lilly would have today. The Matterhorn, the Jungle Cruise, Peter Pan, It's a Small World, Pirates of the Caribbean. Lance grinned at some of his memories—especially of Pirates.

When he heard the words of the Opening Day Speech again, Lance turned back to the older man who had activated it. Walking all the way around the shimmering image, the man seemed impressed and amused at the same time.

Knowing he had to find out for sure, Lance took a step forward. As he did, he then noticed Wolf and Omah standing off to the side, an empty blue scooter between them. Intent on the older man, Lance hadn't been aware of anyone else around him.

Seeing the look of confusion on his friend's face, Wolf came up to him. "I see you brought Lilly for her first visit."

Lance wasn't going to let Wolf off with normal, everyday conversation. "No, no you don't." He waved a hand at the man who was now talking with Omah and gesturing at the Train Station. "How is that possible? Did you know about it? Why weren't the rest of the Guardians told?"

Wolf tilted his head to the side as if he couldn't understand Lance's concern. "What is it you think happened that you weren't told about?"

Lance lifted his hand to again gesture at the man with Omah. When the man turned at that moment, Lance didn't want to be seen pointing. So, instead, he ran his fingers through his hair and turned away.

"Smooth." Wolf seemed vastly amused at Lance's discomfiture.

Several people approached the hologram, forcing Lance to lower his voice to a hiss. "You know what I found under Pirates in 2002... Why are you smiling?"

"That wasn't what you thought." Before Lance could question him, Wolf motioned for Omah. "Could you both come over? There's someone I want him to meet."

The older man pushed his beat-up Fedora off his forehead, his eyes twinkling. "Who's this, Wolf?"

"Peter's father, Lance Brentwood."

"Well, well, pleased to finally meet you. I'm Walt. You have a fine son."

Mouth dry, Lance's hand was shaky as he extended it to meet Walt's. Once he could tear his eyes off Walt's face, he turned back to Wolf. "Doesn't this prove that it *was* what I thought?"

"What are we talking about?"

Wolf turned back to Walt. "Underneath Pirates."

A knowing grin swept over Walt's face. "So, are you the one who found the bells and whistles I planted? Pretty ingenious, if I do say so for myself."

"Planted? I don't understand."

Walt glanced back at Omah. "He's pretty white. Maybe he needs that scooter more than I do."

"Just give him a minute, Walt. He's usually sharper than this."

Lance shot an irritated glance at her. "Then perhaps you can explain all this to me. If I didn't find Walt...him...uh, you know what I mean...all those years ago, exactly what did I find?"

"What you found in that hidden cavern was, basically, a diversion."

Eyes shining, Walt took over for Omah. "You see, Lance, I know my time is shorter than I would like. I set up that elaborate Hidden Mickey quest with your father-in-law so I could be remembered, so my legacy would be preserved." He paused when Lance nodded that he understood that part. "The ones who followed me to care for that legacy had to be dedicated, like Wolf and Omah here. There were many layers to my quests. I understand the two friends who worked with you didn't find that secondary cavern, right? Only you carried on. Only you persisted. That cavern was just another step to test you. It would lead you to my right-hand-man and you would then be taken under his wing. What you saw inside that contraption wasn't me. That kind of end isn't my intention."

"But it looked just like you."

Walt chuckled. "Have you ridden the Haunted Mansion?"

The question, in the middle of such poignant revelations, startled Lance. "Of course, but…"

"Did you see that singing bust at the end, the one that fell over?"

Lance merely nodded, not knowing what to say. The Mansion wasn't finished in Walt's time. It opened several years after his death.

"Even though I'm still going round and round with my Imagineers over the Mansion, some things we've discussed and agreed on. That's one of them. Only that singing head isn't mine. It looks a little like me, but it is really someone else. When the time comes, a copy of that head will be used in that chamber you'll find…did find." Flustered, he turned to Wolf with a laugh. "Gosh, it's hard to talk about something that hasn't happened to me yet, but you all have gone through." His eyes narrowed. "Even though you two refuse to tell me what year this is."

"Still not going to tell you, Walt."

With a good-natured snort, Walt shook his head. "Fine. Be stubborn."

Understanding was finally dawning on Lance. "Then, you're here because of Wolf and Omah?" His hand shot through his gray hair again as he turned to Wolf. "Wow, I didn't know you could go forward in time."

"We didn't, either, until we started experimenting." Omah linked her arm through Wolf's. "Which we did *before* we brought Walt along."

"I blackmailed them!" Walt seemed quite pleased with himself. "Took them long enough to fulfill their promise, but," as he appreciatively looked around, "they did a bang-up job of it. I can't wait to see the rest of it."

When Walt wandered back to the hologram, Lance turned to his friends. Aware of his own age and grayed appearance, his eyes strayed to their unlined faces and dark hair. "This is turning out to be quite a day, and it hasn't even started yet. Can Kimberly, Lily, and I hang out with you? How many people get to go to Disneyland with Walt?"

"Just as long as you don't tell him what year it is. Oh, and make sure he doesn't grab any brochures. We think he sneaked one past us at Disneyland Paris."

Lance nodded his agreement. Now that the shock had worn off, he studied Walt with a more critical eye. "He looks pretty tired. When is it, in his time, that is?"

A look of grief came and went in Wolf's eyes. "Pretty close to the end. It took us a while to perfect this forward movement in time. It's the end of October."

"Oh gosh." Just a few weeks later in 1966 Walt would go to the hospital to have his lungs X-rayed. That was when the tumor would be discovered.

"Yeah."

Lance squared his shoulders. "Then we'll just have to make sure this is a special day for him. We'll show him that it was all worth it." When the Opening Day Speech was activated again, Lance walked over to Walt's position. "So, what do you think?"

Walt just rocked back on his heels and smiled, a twinkle in his eye. "Couldn't have said it better myself!"

Lance glanced once more at his wife who was busy pointing out something in the Disney Gallery's window to Lilly. "You did well." Lance put his hand on the man's shoulder. A little softer, he repeated, "You did real well, Walt!"

—THE END—

HIDDEN MICKEY COVER ART & HIDDEN MICKEY HEART
AVAILABLE AT:
HIDDENMICKEYBOOK.COM/MERCHANDISE.HTML

LIMITED EDITIONS

HIDDEN MICKEY COVER ART CANVAS PRINTS
NUMBERED AND SIGNED

© DOUBLE R BOOKS

LIMITED EDITION
HIDDEN MICKEY HEART NECKLACE

14K YELLOW GOLD VERMEIL
30 CARAT LAB CREATED RUBY
"HIDDEN MICKEY" IS INSCRIBED ON THE BACK
AUTHOR SIGNED CERTIFICATE

© 2010 NANCY RODRIGUE

Enjoy all the books from Double R Books
Hardbacks - Paperbacks - eBooks - Apps

Hidden Mickey
1: Sometimes Dead Men DO Tell Tales!
2: It All Started...
3: Wolf! The Legend of Tom Sawyer's Island
4: Wolf! Happily Ever After?
4.5: Unfinished Business - Wals

Hidden Mickey Adventures
1: Peter and the Wolf
2: Peter and the Missing Mansion
3: The Mermaid's Tale
4: Revenge of the Wolf
5: When You Wish

Hidden Mickey Quest books to play inside Disney parks

Hidden Mickey Adventures
in Disneyland ❖ in WDW Magic Kingdom
in Disney California Adventure

THE HIDDEN MICKEY FAN CLUB BLOG

LOG IN AND GAIN ACCESS TO OUR ARCHIVED NEWSLETTERS WITH BEHIND-THE-SCENES ARTICLES WRITTEN BY PAST AND PRESENT CAST MEMBERS WITHIN THE DISNEY PARKS. FANS ALSO RECEIVE ADVANCE ANNOUNCEMENTS ON BOOK SIGNINGS, SPECIAL EVENTS, AND SPECIAL OPPORTUNITIES TO BUY BOOKS AND MERCHANDISE BEFORE THESE ARE RELEASED TO THE PUBLIC.

BLOG.HIDDENMICKEYBOOK.COM

JOIN THE FACEBOOK HIDDEN MICKEY FAN CLUB

LOG IN TO FACEBOOK AND "LIKE" THE "HIDDEN MICKEY FAN CLUB" TO BE ENTERED IN THE BOOK GIVEAWAY CONTEST. EACH TIME A 100 "LIKES" MILESTONE IS REACHED, A HIDDEN MICKEY ADVENTURES QUEST & GAME BOOK IS GIVEN AWAY IN A RANDOM DRAWING. JOIN TODAY TO WIN!

WWW.FACEBOOK.COM/HIDDENMICKEYFANCLUB

About the Author

Nancy Temple Rodrigue

Nancy lives in the small town of Lompoc, California. Her work shows her admiration and respect for the man who started it all–Walt Disney.

Her love of all things Disney is shown in her *Hidden Mickey* and *Hidden Mickey Adventures* series of Mystery novels.

Nancy loves leaving you with a cliffhanger ending, and the next book picks right up where the last one left off. You get just enough to answer those lingering questions you were left with, yet she leaves you with more that remain unanswered. In this story you may want to keep some tissues nearby as it just may tug on the heart strings a bit. You may also want to note what Walt reveals to Lance in the Epilogue, it will take you back to the *Hidden Mickey* series.

If you love the quests that Lance, Adam, Beth, Peter, and Catie were able to participate in, now you too can do this. You will see your favorite Disney Parks in a whole new way with Nancy's *Hidden Mickey Quests* series. The quests are designed to be played inside the Disney Parks. Bonus questions have you finding Hidden Mickeys. These games and quests will take you on a new, exciting journey.

Nancy actively holds book signings and speaking events. Visit blog.hiddenmickeybook.com to follow the author's blog and learn the locations and dates of her book signing events, or follow her at Facebook.com/HiddenMickeyFanClub.

CPSIA information can be obtained
at www.ICGtesting.com
Printed in the USA
LVHW091600220919
631873LV00001B/22/P